CORRUPTED DESIRES

DOLCE OBSURITÀ #2

CORRUPTED DESIRES

CHELSEA BURTON DUNN

4 Horsemen
Publications, Inc.

Published By: 4 Horsemen Publications, Inc.

4 Horsemen Publications, Inc.
PO Box 417
Sylva, NC 28779
4horsemenpublications.com
info@4horsemenpublications.com

Cover & Typesetting by Autumn Skye
Edited by Kris Cotter

Library of Congress Control Number: 2025942304

Paperback ISBN-13: 979-8-8232-0964-9
Hardcover ISBN-13: 979-8-8232-0965-6
Audiobook ISBN-13: 979-8-8232-0967-0
Ebook ISBN-13: 979-8-8232-0966-3

DEDICATION

If you are related to me, I suggest you either put this book down or agree that we never discuss it.

For the moms who struggle to believe they are desirable and beautiful after having their kids: You are beautiful. Wear your scars like the war paint they are.

We are warriors; we are goddesses.

And to all of us who know a nerd can be dark and sexy.

TRIGGER WARNINGS:

Mentions/threats of sex trafficking
Graphic death
Graphic violence
Mentions of domestic violence
Mentions/threats of rape
Instances of misogyny
Graphic sex
Serious dive into anxiety, depression,
and body dysmorphia

CONTENTS

CHAPTER 1

INGRID

The sound of the keys on my laptop clicking, the hum of the fan cooling the computer, as well as the background noise of some random metal playlist I had curated, were doing a fantastic job of drowning out the sounds of Elliot's conversation in the other room. Just past that door and down the hallway of our apartment, my boyfriend was planning what services I could provide his newest boss. I had known for years the kind of company Elliot kept. He never held down a specific job for long, preferring to work short term for a person he knew from a friend or other such strange scenarios. Usually, the pay was good, but everything about what he was being asked to do was illegal.

I knew that.

I just didn't want to know *how* illegal.

Not that I was the picture of perfection in that department either.

I worked at a club part-time as a bartender and the rest of the time I worked online, finding holes in large companies' security and breaching them, just so I could tell them how to fix it … for a fee.

That's what White Hat hackers did after all.

The beauty of this type of work was that, while it was shady and underhanded, it helped the business, and I got to use these lovely skills I had learned to get me large sums on a regular basis. So much so that I often had companies reaching out to me asking if I wanted a permanent position to maintain their security. At that moment, I could think of no reasons why I'd ever want to do that, especially seeing as how I was planning on getting away from all of this anyway.

Elliot may have wanted me to continue, to be of use to him and his gangster friends, but I wanted to have a legitimate life. I wanted to do work that I could tell other people about. I didn't want dark secrets that I needed to hide in order to remain normal, because I wanted the child that was growing within me to be as healthy and happy as Elliot and I weren't in our childhoods.

A hard feat, but honestly not something that I was willing to budge on, even if Elliot had convinced himself I wasn't going to change.

"Ri!"

The sound of Elliot's yell across the apartment made me flinch. I hated that nickname he had been using since we started dating, and I hated the idea of going out there to look at these men who would not be receiving anything from me.

"Ri! Someone important wants to see you!"

I got up from my chair, belly swollen with the little one inside, trying to reset the grim look I was certain inhabited my face.

Despite my pregnant state, I had secured plenty of money from the last few White Hat endeavors of mine that I felt like—despite not planning on doing any work like that again—I could live comfortably for a time: at least until my child was old enough to be of school age and I could pursue a job that they could tell their teachers and the other parents about. Elliot only worked for his drug and booze money at this point, I made sure we had a roof over our heads and had for the last few years. He was unreliable at best.

I didn't have too much time left, but I would find the last bit of money I felt I needed. Just enough to make sure the baby and I were okay and established before Elliot was shown the door.

Stepping out of the hall into the living room was a sight. There were shoes on my expensive coffee table. The shoes themselves were probably equally as expensive, but that didn't matter. It was the principle of the matter. Who goes into someone else's home and puts their disgusting feet all over their hosts' furnishings? I may have been alone in this world, but I knew what subtleties were employed by people like the man seated in the very center of our sofa. He was putting on a display, one he was very accustomed to portraying, given who he was.

Freddy O'Shea.

I knew his face as soon as my eyes snapped to it, probably annoyance and anger written all over it, while his held amusement. If you lived in Chicago and had any idea of the darker side of the city, you knew Freddy.

The O'Sheas were the ruling Irish Mob of this zone. I wasn't sure how far it stretched, but I had been fairly careful to stay away from any companies that were tightly associated with organized crime. It was essentially impossible to find any of the larger companies within the United States that didn't have some hand in mob or Mafia dealings, whether state side or abroad.

But I had been careful. I wanted no association with O'Shea or any of them for that matter.

Elliot, on the other hand had been trying desperately to get his foot in the door with any group that would take him. For whatever reason, his idea of financial and job freedom was being chained to a group like O'Shea's for the rest of his probably very short life.

"Ri?" Freddy asked.

"Her full name is ugly. Don't worry about it," Elliot said. I glanced at him just in time to watch him take a giant swig of whatever it was he was imbibing this evening. Probably gin or vodka.

"Elliot here says you are good with computers?" Freddy asked, his blue eyes having only left me for a moment to give Elliot a disgusted glance before looking back at me. I would wonder why I was with this fool too if I saw the two of us.

There was a time when we had been in more equal places in life, and it made sense. Two people living lives that were not exactly on the up and up. We were alone in the world and had bonded over loving a life of mild chaos as young people. But we were not those same two people anymore. At least I wasn't. Elliot may have still wanted this life, and if anything, to go even deeper, while I wanted out of it all and to make a good life for the baby that was going to come.

"Elliot might be up for working for you, but I don't deal in your world," I said, crossing my arms over my chest, which was a little hard to do with my large belly. The look that Elliot gave me was an anger I had very rarely seen during our relationship. I tried to stay out of his path, never taking the last of his booze or moving anything of his because of the explosive nature of his anger, so for the last year or so, none of that anger had been directed at me. I had found a way to avoid being the target of his rage and thought I could maintain it until I could find a means to leave him behind once our child was a little older.

Now I knew if I didn't take this, if I didn't do whatever job it was that the O'Sheas needed from me, I was no longer safe. *We* were no longer safe.

"That's surprising," Freddy said, glancing at Elliot. "Elliot made it seem like you'd be happy to help me with whatever it was that I needed."

"What is it you need?" I asked, narrowing my eyes. I already knew it was bad. If they needed my expertise, it would be far worse than the normal work I did. I was a White Hat, I *helped.* I wasn't in the business of ruining people's lives.

"There's a girl we need to acquire, and we think your skills may be able to help us get out hands on her," Freddy said, his smile grim.

My lip curled in disgust, and I opened my mouth to tell him exactly where he could shove his needs, when Elliot slammed the glass he had been drinking from down on the quartz countertop, causing it to break and stalked over to me.

"Give me one minute," Elliot said, voice nearly shaking with his temper as he grabbed my arm, yanking it hard enough I could feel my bones protest, and dragged me back into the bedroom.

Freddy knew exactly what he did to me. He could hear it. There was no way he didn't hear my cries, the way I pleaded with Elliot to stop, or he'd hurt the baby.

This was the moment I knew that no matter what he did to me, good or bad, from this moment forward, I couldn't forget that I had to escape, and I had to put the skills I had built my life on down if I was ever going to know safety for the baby I was bringing into this world.

THREE YEARS LATER

The door closed with a snap; the deadbolt sliding into place right after, like that would somehow keep me from leaving. Elliot thought I was asleep. He was heading out to try to "network," he said, which was really just what he called going to the clubs and bars owned by the various organized crime groups in the city and trying his hand at getting further up the lowest rung he had been on for years. He wasn't even affiliated with any one group, just a lackey they all knew they could use, usually not even paying him in cash, instead giving him portions of drugs or merchandise that he could try to sell on his own—not in their territory, of course, he'd have to travel for that.

The good news was he'd be gone for many hours, plenty of time for me to put my plan in place. I didn't have much left of the emergency cash I had gained and stashed away before Nora was born, but I had just enough to pay for the things I needed, a car and documents, with a little left over to feed us and live on until we got to our destination. The plan was simple. Joe, a man leaving one of the Mafias, who I had come across when trying to find someone to make new documentation for myself and Nora, was also trying to get out of the life. He knew it was only a matter of time before he would be considered of no use, but he knew too much about whichever organization he was in to just be *let go*. He decided to help me, and I would be meeting him with Nora in my arms in exactly twenty minutes for us to go through with stage two of my plan.

Stage one had already begun.

With Elliot leaving, it was only a quick message to Joe on the burner phones I got last week, pulling out the bags I had hidden that held only essentials for Nora and myself, before slipping out the door for stage two.

Nora was still asleep in my arms, noise-canceling headphones in place as they had been when I put her to bed to keep her from being roused. She was a good sleeper, but I didn't need her waking and making this even more difficult. A three-year-old awake and asking questions would only make all of this harder, and I needed these first stages to go smoothly, otherwise we would never get out.

My heart beat against my ribcage like it would rather leap out than stay in the confines of my chest, sweat beaded on my hairline, not helped by the scarf I had tied my hair up in. The red of my hair could be more easily spotted, Nora's too, but as long as anyone passing us by thought I was a brunette at first glance, Elliot wouldn't think anything of it if he caught wind of a woman leaving in the night.

Besides, Chicago was a busy place. Even if there were eyes everywhere, what did one random woman and child need to be watched for?

Joe stood at the abandoned cluster of buildings we had agreed on when setting our final plans in place. He was leaning against a car. Older, perhaps in his fifties, but by no means out of shape, his gray hair almost illuminated him in the yellow streetlight a few parking spaces away.

"You made it," he said, quickly flicking his cigarette away and pushing off the car, face full of surprise as he saw me getting closer.

"I did. He's like clockwork and he would never think I'd leave," I murmured, moving to put Nora in the back seat and buckle her in. There was a moment of panic when she seemed to be stirring, but I put the stuffed animal at her shoulder, letting her head easily slump there, and she went back to sleep in an instant.

"We have about four and a half hours to go before our first stop," he rushed out as I sprinted around to the passenger side of the car and got in.

Stage two complete, with us successfully meeting and not being stopped as we made our way out of the main city and onto the highway that would take us south and west.

Stage three was the drive.

I had never driven for such a long time in complete silence, but it gave me time to think about the next steps. Joe and I weren't friends. This was simply two people, both needing to escape. He had connections to purchase the car; I had skills to make new identities for us online and in systems to be certain we wouldn't have trouble wherever it was we decided to go, while he could leave the city to procure the documentation needed for that as well. This was a partnership for this single endeavor, and I hoped once we went our separate ways, I'd never see him again. Never hear from him again. Because if I did, then something was very, very wrong.

It was at the stop in St. Louis, Missouri, four and a half hours later, that he solidified that for me.

"I'm an old man, Ingrid. If you're hearing from me again, it's not because of something good."

The way he said that made the hair on the back of my neck stand up. No, if he contacted me, that would mean they were after us. I had no delusions that Elliot would lose it when he discovered we had left. I wouldn't have been surprised to hear he got himself killed doing something reckless. But it was the slight against the Irish that was concerning to me. Three years ago, I had turned them down, told them I wouldn't help them, and because of that, Elliot lost out on getting a place within their ranks. If he felt bitter enough about my leaving, he could very well try to sic them after me in order to claim that spot he had lost out on. Because if I was willing to leave him, then he would rather me used and dead.

He had said as much to me before.

"Then I hope I never do," I told Joe, taking the keys from his hands and watching as he walked off down the road away from the gas station we had stopped at.

I watched him far longer than I probably should have, feeling as if this was yet another piece of the old life, the old me, I was letting slip away. That was the last man I would ever trust. The last man I would let know anything about me they could use. Joe was the last string, and we just agreed to cut it. With a shake of my head, I slipped into the driver's seat, adjusting it so my much smaller form could see everything appropriately, before pulling away and heading farther west.

Four more hours or so to go and we would meet our final destination. Not a big city, but a suburb of one. Someplace that was big enough to not be noticed, but small enough to be overlooked as an option for someone who thought they knew me and where I would go. Still had to be in the Midwest, so I could blend in and so could Nora.

I didn't have a job lined up or a place for us to stay, but that didn't matter. I would find a way to get us where we needed to be. I would know it the moment I saw it … right?

Nora woke up about an hour from where we would be stopping, her eyes blearing in the mirror and looking confused as she pulled the headphones from her ears.

"Mama…?" The question in her sleepy little voice was heartbreaking.

"We needed to go, Nora. Daddy had other things that were more important, so we are going somewhere better for us," I said, my eyes flicking from the road before me to the mirror and back repeatedly with concern. I would happily pull this car over to comfort her if I needed to, but I much more liked the idea of staying the course, at least until we got to the suburb, and I could find us a place to stay for the night.

Nora sat, her brow furrowing, clearly her little brain was processing the information I had just given her. After several very tense, long minutes, her eyes shot to mine in the mirror.

"Good. Daddy should stay far away."

The finality of her words as well as the way she crossed her arms and immediately tore her gaze to the swiftly passing scenery told me how serious she was. A three-year-old didn't just say things like that about their other parent. My child had, unfortunately, had to come to know that her father was not a good person very early. He was no great loss to her.

We made it to Lee's Summit, a suburb, but a decently sized one of Kansas City. Gang and organized crime activity were fairly low here, and it was very unassuming with people of all class levels. The motel I had chosen to stay at was cheap, but wasn't nearly as unsavory as some of the ones I knew back in Chicago. This would do just fine until I found better accommodations for us.

I had done research, of course, into the area I wanted to stay and businesses I might try to find a job. Daycare would be an expense, but there were a few preschools in the school district that I could get Nora into late. I just needed an address to be able to enroll her and a job to pay the rent.

A few days of scouting, and I would hopefully be able to find what I needed. That was the first and most important goal. So Nora and I went day after day, looking and applying for job after job in the neighborhood we needed to be in. I noted apartments that were close by that had vacancies, but knew I wouldn't be able to get one without a job to back me up quickly. I still had some funds, but I didn't have enough to feel comfortable about putting in an application for an apartment until I knew I had more cash coming in soon.

I started to feel rather desperate after the fifth day. If I couldn't make this work, I had no idea what I was going to do. I couldn't have done more preparations than I had before we left Elliot, because he would have caught wind of that. I was starting to panic, even if Nora was being an absolute trooper and never doubting me as I took her from place-to-place, day after day.

The one place I seemed to keep coming back to, one I hadn't actually gone in yet, was a coffee shop. It was nestled just beside a little strip mall that held a bar, a gym, and a few other small shops. There wasn't a sign saying they were hiring, but I assumed places like coffee shops usually were, at least for part-time work. I could probably use this as a starting point, keep a little bit of part-time money flowing in while I looked for something else, if they were hiring.

I wasn't sure what kept drawing me back there, especially since I hadn't even set foot inside. Something about the name of the place was familiar, as if it was mentioned to me in passing at some point, but I had no idea when or why that would have been the case. As I sat there, watching the patrons come in and out, the friendly signs in the windows, and the homey feeling it gave me, I couldn't help the urge to get out of the car.

Nora clung to my front like a monkey as I made my way from the car into the shop. A little bell chimed as I pushed the glass door open, the scent of pastries and coffee hit my nose, the air was humid and warm, and a strange rightness fell over me as I moved farther in.

"Good morning!" came the cheery voice of the older woman at the counter. A girl a few years younger than me stood on the other side of the espresso machine, grinning as she was steaming some milk for the drink she was making.

"Morning," I said back, making my way up to the counter.

"What can I get for you?"

I wasn't one who liked asking for help. I took care of myself. I always had, and now I had Nora to take care of too. But other than explaining that I was a single parent to the rest of these jobs I had applied to, something about this woman with her salt and pepper hair that curled around her head, the warm brown of her eyes and the wide inviting smile made me want to spill everything to her.

Thankfully I had enough sense to not tell her *everything*, quickly swallowing the tide of emotion and raw information and clearing my throat.

"I-I was actually wondering if you had a job opening. I know there's no sign, but I was hoping… well, I-I—"

Her brows came together with concern and instead of cutting me off or telling me no, she moved around the counter, taking my hand and pulling me toward the nearest vacant table.

"Carmen, could you get this little one here a treat and a coffee for Miss…?"

"Ingrid," I said, letting Nora settle in my lap and turn around to face out. "This is Nora."

"Hello, Nora. I'm Liliana," the woman said, holding out her hand and waiting patiently as Nora reached hers out with hesitation, before shaking it briefly. "So, Ingrid. You need a job?"

"Yes. I just ran from a bad situation. I don't have anything really. I need a job to be able to get an apartment and get Nora in preschool."

That was enough. I didn't need to expand on it and tell her exactly how bad my situation had been. Right? Hopefully?

The way she looked at me, kindly scrutinizing, made me want to squirm a little, I glanced around, also feeling like someone else was watching me. For only a moment, I glanced and saw a man by the front door, unabashedly staring in our direction.

"You know, I have been meaning to get another full-time person. I need more time to take care of a few other things and bringing you on would help a great deal. Have you ever worked in a coffee shop before?"

"I did in high school. It was quite a while ago, but as long as espresso machines haven't changed much, I'm sure I can pick it up really fast."

"Perfect. You'll start tomorrow. Nora can come with you at first. I'll give you training pay, which will help with putting a deposit down on an apartment, and then we'll make sure to get Nora in preschool here so you can start working full-time once your training is over."

The no-nonsense way she said everything, taking charge, and giving me everything, all the things I needed to make sure this escape was a success in one quick statement, made me nearly shiver. That pull to come in here had clearly been driving me in the right direction.

"I–I don't know what to say," I said, flabbergasted by her generosity.

"You don't need to say anything at all. I can tell that there's something about you. Something that will be the missing piece to our little puzzle here."

Carmen came by with the coffee and the treat for Nora, grinning at me as she did so.

An hour later, Nora and I stood to leave, we were full. All my new employee paperwork was filled out as well as a schedule she had written down for me. I turned around and that's when my eyes locked with the man I had felt staring at me earlier. His eyes were also a warm brown, and he had a similar nose to Liliana's. I could tell, despite him sitting at the table with his coffee and a laptop in front of him that he was tall, and muscular too, despite the dress shirt and slacks he was sporting. His mouth turned up into a smile as well, but this time it was more of a smirk.

His eyes danced with delight as I felt the heat rush to my cheeks, a sure sign of a blush. I forced a better smile than the one I was truly capable of on my lips for his benefit. I had no idea what kind of person he was, but it was much easier to tell myself I could blush and smile back at someone, because I was never going to let anyone come any closer to me than that.

That didn't mean those brown eyes weren't featured in my dreams for a very long time following though.

CHAPTER 2

ENZO

My heart thudded against my ribcage, blood whooshing in my ears as I watched the CCTV footage of Adrian LaMartina being shot in the alley behind the hotel. Time seemed to slow. This whole thing had been chaos. A nightmare. Here we were, infiltrating a mob rehearsal dinner, trying to steal the bride away the day before she would be married to Freddy O'Shea, the heir to the O'Shea clan.

Adrian's body went down like a brick. I couldn't see him from the camera angle anymore and it only made the sick feeling in my stomach get heavier. Not a moment after I watched it happen did I hear my brother, Sal, screaming through our comms, demanding to know if Adrian was okay. Sal was in another location. It was only the LaMartina brothers that had gone into the alley. A last-ditch effort to get Freddy to hand over their sister, Carmen, before us Lupos had to truly get involved. Because once we did this, once any one of us Lupos actually crossed the line with the O'Sheas, we essentially were declaring war.

It didn't matter either way though. We were getting Carmen back. The LaMartinas were ours. Our brothers and sister, perhaps not through blood, but that didn't really matter. And my brother Leo was in love with Carmen. It was not a fleeting love, but one that could never compare to any other. The way he had changed so fundamentally from the joyful and fun boy I had known for his whole life to this monster of despair when she was taken from us made my own heart break.

I couldn't imagine loving someone so desperately, finally having them, and then watching them being torn away by a rival. The fiery, red hair and light blue eyes of the woman I loved flashed through my mind. I envisioned the same thing happening to her, being taken by the Irish or some other group we weren't allies with, pain and fear in her eyes, and me just out of reach to be able to stop it from happening. Ingrid was the woman I loved, but also was someone I could never sully with my life and what came with it. She was outside of this seedy darkness that was organized crime. Carmen also wasn't supposed to be part of the life, and up until then, Leo hadn't wanted to be any part of it either, but it didn't matter. We were all sewn into the fabric of the Mafia, whether we liked it or not. I didn't want that for Ingrid.

Seeing Adrian go down like that was akin to watching Leo himself get gunned down, but it was only a moment later that we got confirmation Adrian was alright. Simultaneously, I saw a strange flicker in the code I had used to access the camera I was watching all of this go down on. I let my eyes barely glance over it for a moment, seeing the clear tampering for access, not to the same footage I was watching, but access to *me*.

I didn't have time to dive into sussing out who it could be that was taking note of my actions. I needed to be watching, helping my brothers navigate the streets of Chicago so they could get Carmen back, because Freddy and his half-brother Jeremy had forced her into their car and were now escaping the back alley, heading… well, we weren't sure where.

This wasn't the first time in this weeks-long mission I had seen something like this. Someone was watching my online presence. It had to be someone outside of our situation, but they were watching as I hacked the Irish and they were watching me as I hacked system after system to have real-time information on Carmen's location for my brothers to follow.

This hacker was probably a White Hat, someone who used their skills for "good." A lot of White Hat hackers would approach large companies with the faults in their systems, perhaps giving them ways to resolve holes in their encryptions and firewalls to make them more secure for a fee. Not much better than blackmail, though I had known some to have transitioned into blackmail hackers since the price tag was often much higher.

But this White Hat was dancing in dangerous waters. Though everything, or most things for the O'Shea clan, went through the legitimate company Stately Enterprises, it was still a cover for their very illegal and much more lucrative business. I assumed this hacker hadn't actually looked at what I had been discovering about the O'Sheas, because if they had, they would have known they should turn away and not come back. Soliciting and blackmailing the mob may as well have been putting a gun to their own head.

Later.

Later, I would find this hacker, pull them off this before they could approach O'Shea and hopefully spare a naïve meddler before they got caught up in something they couldn't get themselves out of.

For now, my thoughts had to remain present. The lives of the five most important people in my life were in my hands. And as I gave the instructions to Sal and Leo, listening to the gunfire and the crash that followed, the hacker fell from my mind.

EIGHT MONTHS LATER

"Why are you here so early?" the familiar voice came from my left and below me, but I didn't stop the screw I was turning to look. I knew her voice, and I honestly had known the sound of her footfalls as she approached, however quiet they may have been. If Ash was here, that meant it was about 6:00 a.m., and I had been here for over two hours.

"Cameras," I said gruffly. I had been awake for roughly twenty-two hours now, which made a lot of sense considering the way my eyes were starting to strain as I had been working.

"You could update the cameras anytime, you know," she said, a bit of a bite to the humor in her voice.

Ash was the main trainer at the gym that my older brother Sal and his best friend Adrian owned. She had been given a raise and more responsibilities lately, given the two of them had been a lot busier. In the past, Adrian would have been the first person there, but now Ash had that honor. She seemed happy with the arrangement at first, but now I could tell there was more weighing on her. Was it the added pressure Sal and Adrian put on her, or something else?

I wish I had time to check up on it, but I already had too many irons in the fire to go snooping around employees' lives to make sure they were doing okay.

"It couldn't wait," I said, finally looking down at her from the ladder I stood on and giving her the tired version of my cheeky grin.

I wasn't going to tell her the cameras went down across our network just as Adrian and my younger brother, Leo went into a meeting the night before with a representative from a small group of men within the Italian Mafia wanting to take over the territory now that it was in a sort of limbo.

The system came back up in time for me to witness quite a beatdown, nothing in the system had been breached, but the gym cameras remained unresponsive for some reason, and I wasn't one to sit by and let a hole in our security remain there until operating hours. Adrian and Sal kept some sensitive information in the office, not to mention there was no way to make sure our employees were safe upon arrival.

I had done a sweep of the property with Paolo, one of our guardsmen, and then set to work replacing the now fried system.

Ash didn't seem like she cared to ask any more questions, and for that I was grateful. The last thing I needed was Sal's and Adrian's anger because I revealed too much to her, even if I knew she was fairly aware of the type of business we were involved with. Ash wasn't stupid. She knew what went down with Carmen, that she had been stolen by a rival, but Ash was choosing to stay just on the fringe.

I may not have been as much of a figure within our *community* as my brothers were as far as our family business was concerned, but that didn't make the safety of our people outside the realm of my responsibilities. Even replacing cameras was something I'd never bat an eye at, especially since I didn't particularly trust anyone else to do it for me.

In fact, it was my whole job to maintain the security of our assets, our money, and our people. I was head of cyber security and all the online and computer dealings for the whole of our businesses, the main business being my brother Sal's position as *almost* Caporegime for the big boss of the Italian Mafia in the United States, Manzo Morelli. As such, I could have sent someone else, Paolo, even, to replace these cameras, but since Sal had been trying to secure this position as Capo, it felt wrong to see trouble and not be physically there for it. Everything needed to run as smoothly as possible, or we could be facing catastrophic failure. In our line of work, that meant death.

And yet, part of my haste to get the cameras replaced was because one particular camera on the exterior aimed directly at another of the businesses we owned. The coffee shop. Not only was the coffee shop run by our mother, but I may have had a particularly vested interest in a certain woman who worked there. I wasn't deluded, thinking I didn't have an obsession. I certainly did, but that obsession kept me simultaneously keeping as close an eye as possible on her, as well as keeping my distance.

Ingrid Jacobs was a single mother and a dedicated worker who had escaped a bad situation before coming to the suburb of Lee's Summit three years prior with her toddler. I knew from the moment I lay eyes on her, no one else would ever compare. And thus far, no one had. But because of her closed-off, hesitant nature—which was completely understandable—I only allowed myself to be there for her at the distance she set, which, apparently, meant making sure even when she parked in the lot adjacent to the shop or the alley behind it, I had unfettered video evidence that she was alright.

I made the finishing touches, climbing down from the ladder and folding it up to put it back in storage, when the two men we had scheduled to watch over the gym pulled up in front.

"If Ash is already here, you're late," I said to Roman, who had the unfortunate luck of being the first one to the door.

"She gets here so early," Roman whined, pausing in the open doorway as Joey breezed past him, clearly avoiding me. I wasn't as scary as my brothers or Adrian usually, but apparently, the seriousness in my tone, and perhaps the way I looked, given I was still in sweats and my hair was rumpled from racing from my house in the early hours of the morning to change these cameras, was enough to make them cower. I didn't normally dress this way, but since our father's death, the requirements now on Sal and therefore the rest of us, made many things abnormal.

"I don't care, Roman. If Adrian or Sal knew she walked in here alone, how do think they'd react?"

The color drained from his face, eyes going wide at the possibility there. Yeah, if either of them knew this had occurred, Roman and Joey would be in an unfathomable amount of trouble, especially given who they were supposed to be protecting. It was one thing for the guards to not pay as much attention when Sal and Adrian had been regular fixtures at the gym themselves, but now that the business was taking them both to Kansas City more often, they were counting on their men to be as present as they would have been.

As if my thoughts had summoned him, Sal pulled up in front of the gym too. He also looked like he hadn't slept, but then again, when two of ours were out in particularly harrowing situations, it was hard for any of us to sleep.

"I assume they made it back okay if you're here?" I asked, looking over at my brother as he strode to where I stood, his suit rumpled, presumably from wearing it all night and his hair more mussed than usual.

"They did," Sal said tiredly.

"So why are you here?"

It was a little unusual for Sal to come to Lee's Summit alone, especially this early in the morning, and I was usually told about all his plans for security or scrubbing CCTV footage reasons.

"I just needed to check something," Sal said, his eyes flicking to where Ash had just come out of the office holding the till that was kept in the safe. I remembered when she first was being allowed to open and close, that she questioned the safe within a safe, but had since dropped it. The big safe held the important documents for the gym, the smaller one within it held documents that were better left secret.

It could be a rather tricky thing, making sure the people who worked for us but weren't in the life were kept in the dark about our dealings. I was very certain that Ash knew enough to put the pieces together, and certainly how Ash met Sal gave away who we associated with regularly. In the past, she had made comments here and there and clearly knew that there were things she was kept out of. That was for the best, even if she didn't see it that way.

"I'll be right back. I want to hear about the surveillance system outage, so don't try to slip away," Sal said, focusing back on me with a look that would have struck fear in almost anyone else, but I had grown up with this man, that look had been honed after years of being dominated by our terror inducing father. The worst I would ever get from Sal would be harsh words and perhaps a punch, if I really deserved it.

"I'm surprised to see you here so early, Sal. Has Adrian been slacking enough that the boss has to come get his hands dirty?" Ash asked as he walked past the counter where she was setting up for the day's business.

"Just need to make sure none of our employees are trying to land a rabbit on us," Sal said, slowing enough to give her a pointed look. Well, *that* piqued my interest. Sal using fighting slang in front of our martial arts instructor to suggest something was up with her, was very interesting indeed.

Normally, Ash was the one saying clever things that shut up Adrian and Sal. She knew they both had something of a crush on her and loved using their frustrations against them. But this time it was Ash who closed up like a clam. Something was going on with her, and him mentioning a rabbit punch with that meaningful gleam in his eye, let her know Sal knew about it.

He disappeared into the office, leaving Ash to let out a long breath, resuming her organizing of the counter for the day; but I couldn't let that go.

"What was that, Ash?" I asked, coming up to lean on the counter. Unlike my brother and Adrian, Ash had no superpowers to lay against me.

"Nothing. You Lupos and LaMartinas should remember not everything, or everyone, is under your purview," she snapped, glaring at me.

Ash was a formidable fighter. It had been Sal and Adrian who saw her at an underground fight club years ago and offered her a job training at the gym. She hadn't been fighting since then, except for exhibition matches that were set up through the higher-end clientele of the Italian Mafia. Such fights were much better at protecting the fighters than underground matches, but the frequency was less, so despite the large payouts from fighting and winning in those matches, I could tell Ash had been itching to get back into the rings that she knew before.

"I'm not asking as a Lupo, Ash. Or at least, not a *Lupo.* I'm asking as a friend and as Sal's brother," I said, putting my more comical demeanor aside. Her hard look softened a little, but she shook her head, clearly not wanting to talk.

"What about you? Rushing over here first thing in the morning to fix the cameras? Couldn't be that one of those cameras points directly at the coffee shop, could it?"

Ash seemed to be able to pick up on things much better than everyone assumed. It was silly, honestly, given her fighting background, that anyone would assume she didn't see the subtle clues about our more lucrative business quite well. But it wasn't like I kept my feelings for Ingrid a secret. Everyone seemed to know how I felt about her, except maybe Ingrid herself.

"I don't know what you're talking about," I said, letting a little smirk quirk up in the corner of my mouth. She smiled back.

"She's not defenseless, you know. I've been giving her and Nora a little training here and there."

That surprised me. Not that Ingrid being active was a shock, her body was amazing, if anything I wanted to unwrap her from those clothes to see the beauty of it even more, a fantasy I had been having since I saw her and a frequent start to some of my most treasured dreams. What bothered me was that I hadn't known about it.

"What?"

"She gives me free coffee and I give her and Nora lessons at the gym after hours sometimes. It's not super frequent, because she has that other job now, but we've been practicing for a couple years," Ash said, glancing over at the mats and hanging bags, as if she was imagining Ingrid's fist hitting that bag. I certainly was.

"You get free coffee anyway, Ash," I said, trying to get her to keep talking about it while I tried to make sense of how I didn't know this before. I kept a pretty good watch on all the cameras. I supposed after hours I didn't often look too closely, and Ash staying late wasn't abnormal.

"Yes, but I always tip anyway. You tip, don't you, Enzo?"

My gaping mouth expression was enough to get her to laugh, and despite my wanting to ask her more questions, and avoid the fact that, no I had not been tipping for my entire life getting free coffee at my mother's shop, it didn't matter much anyway, Sal reemerged from the office, tucking something in the inner pocket of his suit jacket.

"Have a good day, boys," Ash said, her expression going back to its usual tease as she looked at Sal.

"Oh, I will," I said with a wink, making Sal scowl before we made our way out to the parking lot. Teasing and play-flirting with Ash was spectacularly fun to do in front of Adrian and Sal. It always made both of their faces tense with pent-up frustration that they apparently had decided to do nothing about. I just simply couldn't help myself when the opportunity arose.

"So what happened with the cameras?" Sal asked as we walked toward the coffee shop. There was no need to drive there. The distance wasn't too far, and it gave us an opportunity to talk without many ears around to listen.

"The outage was an attack. I haven't traced it yet, because by the time I got everything back up and made sure we weren't breached further, I noticed the cameras at the gym weren't coming back up," I told him, feeling the weight of his eyes on me as I pressed forward a little quicker.

"Is that what your plan is today? To track it?"

"It's on the list. I still have to scrub the footage of Adrian, Leo, and the cleanup crew. And I need to keep up with the O'Shea's new person," I said, gritting my teeth a little as I thought about my latest obsessive task.

Whoever had been O'Shea's cyber security last summer had probably been *dealt* with following the initial breach I made to get into their systems. It had been one of the biggest reasons that we got Carmen LaMartina back. Carmen was the youngest of the three LaMartina children who we grew up with. Adrian, Benny, and Carmen were essentially our bonus siblings, since our mothers were best friends, and we grew up next door to one another. When Carmen was taken last year by the Irish to act as some sort of sacrificial lamb for an alliance between our father and Colin O'Shea, we decided enough was enough, and did whatever we had to do to bring Carmen back to us, and to my little brother Leo, who she was now engaged to. We even killed our father for it.

But now O'Shea had a new person running their cyber security, someone who had previously disappeared from the web for three solid years. Before they disappeared, I had been obsessed with how good they were, watching in amazement at how flawlessly they could hack into something, seeing weaknesses in code I wouldn't have caught back then. I had watched and learned from this hacker, my skills getting much better over the years they had been away, and now here we were, going toe to toe against one another on a regular basis. To say I wasn't pleased to be testing my skills against one of the most renowned hackers on the dark web would be a complete and utter lie, but it also came with quite a bit of frustration.

"Ah, yes. No wonder you look like you never sleep anymore," Sal said with a grin, his eyes sparkling with restrained laughter at my expense.

"You don't look much better," I shot back with narrowed eyes, gaining a chuckle from him.

"We just need to secure a few more things and I think it will be irrefutable that I should be Capo," Sal said, running his hand through his hair nervously.

We just didn't need anything else going wrong for us. One attack or loss in our growing power could be the small pin that tipped us from being on top to costing us our lives and all the people we held dear. No one was safe until we firmly established Sal's leadership and received the full backing of Manzo Morelli.

"We'll do it. But maybe we could all work a little sleep in here and there," I said, slinging my arm over his shoulders as we finally made our way to the front doors of the shop. He gave me a tired smile and leaned into me a little more.

My heart hammered in my chest at the proximity. I knew what would be waiting on the other side of this door, a woman who I couldn't get enough of, even if she gave very little. I'd take anything she had to offer me though. And that feeling only solidified as the bell chimed and we walked through, only to have my vision obscured by the line of people clustering close to the counter. Sasha was there, smiling brightly as she took orders, but she wasn't the woman I wanted to see. No, it was that fiery red hair that was peeking over the top of the machines she was using that caught my attention.

CHAPTER 3

INGRID

"That color looks beautiful on you."

I looked up, expecting the person to be talking to Sasha, my coworker, who was in her early twenties, fresh out of college, and, of course, stunningly beautiful. She was at the register, getting the orders while I was busy behind the espresso machine, making the actual drinks. This was my preferred station, even when Carmen had worked here. I liked being the one making the orders, instead of the one talking to customers. Not that the regulars didn't talk to me anyway. After three years of working at this coffee shop, it was easy to speak to the ones you saw every day, whose orders and preferences you knew like the back of your hand, but I wasn't very personable otherwise.

But it wasn't Sasha who the man was speaking to, but me.

My eyebrows shot up in surprise as I looked at him. Business suit, well put together in his attire for work on this early morning. He was nice enough to look at too, probably my age or a little older, but even if he was someone in the right demographics to give a second glance to, I was not wanting attention like this. I didn't have time, nor did I care to dip my toe into the risk involved with letting another person into my life.

"Thank you," I murmured stiffly, turning my focus back to the latte I had been making. His latte, I assumed, since he wasn't at the register anymore.

"You know," the man started, leaning against the counter, clearly trying to get closer to my general vicinity. "I feel like I know you from somewhere."

I fought the instinct to roll my eyes.

"Interesting. I have no idea where," I deadpanned, keeping my eyes on the slow drip of espresso into the shot glasses instead of his eager gaze.

"Well, maybe I could get your number, and we can chat about it later when you aren't so busy."

"I don't give out my number to strangers," I said, making the mistake of looking up at him, only to see him smile widely. It reminded me of the way a predator would stare at his prey. I had seen that look before. I could see how some women might find it disarming, but it just put me on edge. I wasn't some lamb to be taken care of or taken advantage of, but my meek appearance often had people misjudging me as weak.

"Greg Thompson," he said, reaching his hand over the counter and espresso machine awkwardly to shake. "And you are?"

I turned the steamer on, the sound drowning out everything else around me. I didn't acknowledge his gesture, but he didn't seem to care, continuing to hold out that hand and smile. As soon as the milk was steamed, I turned away to finish the latte, but he was still there, not taking any of my not-so-subtle hints.

"Your latte, Greg," I said, placing it on the counter. Thankfully, he had withdrawn his hand, but he still had that stupid grin on his face.

"Ingrid, right?" he asked, gesturing to the name tag on my apron. "So we aren't strangers now. You know my name and I know yours," he said as I withdrew my hands from his cup before he could try to touch me. It was too busy in this place for him to try anything overt, but he was making my skin crawl. Why was it always the aggressive and creepy men that seemed to be attracted to me? It was like they had some sixth sense that I was going to say no, and they saw it as a challenge.

Unfortunately for them, that was a challenge they would never win.

"I'm good. Have a nice day," I said, trying to force a smile, but I was certain it came out less friendly and more like a grimace. His smile seemed to melt from his face, a scowl quickly taking its place. I knew I was going to have to start being overtly rude if he didn't drop it. Not something I wanted to do, given I had to come back and work here, but Liliana, the owner of the shop, wouldn't bat an eye at me defending myself from a pushy man like this.

"Why don't you just—" he began, his voice clearly gaining an edge with his frustration, but he was cut off by a voice just behind him.

"I think you should just take your drink and head out." 6:30 a.m. was a little early for Enzo Lupo to be in the coffee shop, but he came in nearly every day. As regular as the sunrise, that one, and I found I counted on it, which was not a good sign.

Greg whipped around at the sound of Enzo's voice, finding the imposing figures of the oldest two Lupo men behind him, towering over his frame. Both Sal and Enzo had to be over six feet tall, and so was their younger brother, Leo. Enzo was the shortest of the three, but that didn't mean he didn't tower over me. He wasn't as bulky with muscles as his brothers, who clearly worked out regularly; he was leaner. But he was in no way out of shape, I realized as I took in the tighter-fitting knit shirt and loose joggers he was sporting instead of his normal attire. The muscles in his arms may not have been huge, but they were defined, so was his chest.

Between the fiery look in his eyes as he glared at Greg and the just-rolled-out-of-bed attire, I was surprised my mouth wasn't hanging open in shock and immediate desire. I felt the blush creeping to my cheeks and forced myself to look at the back of Greg's head instead. It didn't matter if Enzo had been the subject of my fantasies for years; *he* couldn't know that.

"I can do whatever I want," Greg snapped back at Enzo, clearly irritated, but instead of walking away as a smart person would have, he merely leaned his back against the counter, crossing his arms and taking a sip of the latte in his hand.

"Well, Greg, I'm fairly certain that this lady didn't want to talk to you. I'm not sure what country you're from, but here, we listen to the ladies when they try to end a conversation. Clearly, if you didn't pick up on that, you're a creep," Enzo continued, stepping more into Greg's personal space.

"I wasn't being creepy. I just wanted to get to know her better. Isn't that right, Ingrid? We're just becoming friends?"

I let my eyes travel to meet Enzo's. He was looking at me with those deep brown orbs, an eyebrow raising in question, clearly asking me if I wanted him to take this further. I could only shake my head no, because I wasn't sure I could form words now.

"I don't think she wants to be friends," Enzo said, the corner of his mouth quirking up, giving me a wink that made my blush that much deeper when Greg turned back to me.

"Ingrid, if you'd just give me your—"

"She's not giving you her number," Enzo snapped, stepping even closer, so now the height difference was far more noticeable, since Greg, having turned back to look at him, had to crane his head up to see the fuming Italian. "You need to go."

"I—"

"We own this establishment, and you're pissing off my brother here, so I think—if you don't want blood all over that nice suit of yours—you should probably make your exit and get to work. That's where you're headed, isn't it?" Sal asked, his words both cutting through and adding to the tension that had now caused the whole shop to go silent. The line had come to a standstill and Sasha was gawking at the four of us just as much as the rest of the customers.

"I-I'm sorry," Greg stuttered, pressing his back to the counter and sliding to the side to get away from the imposing figure of Enzo. "I'll just—"

"Please, just go," Sal said, now reaching up to pinch the bridge of his nose, as if the man being flustered irritated him more than anything.

The jingle of the door opening and closing echoed around the quieted shop. Enzo and I stood there and looked at each other for a few long moments as the noise picked back up with Sasha taking orders and customers going back to their conversations, but I couldn't be bothered to look at the orders I should have been making, not when Enzo, sweet, funny Enzo, was looking at me like he wanted to both wrap me in his arms and protect me, while simultaneously devour me … in a good way.

It was a look I had only gotten in fleeting moments before. Now, it seemed like it would last forever if I let it. Even though I shouldn't have, I wanted him to look at me that way.

"Thank you," I said, finally finding my voice and glancing at Sal for a moment. Sal nodded at me before I turned my eyes back to Enzo. The break in eye contact usually was what made that look fall from his face, but this time, when I looked back into those brown orbs, it was still there. A deep hunger woke something buried inside me.

"We just thought we'd grab a coffee. We're getting back in line, aren't we Enzo?" Sal asked, though his tone let on that it was not a suggestion, grabbing Enzo by the t-shirt sleeve and tugging him toward the now very long line. Enzo's gaze fell away, and I took in a deep, shaky breath, trying my best to get my heart to stop pounding as I began making the drinks Sasha had rung up.

While advances like Greg's were irritating and disgusting, any attention from Enzo seemed to set me on fire. I wasn't sure what it was about him. Perhaps it was the fact that since I had moved here and started working for his mother, Liliana, he had been present and attentive, but never pushy.

And he flirted with me.

At first, it was just jokes, clear attempts to make me smile and get to know me better, but as time passed, it had moved to overt flirtation. I flirted back, of course, but I couldn't delude myself into thinking this would ever become anything more than the back-and-forth it had always been. At least, I hadn't thought so until he looked at me the way he had been just moments prior, defended me against the sleaze-ball, and got my heart rate up in a way that made the breath force its way through my lungs into a pant as I tried to engross myself in my job.

I was just tired.

That had to be it.

My reactions were like this because I was exhausted, more so than my usual, and it couldn't be helped.

I had too much to worry about in my own life to bring another person into it. It was me and my daughter. No one else needed to be part of our little duo. We had already dealt with that. We had already escaped that. Enzo would have to remain a fantasy, because nothing between us could ever go further than what it already was.

The line dwindled until, finally, it was just Enzo and Sal's orders we were making. They both ordered black coffee, which I suspected was Enzo's usual when he wasn't here. On regular days, when he came in for coffee, he would order some strange and complicated monstrosity but would barely touch it. When he started ordering it, I had found it so odd and not in the character I had created for him in my mind, but now that I was pouring the steaming black brew into a to-go cup for him, I realized he must have had an ulterior motive for ordering those complicated espresso drinks from me.

That man always had some rationale behind everything he did.

"Not staying today?" I asked, having finally calmed myself down enough with staying busy, that I trusted myself to talk to him again.

"Unfortunately, I pulled an all-nighter, so I'm going to get a few more things done at home and then try to get a nap in." The darker-than-normal circles under his eyes and his attire and general tired appearance made a lot more sense. I knew he worked with computers—he always had his laptop when he came into the shop—I just wasn't sure what exactly he did. I assumed it had something to do with Sal's business, though that was fairly broad, given that Sal seemed to have inherited the ownership of several businesses from his father after he passed. It would be a lot of work to run the tech for all of these companies they ran. Cyber security alone was quite a job, let alone all the other things one had to deal with for a business.

"I know how that is," I murmured, having not gone to bed myself the night before. Just thinking about my other job and the fact that I had just murmured that out loud made me cringe.

"I'm sure Sasha could handle the rest of the day, if you wanted to skip out early and take a nap before picking Nora up from school." His words and expression were full of concern and sincerity, while my mind seemed to immediately go to a dirty place. Somehow my tired brain started running images of the two of us cuddled up on my couch, just intending to rest, but instead…

I'm certain I was blushing. His eyes twinkled, lips widening into a smile as he watched the color crawl up to my cheeks.

I felt like he could read my mind.

"I'll nap while Nora has her snack," I said with a nod, taking a step away from the counter that was between us, needing to physically distance myself from him. Whatever his appearance and that altercation with Greg did to me was crumbling very carefully laid walls that I had built up to protect myself and Nora. I definitely needed to get more sleep.

"You do that, Ingrid," he said, finally grabbing his cup with his large hands and uncharacteristically slipping a twenty into the tip jar before turning with Sal to head out the door.

"Oh my god, Ingrid," Sasha squealed before the door even closed. The shop was mostly empty now; the only few remaining stragglers were regulars who usually stuck around for an hour or so.

"Don't, Sasha," I said, already knowing what she was going to start babbling on about. She, like most people it seemed, based on the smiles on the regulars' faces—most notably Mary, who had put down her romance novel to watch—had immediately noticed how Enzo and I interacted with each other and was now going to be incessant about telling me how she felt about it.

"It's honestly like some regency romance. You two talk and flirt, he gets *jealous*, defends your honor, but you never touch," Sasha said with a sigh, following me back into the kitchen where I faked checking on some cookies that were not yet thawed enough from the freezer to throw in the oven.

"There's not some great romance going on there, Sasha. And it can never turn into one," I said, turning again, trying to get away from her back to the front, but she just followed, bouncing right along behind me with all the energy in the world.

"The way he looks at you, Ingrid!"

"It's not going to happen! Even if it did, one look at my naked body and he'd run for the hills," I said, gesturing to my wide hips, the extra weight at my stomach. I was curvy and, under the clothes, there were stretch marks and some loose skin from when I was pregnant with Nora. This wasn't a body that was desirable, especially not to a man like Enzo, who could have had any woman he wanted and probably did. That thought alone made an inferno of jealously rise up in me that I had to tamp down on before I looked at Sasha again.

"I think he'd like your body just fine," Sasha said with a wink, making my blush creep back and my momentarily imagined nap with Enzo return with a vengeance. At least he wasn't here to watch me this time.

"Not going to happen," I grumbled, trying to push that from my mind as I grabbed a rag to start wiping things down.

"We'll see!" Sasha practically sang as she skipped back into the kitchen to start getting things ready for the lunch and afternoon rush.

CHAPTER 4

ENZO

I did nap, but only after I had triple-checked that all the cameras were in working order and that I hadn't missed any breaches in my haste to rush to the gym that morning. My nap was brief, only a few hours, before I took a shower and decided that, though I had plenty of work I should have been doing with all of my monitors and tools at my disposal, the blush on one particular redhead was something I had to see one more time today.

So there I was, in my spot in the coffee shop, the table closest to the door, but facing it, with the window right beside me so I could best see the exterior and parking lot. I sat here for a reason; I had for years when I chose to spend time here. I needed the vantage point. In my and my brothers' line of work, it was, unfortunately, very possible that someone could come to any of the establishments we owned and wreak havoc on our employees and family members. But this had been a regular habit of mine for years. This spot had been mine for almost as long as I could remember, the bonus to having a "spot" in a coffee shop was the coffee, but for the last three years my frequent appearances here had been for a different reason, or partially a different reason.

I glanced over at the counter. Ingrid and Sasha were in the throes of the afternoon rush. Between 1:00 p.m. and 2:00 p.m. the coffee shop was brimming with customers before it dwindled down for the last few hours of the day prior to closing. Sasha was young and classically beautiful, but that wasn't who I could barely keep my eyes from gliding back to.

That red hair drew my gaze immediately for the second time that day. She effortlessly made drink after drink. The curls starting to escape the clip in her hair at the back of her head were absurdly attractive. I loved the way her blue eyes lit up when she smiled, but even more the sparkle of mischief in them when she smirked and teased me. Or the way that blush would move over her pale cheeks.

After that delicious blush earlier that morning, I couldn't stay away. I should have, but there was no resisting the draw I had to her.

For some people, love grew on them slowly over time, but for me, it had been like a thunderbolt of lightning the moment I saw her. She had captivated me from that very first glance and every day since then, I had been lost in it. Which was why I came here nearly every day, especially when I knew she was working.

Ingrid's eyes found mine past the crowd waiting for their drinks, pink blossoming on her cheeks when she saw me looking. I could only smirk in response. I didn't mind that she caught me. I felt like I had made my feelings rather clear over the three years I had known her, but she was the one always pushing me away.

It was probably for the best. Ingrid was a single mom who had more than her hands full, and I was a reformed playboy who was in the Mafia. Not quite the safest match for a woman like her. I also knew she had left her old life behind because she wanted a safer place for her and Nora. If I ever tried to cross that line or break that careful boundary she put in place, it would make her and Nora less safe, not more. She was already in jeopardy by simply being associated with my family by working at the shop.

I turned my head back to the computer in front of me, forcing myself not to watch her as I wanted to. I had plenty of work I needed to get done, and now that I was seeing how little I had accomplished during the daylight hours, I knew I'd be up all night again working on it. That wasn't the worst thing in the world. It would give me a little time to watch my other addiction, though this one was behind the screen, hiding in coding and on the dark web.

My phone rang from where it sat on the table beside me, Adrian's name popping up on the screen. Adrian, the oldest LaMartina, was essentially my brother anyway. We were all raised together, practically as one family with how close our moms were. Adrian and Sal were only a year different in age and very close, Adrian being Sal's second, and my younger brother Leo was the same age as the LaMartina's middle child, Benny. Growing up, I had always gone between the two groups. I learned to be extremely charismatic and funny in my youth because, unlike both of my brothers, I didn't have a built-in best friend like they did.

Not that I ever felt lacking, but that was probably at least part of the reason I turned to computers when I was younger. I dove into the internet headfirst as soon as I could, learning everything, and now there were very few in the world who could hold a candle to what I knew how to do with a code.

"Hey Adrian," I said after popping my Bluetooth headpiece in my ear and setting back to the algorithm I was working on. It was a trap essentially. Anyone who tried to get into my systems or track my actual activity on the dark web would end up exposing themselves to me. I needed a way to find out exactly what groups were targeting us. We already knew the O'Shea clan of the Irish Mob was after our heads—that was obvious after what we did do them last summer—but now that Sal hadn't been officially declared the Capo for this territory, we basically had a bullseye on all our heads. The territory was up for grabs, not only by other organized crime groups, but by those within our own organization wanting to secure a higher position.

"There's a meeting tonight. We're going to need footage scrubbed," Adrian said.

"I can do that. I'll be up working on something anyway," I said, suddenly wishing I had a second screen here so I could pull up the CCTV cameras at the site now instead of later. Coding in the middle of the coffee shop with my laptop was one thing; setting up a whole desktop situation so I could illegally look at security cameras was completely different.

"Anything new with the Irish on the internet side?" Adrian asked. He and Sal always asked, and I talked to one or both nearly every single day.

"Still no. Can you drop this subject for at least five to ten business days? I'm so sick of saying the same old thing over and over again," I grumbled, getting a light chuckle from Adrian on the other line.

"Five to ten?" Adrian asked through his own chuckles.

"I have more than one iron in the fire, and I'm at the shop right now," I said quietly, realizing the volume surrounding me had decreased, indicating that the afternoon rush was over.

"Always at the shop these days. It's almost as if you like someone there," Adrian teased.

I loved and hated that he was right. We all relentlessly teased him and Sal about their obvious crushes on Ash. The three of them fought like they hated each other, but deep down, everyone knew they both had hearts in their eyes for that girl. It was only a matter of time before one of them would break down. I wondered who Ash would end up choosing in the end, or if she would just completely wash her hands of both of them and their nonsense.

"I have to keep an eye," I murmured, glancing up to see the line had indeed died off and now there were only a few people left lingering within the shop, Ingrid clearly switching over to cleaning mode, instead of barista.

"Don't you have cameras in there?"

"Well, since none of the guards come by now that you're in the city so much, I'd rather not take chances, especially when Mom is here. It's too—"

Exposed.

Dangerous.

Reckless.

But I couldn't say any of those things right now. I was already speaking too loud for how quiet this place had become.

"I didn't realize the guard detail had been slacking," Adrian said, his voice apologetic. It was his and Leo's jobs to maintain the physical security teams. Most of the guards came with Sal to Kansas City, but since this was where so many of our businesses were, not to mention people working in those businesses that were family and friends, it would have been better for them to keep some guards back than the sparse handful they left for the whole of Lee's Summit.

"You haven't read any of the emails I sent you?" I asked, my voice perhaps a bit thicker with my frustration and condescension than I would have liked.

"I—"

"I made new schedules that you were supposed to send out. *My* plan would better divide our resources, especially now that we gained—" I cut myself off. I couldn't be saying so many things out loud in this public place, especially not with Ingrid and Sasha so close by to potentially hear what I was talking about. I almost said the name of the Kansas City gang we had just recruited as soldiers and associates. I really didn't need Ingrid hearing those words from my mouth and running for the hills.

While I logically knew that Ingrid probably *should* run from us, there was the very selfish part of me that wanted her to stay forever, even if I couldn't have her the way I wanted to. I liked justifying it by thinking there were too many roots she had already put down here. She and Nora built a life that would be so difficult for her to rebuild. Given a good enough reason, I knew she had done it once before and Ingrid could and would do it again.

"I'll look them over now. You going to be ready to scrub that stuff tonight?" Adrian asked.

"I always am," I said, closing my laptop with a snap. "Text me the details."

"I will. Talk to you later, Enzo," he said before he hung up. It may have been unceremonious, but I didn't mind. I knew Adrian just as well as I knew my other family. We were affectionate and loving, but also busy people. No one begrudged another for abruptness or being blunt.

As I stood, slipping my laptop back into my bag, I noticed Ingrid coming around the counter, that small blush on her face again as she came closer to me.

"I'm about to head out. Have too much to do and you're distracting me," I said with a smile as the blush deepened on her cheeks.

"I thought you might want a coffee to go. You look about as tired as I feel," she said, a little smirk playing at her lips. I took the to-go cup from her, winking and making her shake her head and roll her eyes, but it was what she said that really struck me.

She did look tired. Far more tired than I had seen her before. It had been creeping up and everyone around us seemed to be noticing it. She had lost weight, those dark circles under her eyes growing deeper and more pronounced, and there was a definite slump in her shoulders, like a heaviness was resting there, some burden that she wasn't letting any of us know about.

It brought me back to the conversation I had with the moms just a few days before, Monday. I went by their house to check in. It had become a sort of tradition for me since I moved into Maria's old house next door to my mom's. "Monday Mom Check-Ins" were expected now, and I usually filled in my brothers and Carmen about how they were doing afterward. Maria was in remission from cancer she beat a few years ago, but they were both getting older and we all worried, even if they were living together now.

"So what's the plan for the week?" I asked as Maria filled my plate with another helping of eggs. Perhaps Monday check-ins weren't just for the moms. It gave me, a middle child, the sole attention of both of the women who raised me for a few hours every week.

"Maria and I are going up to the elementary school to read to kids, then making sure Peter gets a new suit.

If he's going to be watching us all the time, I don't want to see that ugly brown thing ever again," my mom said. I grinned at the way her nose crinkled thinking about Peter's suit. It was, in fact, ugly. He didn't even have to wear a suit at all, but for some reason, he donned one, usually the brown one, every Tuesday and Thursday that he came and guarded the moms and clearly my mom was finished seeing it.

"He needs navy or black with that complexion, or maybe a brown that doesn't have so much green in it," Maria continued for my mom, her face equally disgusted.

"I'm sure with your guidance he'll be looking much more dapper," I said with a mouth full of eggs, grinning like the childish thing I am.

"You better not talk with your mouth full like that at family dinner this week. We're having guests," my mom snapped at me, her irritation at Peter's attire turning on me now. That was my intention.

"Guests?" I asked, now rather intrigued. Rory and Daph, Carmen's best friends, were not "guests." The moms referred to them as "the girls," so whoever was invited was not someone who normally had an open seat at the table.

"Liliana invited Ingrid and Nora to family dinner," Maria said, the corner of her mouth twitching as she watched my reaction. I wasn't sure what my face looked like, but I felt certain it was somewhere between elation and embarrassment. I swallowed my bite thickly.

"Ma must have laid it on thick. Ingrid never says yes to family dinners," I said, having been rather dejected the first few times she had been asked and the two of them never showed. She had come to other gatherings over the years, usually bigger events, like Thanksgiving and New Year's Eve, but never the intimate setting that

was family dinner. The fact that she would be coming now made a different sort of anticipation bubble within me. It was a sense of excitement I had never felt before.

"I didn't have to 'lay it on thick,'" Mom said as she came in from the kitchen with her refilled coffee, sitting beside Maria.

"Ingrid has been working so hard. She's doing that transcription stuff at night. I don't know if she's taking on more jobs because she and Nora are hurting for money or what, but when she dropped Nora off Friday morning, she looked like she hadn't slept at all. I hope she got some sleep over the weekend, but I doubt it," Maria said sadly.

"If I didn't know better, the way you look, I could almost assume you two were keeping each other up late," my mom added. I both loved and hated that com-ment. Loved the images it brought to my mind, hated that it was my mother saying it.

"Oh Liliana," Maria said, brows drawing together with concern. Carmen and Ingrid had become rather close since it had been the two of them working together at the shop for years, so like my mom, Maria had grown quite attached to her. Everyone had folded Ingrid into our lives, accepted her as family, but she still kept us at arm's length. "I don't know why she won't just let us help."

Seeing Ingrid's obvious physical exhaustion before my eyes was enough to make me wonder what she would let us do to help.

What kind of transcription jobs was Ingrid taking that would keep her from sleep?

How hard on money were they?

For over a year, I had been thinking of how I could somehow get her extra money without her realizing it. I had very nearly gone so far as to hack her bank account information and just start depositing here and there throughout the month in the hopes she wouldn't notice. But Ingrid *would* notice. If I knew nothing else, something like that wouldn't get by her. She may have been closed off, but she had a way of picking up on subtleties that rivaled me. I always attributed my own eye for detail to my computer work, but it could have been whatever life she lived before coming here that honed that particular skill for her.

I also knew if I tried to pry out the details from her, she would close up like a steel trap and I would only serve to push her farther away. That had already happened about two years ago when I tried to find out what she had been running from. It took everything in me not to search for her online myself and find out. The fact that I stopped myself was odd. With anyone else, I would have immediately gone and searched for them, to hell with what they said or how close they were to us, but with Ingrid, I wanted to leave that to her. I would have much rather had her tell me what happened before coming to Lee's Summit than to know without her consent.

I thanked her for the coffee, even though I desperately wanted to ask her the questions that I knew she wouldn't give me the answer to, and forced myself to leave before I put myself any further behind on what I needed to get done.

CHAPTER 5

INGRID

2:00 A.M.

Late, but not bad.

I had been working on shoring up the firewalls for the other company I worked for over the last two hours. Nora was snuggly in bed and asleep by nine, I cleaned up from dinner, then got everything ready for the next morning, before showering and sitting down to the computer by midnight.

It was something I hadn't wanted to do since before Nora was born. The money was always good, but the price? I wasn't so sure.

In my previous life, I had been a White Hat hacker. I didn't hack things and steal information to sell to the highest bidder, instead I would hack into companies or watch and study how another hacker did, then approach the company with how the breach occurred and how to fix it, for a price, of course. It was still blackmail, but it was less harrowing than true blackmail, since the only information I was stealing was how to get past their securities. Other hackers may not have been so kind. Or at least that's what I told myself.

Long ago it had been such good money it supported me and Nora's father quite well. That money was the reason Nora and I got away from him. It was the reason the two of us had the life we did now. But being a White Hat was still potentially dangerous. I wanted better for Nora. I wanted her to have a mother who worked a regular job, provided her with a regular life, and that's what I had done for the last several years. Only when the shop closed and no money was coming in had I even considered falling back on those old skills. Because what else could I do?

But I had pigeon-holed myself into an actual position for a company. Last August I was lurking the dark web, trying to see if I could find any action that would indicate a company of substantial wealth was being broken into and boy, did I find it. Stately Enterprises was being attacked. Their firewalls and encryptions were good, but this hacker, W01f, with the help of another person whose online presence had been nothing more than a string of seemingly random numbers, had been actively pushing to break through for nearly two months.

At one point I had thought to step in, to reach out to Stately and suggest some things or let me help them for a flat quick fee, but instead I watched, transfixed in the chaos and beauty of what I was witnessing W01f do. It wasn't until he actually broke through them completely, gaining access to what information he had so desperately wanted—I didn't investigate what that information was, I didn't care to find out—that I knew I should approach. But instead of reaching out and being paid for a one-time service, somehow the owners of this organization had convinced me to take a position.

Perhaps it had been the uncertainty of the shop's reopening or maybe the thrill and the familiarity of diving back into skills I had shelved, but either way, I had landed myself a lucrative job.

The beauty of it was they didn't have my true identity. Since Stately Enterprises was based in Chicago, I didn't want the old me being associated with that place again. As far as the city was concerned, I was dead. Despite that, with each passing month, the attacks from outside sources grew and so did the need for my services. I had trapped myself working for this company in a way, because even if they didn't know who I really was, they certainly knew enough that someone skilled, like me or this hacker, W01f, would be able to find out.

What had I done?

Now I was back to working at the shop for Liliana and doing this work at night. I was barely keeping my head above water with how busy I felt on top of raising my daughter.

It was in this stressful spiral of thoughts as I navigated the dark web and started to put together an algorithm that would actively create new encryptions for some of the more sensitive materials the company wanted me to keep sealed, that I heard the distinct ringing of a phone I hadn't used in three years. I kept it charged, taking it out of its little spot in my closet every few days to check it, then putting it back. I had been thinking more recently that perhaps I would never get a call, that I could just get rid of the burner phone soon, but I was very wrong.

Heart in my throat, I quickly got up from the chair in our combined living and dining room and went to my bedroom. I didn't have to turn on the light to find it. I knew exactly where the phone was stashed; tucked into an inner pocket of a purse I had never used was the brick. The ring was just as piercing as seeing the screen illuminating with the phone call. I answered it, putting it to my ear and waiting.

"Someone reached out. They're looking for you."

I knew that voice. Of course I did. But hearing it again when I had felt like I let him take the last pieces of the old me when I left him in St. Louis was a strange feeling.

"Why me?"

"Unfinished business? That man of yours causing trouble? Who knows?"

Joe's voice actually sounded a little gruffer than it had three years ago, like he had become a chain smoker in our time apart. I didn't blame him. We had successfully run away, but the fear of being found was always looming in the back of my mind, as I'm sure it was his.

"And you?" I asked, moving back to where my computer was and quickly pulling up another window so I could do some searching of my own. Someone familiar enough for Joe to use the term "they," most likely the Irish, was looking for me. I needed to know how easy I was to find.

"Not yet. Just be warned. You might want to make other plans."

As he said that, an email came through. Colin, my boss with Stately often emailed me at all hours. I didn't always reply right away, especially when he emailed this late, and most of the time I ignored it until later, but I had the strangest urge to look at it.

"Are you making plans?" I asked, eyes skimming over the words on the email. Colin wanted to meet me in person. He had a proposal for me, a different project that he wanted me to tackle. Someone else would be taking over my other duties and if I did this last thing for his company, he would let me go, as I had asked for several times over the last few months. The meeting was for Sunday, since he knew I worked another job during the week, and I didn't live in his company's area.

"I have a few things in the works already. I can help you too, if you want to get together. I don't want to discuss it, even on the burners. You know someone can be listening anyway," Joe offered.

"I could come this weekend. I have a meeting on Sunday I need to attend. If you could watch Nora for a day so I could take care of that, we can discuss plans when I return."

I knew I should have thought about meeting the owner of Stately Enterprises a little more, but the idea of being able to get out cleanly from him as well as get a last boost in funds before needing to disappear again was far too appealing. I didn't particularly love the idea of leaving Nora with Joe. I didn't know him well, but I couldn't exactly go to Liliana and Maria and ask them to watch Nora so I could go meet with my other boss last minute. It would seem far too suspicious if I did that.

"You want me to watch your kid?"

"There's really no other option. I can't bring her with me to this meeting, we need to talk, and the outcome of this meeting could be the funds I need to get away before they catch onto me," I said, pulling up information on Airbnbs close to the location Colin wanted to meet.

"Fine. I'll text my address. Delete it after. When will you be here?" The annoyance in his voice almost made me smile. If I didn't know I was going to once again be running for my life, I would have.

"I have to work tomorrow morning, and this works better if Nora is asleep for the ride. I'll probably get to you about midnight, maybe one in the morning," I told him.

"I'll be here," he said, quickly hanging up the phone.

My mind was racing now. The burner phone sat beside my laptop as I replied to Colin's email. The adrenaline was spiking, making my heart pound as I moved on to book the Airbnb, thinking of all the things I would need to do before we left the very next night, and of course the additional plans I would need to make on my return. Would I have enough time to give Liliana two weeks' notice? The idea of hurting her after everything she did for us hit me, causing me to pause.

And it wasn't just her. It was all of them. It was Enzo.

The life I left behind before, the only person I was really leaving was Elliot. I was escaping him, and him alone. I had no friends or family. Family had all been gone long before I met Elliot, and any friends I had when we started dating disappeared when his narcissism deemed them too influential on me for him to hold on to. I was alone in that life, with only Nora, and now I wasn't.

I had people who cared about me and people I cared about, and I didn't want to leave them.

My breath caught in my chest as my fingers stilled against the keys of my laptop, eyes welling with tears. How would I be able to do this? How had I let myself get so attached, so invested in being part of these people's lives? How would I ever rebuild a life for Nora like I had here?

I let myself feel it for a few moments, taking deep breaths and letting the tears stream down my cheeks silently, before I wiped my eyes and went back to the algorithm while simultaneously digging into my old self. Someone was searching for me, and I wanted to know who, because not knowing could mean making mistakes that would lead them to me when we left again.

[W01f: Isn't it about your bedtime, Red?]

The message popped up in my field of view. At some point in the last eight months of watching W01f, I had opened up a little avenue of communication between us. They had certainly noticed me, but weren't going to make the first move on touching base. I couldn't help myself, of course. There was some teasing part of me, as I suspected was in most hackers, that wanted to be able to goad the competition.

[R3d2: You don't know where I am. Who's to say what time it is here?]

[W01f: This is just usually the time your activity shuts off. Pulling an all-nighter? Or I suppose an all-dayer?]

Just that comment alone made me want to close everything down and jump IP addresses, but if I did that, everything with the algorithm would be lost, and it was—I snapped my eyes up to the clock on my computer—4:40 a.m.

Shit.

I needed to be getting Nora up in less than twenty minutes so I could get her to Liliana's. Since I opened the shop but had no one to take Nora to school during open hours, it had become a ritual that Liliana would bring my six-year-old to school for me so I could go to work. Maria loved feeding Nora and the two older women had definitely become grandmother figures in Nora's life. Another sucker punch to my heart at even thinking of taking Nora away from those sweet women almost made me double over.

[R3d2: I was only waiting for you to get here.]

[W01f: Oh, I've been here, Red. I know what you're up to. I'll get through anything you put up eventually.]

I wondered if the new person Stately Enterprises had hired would be able to keep up with the relentless nature of W01f. I was so tired and overworked because he had quite a way of making even the most complex defenses I put in place seem like barely a chore. There were times we had been actively battling, him pushing in as I tried to keep him out. While tiring, I couldn't deny it was exhilarating to have such a challenge thrown my way. It made me feel almost invincible when I somehow managed to keep him out each and every time.

[R3d2: I'd love to see that, nerd. There's a first time for everything, I suppose.]

Just as I sent the message, everything populated. I didn't even give them a moment to make a quip back at me, simply closing everything out, turning off my online access, heading straight to my room, where only a moment later my alarm began going off. I moved quickly to Nora's room, opening the door softly and climbing into her bed with her.

Each morning, I would just take in her sweet sleeping face for a moment, basking in her innocence and beauty, before I had to rouse her. If I could, I would keep her happy here, but now that didn't seem like it could be a reality. This time, leaving would be so much harder on her, and I would have to find a way to explain to a six-year-old exactly why we were leaving everything and everyone we cared about behind.

"Nora, my sweet. It's time to wake up," I whispered, sitting on the side of her bed and brushing an unruly red curl from her forehead. She stirred a little, brow scrunching adorably as her brain tried to reacquaint itself to the waking world.

"But I liked my dream," Nora murmured, her voice still thick with sleepiness.

"I'm sorry, baby, but we have places to be."

"We were at a big garden, and I wanted a flower, but you said I couldn't have one," Nora began, her eyes still closed. She loved telling me her dreams, and in the past I would have let this go on, but we didn't have time, not today, not lately. "And then Enzo made a flower that I could keep forever. He made you one too, Mommy."

My heart thudded in my chest at the mention of Enzo's name. Odd that when I did get an opportunity to dream, Enzo was usually featured, but now my daughter was dreaming about him doing sweet things he would very likely do in real life, and I was not prepared for the way it seemed to fill me with longing. I couldn't afford to long for someone, especially not him, and especially not now.

"We've got to get a move on so Liliana can make you breakfast before school," I said, trying to push the warmth her dream gave me to the side. I would need to squash those feelings for this family within myself, and quickly.

The sound of Liliana's name seemed to rouse Nora more than anything. She sat up, eyes bright for having just woken up.

"Do you think Maria will be there too?" Nora asked, scooting from the bed and trying to reach for her clothes that were still just a bit too high for her to reach when placed on top of her dresser.

Maria was Liliana's best friend and the mother to the LaMartinas. For the longest time the two families seemed like one, what with their joint gatherings and how close they all were, but that was about to become official with Carmen LaMartina and Leo Lupo's wedding that was set for just a month away in May. The youngest of each family were getting married. It was a match everyone else could see coming a mile away.

It wasn't long after Carmen and Leo finally got together about eight months ago that the Lupo's father, Salvatore, passed away, and Liliana felt safer having her best friend come live with her in her house rather than just simply be in the house next door. Maria was always there when Nora came in the mornings, but I wasn't going to say that. Nora's questioning just meant she was still filled with childlike wonder. I wanted her to hold on to that a little longer before the world proved to her than it was not a good place.

"I'm sure Maria will be there," I said, pulling the clothes down for Nora to snatch and watching as she raced to the bathroom, all traces of sleep gone.

I went to grab my clothes, pulling on jeans and a T-shirt before glancing at myself in the mirror. My eyes were still a little puffy from crying, the dark circles only accentuated, and the expression on my face seemed haunted, tired and sad. My own red hair was quite a mess from where I had raked my fingers through it all night. I didn't have time to fix the curls, deciding just to quickly braid my hair back as I moved to the bathroom where Nora was finishing brushing her teeth.

"If Maria is there, she'll make *bikooti* with her peach jam!" Nora said around her toothbrush.

"Biscotti?" I asked, not exactly sure what the garbled word had been, but guessing. Nora nodded enthusiastically, her unruly curls shaking with the sharp gesture. "Only if we're out the door in five minutes." With that, Nora's brushing became much more vigorous while I stepped up to the mirror to brush my own teeth and then slap makeup over my skin to try to mask the horror show beneath. But no matter how much makeup I put on, it wouldn't hide the dread in my eyes, and that was something I would have to keep at bay from Liliana and Maria.

CHAPTER 6

INGRID

The drive to Liliana's was quick. We pulled up into their driveway, taking in the sweet neighborhood I wished Nora and I could have moved into. Working two jobs, even if the pay was good, did not mean I could even remotely afford to purchase a house, let alone one of these beautiful homes. Not that it mattered anymore. Maybe if Joe hadn't reached out, and no one was looking for me, I would have eventually made enough money to buy a very small house for the two of us at some later point, but now none of that mattered.

"Liliana!" Nora squealed as I opened the car door for her and she jumped out, racing toward the front porch where the woman sat. The cool spring morning didn't seem to be deterring the woman who was leisurely sipping her coffee with her robe and slippers on.

It was easy to see how all three of her sons got such good looks. If I hadn't known their father before he died, I would have assumed they all got their beauty from her, but Salvatore had also been quite the dark Italian god, even if he had been older and meaner. Liliana and

Maria had both aged gracefully, looking older, but like fine wine. Laugh lines and a peppering of gray in her otherwise dark hair were the main giveaways.

"Good morning, Nora!" Liliana said, eyes sparkling with joy. She was eager to have grandchildren of her own, that much was clear with every grumble about her unwed brood, but what she lacked in little ones of her own to take care of, she made up for with having Nora in her life. My heart surged with appreciation and heartache at the way Nora effortlessly folded into Liliana's arms as if she were actually her grandmother. Nora needed people in her life, and I was about to take everyone who meant something to her away.

"Sorry I can't stay. We're running a little behind this morning," I said, smoothing Nora's hair down a little.

Liliana's eyes took in my face, scrutinizing the sleep deprived look I couldn't quite hide with makeup.

"Ingrid, if that transcribing job is keeping you up all night, you can't keep going. I'm sure I can talk to Sal and we can find you something else that would pay more or—"

"No, no. You've already done too much for us, Liliana," I said quickly.

She had been trying for the last few months to convince me to leave my other job. Sal, her oldest son, who had taken over the family business, would certainly find me something that would help without upending our lives. At the time, I had no good way of getting out of working the job, or at least I hadn't found one yet. Now, I not only had a way out, but I had to make us disappear too. No job Sal could give me would spare me from what was possibly coming my way if I didn't heed Joe's warning.

I hated lying to her, to everyone, but that was what was necessary. Just a few more lies, and they would never see me again anyway, so what did it hurt? Nothing, other than my heart, and probably Nora's too, when we were gone and the family we had slowly acquired became nothing more than memories in her sweet child-like mind.

"You're good with computers, I'm sure Enzo could—"

"I have to go!" I said, my whole body going tense at the mention of her middle son's name.

Twice in one morning I was reminded of him by others, and of course the thought of leaving him behind seemed to tear at my insides a little more than anyone else. We weren't anything other than flirtatious acquaintances, perhaps even friends, so why did the idea of leaving him, losing him, make tears sting my eyes far more than the thought of leaving anyone else?

"I love you, Nora. Be good for Liliana. I'll pick you up after school," I said, stooping down to kiss my daughter's soft cheek as well as hide the blush I was certain was staining my cheeks and the tears that may have formed in my eyes.

"Bye, Mama!" Nora called after I hurriedly went back to my car, jumping in and taking the short drive to the coffee shop.

The whole way there, I couldn't stop thinking about how strange it was to feel so connected to someone I kept at a distance. Enzo wasn't mine, and I wasn't his. The last time I had let a man mean anything more to me, I had to run to get away.

Images of Elliot's face as his fist came down on me flashed through my mind, and I braked a little harder when I got into my parking spot than I needed to. It was too early for anyone else to be here, a fact I was thankful for, since I looked like a shaking mess as I walked up to the doors of the coffee shop and struggled to unlock the door. Even if I knew that Enzo would never do such a thing to me, that he was far different than the man I had escaped, it wouldn't matter now anyway. Nora and I needed to leave again.

Despite the way it began, the day went by smoothly. The busy rush of the morning tapered to its normal, slower pace in the afternoon, but my tired brain couldn't seem to purge all the thoughts that were nagging at the back of my mind. It didn't help that the reminder of that brief conversation with Liliana kept playing over and over in the back of my mind. Some of these thoughts were not helpful.

Why hadn't I reached out to Liliana when the shop was closed? I'm certain if she had been reminded, she would have helped me, or found me something to do for Sal or someone else that wouldn't have put me in the position I had been in.

Maybe if I hadn't been working for Stately Enterprises, someone wouldn't be searching for me. Did I oust myself by doing what I had been for the last eight months?

And of course, the most unhelpful thought continued to pop into my head as the morning pressed closer to afternoon.

Enzo.

It was strange that he hadn't made his usual appearance in the shop. The near constant customer sitting at the table by the window all day, every day, was nowhere to be seen. It wasn't completely unheard of for him to come in closer to eight, perhaps later if he was doing something with his brothers, but now that it was well past noon, I found myself anxious and disappointed.

For years Enzo and I had done the dance, little jokes and teasing, but knowing it would never go anywhere. I was a single mother working two jobs to make ends meet who looked exhausted ninety percent of the time and never at all put together; whereas Enzo was well-off, a genius with computers, and beyond that he was … well … *hot.*

Like the rest of the Lupos, he had those dark Italian features. His eyes were brown, he had thick dark brows that were so animated, often to make me laugh or blush, and he had a dimple in his cheek that popped out, especially when he gave me that cheeky, lopsided grin. I could almost see him sitting at that table, as if he were there, his laptop in front of him while his fingers moved quickly and steadily over the keys. Despite being constantly in front of a computer, that man was muscled. None of those men seemed to let their lives get in the way of staying in shape. It helped that they also owned a gym.

I rarely had time to work out. I had extra weight from my lower belly all the way to my thighs, and stretch marks littered my skin from where I'd gained weight when I was pregnant with Nora. I may have been able to cover it up well, but this body wouldn't hold Enzo's attention if he ever laid eyes on it. Not that he ever would.

Enzo and I may have been of compatible age, but there was no way I could continue to delude myself into thinking our playful flirting was ever going to turn into anything more, especially not when I had myself and Nora to protect, and my own little secrets to keep.

My fantasies of Enzo would have to stay just that. Fantasies.

I shook my head at my own ridiculousness. There was certainly not going to be any way of entertaining those fantasies when Nora and I had to disappear. Nora would lose a support system and grandmothers, and I would lose…

My breath hitched.

It was better for me to focus on the cut and dry plans, not think of how much I wanted a certain Lupo that I could never have. It was clear that the Universe, God, or Fate had decided that I didn't deserve real love, otherwise why would I have had to run away from Elliot?

"I'm going to start on tomorrow's batches. You okay out here alone for a minute?" Sasha asked, pulling me back to reality. I had been going through the motions, clearly, because the look on Sasha's face was that she wasn't completely sure I *could* watch the front alone now.

"Of course," I said, nodding my head as I looked over at her with a forced smile.

Sasha leaving me alone up front was essentially just giving me time to more thoroughly work myself into an anxious frenzy. Yes, it was better for me to think of all the things I needed to get done, to plan my next steps for scrubbing Nora and I clean and to become new people, but it wasn't like I could do any of it while I stood behind the counter waiting for people to come in and order coffee-based drinks from me. I limited my musings to a small portion of my mind and perhaps a piece of scrap paper, but once the number of customers coming in slowed to a dribble, scrubbing the counters and machines was not doing enough to keep the anxiety from slipping in and overwhelming me.

Considering that, my thoughts went back to Enzo and how it was so strange he hadn't made an appearance. And then I noticed one of the men that usually stood around the gym standing and leaning on his car outside the shop. I hadn't really registered the guard's presence until this moment, probably because I had been lost in my own pity party, but I was fairly certain that was Travis, who usually stood guard at the gym. Or he did before Salvatore died. I hadn't seen him there in months either.

It seemed like an odd thing, but I felt confident that Enzo had made Travis come watch out front. Why? I wasn't sure, but it was something I could imagine Enzo doing.

As if my thoughts had called him, Enzo waltzed up to Travis, the two of them exchanging words for a moment or two, before he turned his attention to the front door. In an effort to not be openly gawking, I turned back to my scrubbing of the exterior wall of the counter, trying to keep myself occupied. Plenty of scuff marks over the years from the toes of people's shoes, a dog, and the occasional bicycle tire.

Enzo walked through the door of the shop, laptop bag slung over one arm, stuffing his phone in the pocket of his black jeans with the other. He looked as tired as I felt, though it didn't take away from how beautiful he looked. Like his brothers he had that lovely sharp bone structure, his Roman nose suited his face, and his hair had started to grow out rather long, making him look a little more like his true laid-back self, than when he slicked it back and dressed formally in a perfectly tailored suit. Just the memory of that image of him had my breath quickening in my lungs. The suited Enzo may have been a version of him that wasn't the funny, sweet one I knew, but it was still drool worthy.

I was staring into his brown eyes that danced with amusement as he approached. There wasn't a counter between us like there usually was, and I stood from my crouched position, taking in the way I had to crane my neck to look up at his face.

"Does anyone work here?" he asked playfully, stopping just short of me and leaning on the counter, blocking my path to go around and take his order.

"They all hid when they saw you coming. They must be afraid they'll get eaten by giants." My lips twitched with amusement, while simultaneously being irritated with myself for the childish book reference. Nora and I had been reading about Jack and the Bean Stalk just a week before, and the obvious difference in our heights brought the word giant to mind. I wondered if he was giant sized in all aspects.

"Bone bread isn't really to my taste," Enzo said without missing a beat, making me grin before I pulled my face back to serious.

"Well, I suppose since no one else can assist you, I'll have to do," I said, moving around him to go behind the register.

"Anything good here?" he asked, shifting to lean even farther across the counter, so our faces were closer to level.

"You'd have to ask a regular. I just work here," I said back, watching the corner of his mouth lift a little before he turned to look around the empty shop. No one was there. That fact seemed to sink in as I watched the side of his face while he made a show of looking for a regular customer to ask.

So rarely were we ever truly alone, and I found that since these may be the last times I'd ever get alone with him, I wanted to savor the undivided attention I was getting. I wanted to bask in the glow of his eyes on me and his words only meant for my ears.

"Hmm. Doesn't seem like there's anyone to ask," Enzo feigned, letting his eyes fall back on me. Those dark brown depths seeming to punch through me each time they locked with mine. Those eyes were hungry, as they had been when he looked at me after the scumbag wouldn't leave me alone. They were hungry for *me*.

"Well, our most consistent regular usually gets here much earlier, but I have it on good authority he's going to show up at some point."

"Who is this mysterious regular?" For some reason this back and forth between us, while very much like us, wasn't being held back as much because we weren't surrounded by others. And with that lack of supervision, I found myself almost feeling like I did when I bantered with W01f online. But that was absurd, because Enzo couldn't possibly be W01f.

"He's some nerd who always has his computer with him," I said with a grin as I turned to start making his regular drink, just barely catching the little glimmer of a challenge in his eyes before I wasn't facing him anymore. For some reason, I decided to play into this. To feed this feeling that I was getting quite the thrill out of.

"I wonder if you can so easily spot a nerd, because you're one too?" Enzo asked, drawing my eyes back to him as I put the second round of espresso on the machine to brew.

His words had my heart rate spiking with lust and fear. I knew he did security work for their company, which meant he probably was doing a lot of similar things I was doing for Stately Enterprises. Suddenly, I wondered what his call sign was, what breadcrumbs he left behind, who he was behind the screen. Did he believe the lie about being a transcriptionist, or did he *know?*

Not that it would affect him at all. I was just working in cyber security for that company, there was nothing bad about that, per se, though lately I was getting the feeling that the company I worked for may have had their hands in far darker things than I thought they were initially. That wasn't unusual for wealthy corporations and would explain why there was a hacker consistently trying to break into their information, but I wasn't on that side of things. I worked on the light side, the good side, and purposefully kept my eyes away from documents and files so I wouldn't find out.

I inspected Enzo's face, looking for any sign that he felt animosity or hatred, and all I saw that was desire and joy. He found happiness in our conversation just as I did, and I was ruining it by thinking too much about everything. My specialty.

"Now that I think about it, you look an awful lot like him," I said, raising an eyebrow and making sure my face stayed playful, even if I was running through every time we came across each other recently in my mind and trying to determine if something he did or said seemed suspicious or just him being his odd self.

"Ah, then he must be pretty handsome."

I let the grin spread over my face as I turned away to pull the milk from the fridge for steaming.

He couldn't know. If he did, there was no way he would behave this way around me or joke like this if it was a problem for him.

"Full of yourself too," I said when I turned back. As the steamer sounded, not allowing Enzo any sort of retort, a yawn escaped me uncontrollably, making the flirtatious smile on his face falter slightly as he noticed my tiredness. I was a single mom, tired was over half of my existence, but I must have looked worse than usual because as I slid the cup across the counter to him, he grabbed my hand.

The intensity of the feeling of his skin on mine was like a bolt of electricity going through me. Any exhaustion I felt seemed to melt away in favor of heart pounding.

"What can I do, Ingrid?" he asked, his voice so much softer now, deep with feeling as he looked me in the eyes. I blinked back the tears that prickled at the corners of my eyes, at the sincerity in his tone.

"Nothing," I whispered, pulling my fingers from his grasp. "Just don't make me worry."

I hadn't meant to say the last bit. Maybe it was my own exhaustion, maybe it was the concern and vulnerability in his eyes, but I let it out, anxiously looking up into his eyes once more briefly and seeing the surprise there. The worst part of seeing the surprise was how much I knew he would worry about me. Because despite what I may have said to myself, I knew Enzo had cared about me for a very long time, and he would be upset and concerned when Nora and I disappeared.

"Ingrid … can I—" But the bell over the door chimed and Liliana came through the door, cutting Enzo off before he finished the sentence, which I was certain I both desperately wanted to hear, and didn't, for the sake of my willpower.

CHAPTER 7

ENZO

"Enzo!" my mother's voice sounded right after the bell that made Ingrid snap up straight as a board and step away from me, effectively taking herself far enough away that I couldn't touch her, let alone dive a little further into this conversation. Her little admission to worrying about me had cracked that thin boundary we had between us, but only just a little. I wanted to talk to her, really talk to her. We'd had a few conversations over the last few years that I would consider real, several of them happening over text messages instead of in person, but most of our interactions were short ones here at the shop that could only really be playful, never truly serious.

Limerence, I realized, was what I felt for Ingrid. She captured my fantasies the moment she came into our lives three years ago with little Nora in her arms. I had been grabbing my standard mid-morning coffee the day she walked through the door, Nora on her hip. Both of them were so striking, shockingly beautiful, with that pale skin and fiery red hair. Ingrid's eyes didn't meet mine as she moved toward the counter, but I saw the haunted look in them, not distracting from the devastatingly beautiful light blue.

She looked like some sort of goddess, but it was when she started talking to Ma about a job, while effortlessly comforting little Nora, that I knew she was a warrior. Haunted eyes and all, she wasn't a quitter, and I admired that.

I wanted to make this woman happy. I wanted to see a smile on that face that wasn't forced. It took a few weeks, maybe a month, but I managed that first true smile. I can't even recall what I had said that she found so funny. My mind was immediately blown away at how breathtaking she looked with those blue eyes alight. And the way she started to banter right back at me, I almost grinned like a fool just thinking about the memory. She was also incredibly intelligent and witty.

I couldn't get enough.

But for all the time I had spent in her company, mostly here at the shop, she was still a closed book; a mystery wrapped in a very unassuming package. A mystery I would love nothing more than to dive into and unwrap.

"Hi, Ma," I said, turning around and greeting my mother with a kiss on the cheek and a hug. Nothing like hugging your mom to turn your hot blood to ice.

"I'm glad you're here. I won't have to text you," she said when we broke apart. "Family dinner is postponed until tomorrow. Carmen and Leo will be able to make the trip if we wait, since she only has tomorrow's classes left."

"I wonder if she's going to bring anything tasty to try," I mused, thinking of her spring break when she spent the whole time baking new things she had learned for all of us. I thought her tiramisu couldn't be better, but I had been very, very wrong.

"Only if you come," Ma said with playful, narrowed eyes. "Ingrid, I still want you and Nora to come too."

"Oh no," Ingrid said, snatching a rag and scrubbing a spot I could have sworn she had been scrubbing when I came in the door. "I don't think dinner tomorrow will work."

"You and Nora are always welcome! Aren't they, Enzo?"

I waited a beat or two until Ingrid met my eyes. I hoped my face showed how I felt that I would love nothing more than her and Nora to come to every family dinner, but instead, I managed a slightly choked, "Of course," as I saw a sadness in her eyes.

"That's settled then. Tomorrow night at 6:30 p.m.. I'm still waiting to hear back from the other boys, but if Nora is coming, I know what I'll be making," my mother continued, as if Ingrid and I hadn't had a loaded look right before her eyes, moving around the counter and heading back toward the kitchen and office.

Ingrid still hadn't agreed, but that meant nothing to Liliana Lupo. That woman was a force. If Ingrid truly couldn't make it for some reason, it wasn't worth bringing it up until the day of the event. My mom would come up with every reason why or how it could be arranged that Ingrid and Nora could make it if she had enough time to work on it.

I pulled the latte Ingrid had so carefully put together for me, snatching a to-go lid and snapping on.

"You aren't staying?" she asked, her voice still quiet.

"I have too much to do today. And if I'm making it to family dinner tomorrow night, I'd better start now," I said apologetically.

"I understand that," she said with a nod, a wave of fatigue passing over her face that brought up the intense concern I had been feeling earlier when I saw her strained yawn. I wasn't sure what was causing her to lose sleep, but I didn't like it. Not a bit.

"I'll see you at dinner, if not before. This nerd might need a pick me up," I said, trying to lighten the mood.

"I'll be here ready to make my regulars their overly complicated drinks tomorrow too," she said with a little smile.

I was still thinking about that smile hours later, when the half of the latte she made me sat cold on the table beside my second screen and the hum of the computers was the only sound that could be heard.

"Did you scrub that footage?" Adrian's voice came through the earpiece in my ear as I tried to multitask. We had been talking about new schedules for some of our men, adding guard details in so that we could ensure all the important people in our lives were continuing to be watched over. I was certain from some of the people gaining guards there would be some push back, mainly Daph and Rory, Carmen's two best friends. But I was also looking at footage of our warehouses and properties that had motion detectors tripped the previous evening, and searching the cameras around our building, while simultaneously running a test to determine if I could find any weaknesses in the new algorithm R3d2 had put up the night before.

"Working on it," I said through gritted teeth.

"We can't catch heat for that, Enzo. Too much is riding on each move we make. The cops getting involved now will just make a mess of things," Adrian said, and I could picture his scowl.

"I know," I snapped, pausing at a frame that may have shown Leo's face. It was hard to tell with the lighting at the current magnification, but if I could recognize him, the police might, and I couldn't take that chance. Leo may have been our enforcer now, but he was also a decorated, honorably discharged soldier with connections. He, of all people, having the police catch wind of his activities, would only cause us to lose potential assets and allies in the future. If it were simply a grunt, we could deal with the bail or pay off the police to keep it quiet. For Leo, it was a whole different game.

"I know we're putting a lot on you, Enzo, but—"

"Don't even start. I'm not backing out and I wouldn't quit on any of you, and you know it. Little overwhelmed? Maybe. But don't doubt me."

"Noted," Adrian said. It seemed like he wanted to say more, but the distinct sound of the gym in the background could be heard. He hadn't been at the gym for a while, and I wondered if both he and Sal showing up at the gym within days of each other was a coincidence or not. They both gravitated to Ash, but it was almost like they orbited each other too.

"Coming to dinner tomorrow, since you're in town?" I asked, smiling a little at the sigh I heard while I wiped the evidence of my little brother from the footage.

"Couldn't get out of it, even if I had a meeting," he said, to which I grinned even wider.

Adrian and Sal had been notably absent from the last month of family dinners. They were lucky they had good excuses. Trying to secure their place as Caporegime and second in the territory to keep all of us safe was a fairly good reason to miss dinner with the moms. However, there was only so long that our Italian mothers would allow them to miss. Dinners together were an essential part of our family. Being together was what made the LaMartinas more than just simply family friends.

"I don't want to keep hounding you about O'Shea, but you know that he's planning something. I just don't know what yet."

"Of course, he's planning something. We killed his sons and thwarted his plan. He's not going to let that one go without reciprocation. I just haven't seen anything yet."

Well, other than the blocking work R3d2 had been doing, but, nothing large had been moved, no big sums, everything, for the most part, seemed to stay on the books of their legitimate businesses, and I was just waiting for the other shoe to drop. Colin O'Shea didn't suddenly go strait-laced because his sons were dead. If anything, it made him even more of a contender. He had nothing to lose, and we definitely had plenty.

I was missing something, or probably several somethings, and was getting very worried that we were going to have quite a mess on our hands before it was all said and done.

"Let me know if there's anything I can help with. I know we're always asking you for things and you have so much going on. I'm not great with the computer stuff, but Leo's not bad, and we can always see if Kia would be willing to—"

"I'm fine, Adrian. We don't need anyone else," I said, though I knew that wasn't true. Kia and I had worked well together when we were searching for Carmen, but she had no interest in long-term work for us. Kia was deadly with a computer and a sniper rifle. Out of the military, she was loaning her services out to the highest bidder for the time being while she decided what other ways she'd like to spend her time. She'd help me in a pinch, but what I really needed was someone reliable who could help in all aspects, not just briefly, so I could catch up now.

"See you tomorrow," I said before Adrian ended the call with a grunt.

I was busily scrubbing footage, my algorithm running, when I saw the familiar little codes that indicated R3d2 was online and doing what they did best, digging for information and putting up walls so high and thick, that only the bravest would even consider trying to break through them.

I glanced at the time. 1:00 a.m. Right on time for them.

I might have become a bit of a stalker, knowing when they usually got online and back off. I tracked all their normal IP addresses or the ones they bounced their signal off of to obscure their true location, so I had no idea where they actually were. I could have dug more into who they truly were, but that wasn't the priority. Gaining the information I needed, and making sure our people and information were guarded were my objectives normally, and that wasn't going to change, at least not tonight.

Getting through R3d2 was a battle I didn't have in me with the other tasks I had to contend with. I wanted to push, to make some sort of dent in the ever-growing security surrounding the Irish clan that had tried and failed to tear my family apart, but I knew it wasn't worth the energy.

R3d2 had been a name synonymous with some seriously high-level White Hat hacking and dark web predator flagging, then like a phantom, R3d2 was gone. Just as swiftly, they were back. I admired them; that was rather obvious. R3d2 was the king of getting companies and wealthy individuals alike to beg on their knees and with their wallets for help when they tore through their securities. And as for the dark web... Well, some very bad people were caught because of R3d2.

It made sense that if a White Hat were to ever switch sides, they'd be someone to contend with. Knowing exactly what they would do to get through code and dig into the dirt on an organization meant that R3d2 knew how to protect that information from others.

For years, I would have loved nothing more than to go toe-to-toe with R3d2 and see which one of us would come out on top, but I certainly wasn't happy that it was happening now. My family and all of our lives were in jeopardy. This wasn't exactly the time to be playing games with an infamous hacker.

But it was strange to me that R3d2 was assisting a mob boss, instead of pulling apart all their illegal dealings and making them pay. This told me that something in R3d2's personal life had pushed them down this path, something that was either making the reality of who they worked for a moot point, they didn't care to even find out, or O'Shea had something on them that would utterly destroy them. Either way, I hated to see someone I had revered work for the man who might very well be what kills us all.

[W01f: don't stay up too late, Red. You'll be too tired to play.]

[R3d2: And who would I be playing with? I don't see anyone online right now who could even stand a chance.]

[W01f: Oh, Red. If I really had time to go after your little algorithms, you wouldn't know what to do with yourself.]

[R3d2: Only because you don't have time?]

[R3d2: Too tired?]

[R2d2: Or too scared?]

Something in the way they sent those successive messages was familiar to me. It didn't make sense, because it was in message form, not actually said with words, but it definitely gave me an impression of how it was to be said, and it reminded me of someone.

[W01f: Do you have time?]

There was a pause, long enough to feel noticeable, before the next chat popped up.

[R3d2: I have a lot to do tonight and you're not ready to play with me, wolf.]

So tempting.
That felt like a theme for me. Temptation.
My mind went back to the woman who tempted me with simply a look in my direction. Odd that I had been reminded of her not once, but twice. But R3d2 was right. I didn't have time tonight to lose myself in those sorts of games, with R3d2, or Ingrid. Too much work to be done.

[W01f: Too tired tonight. Maybe tomorrow?]

[R3d2: You think tomorrow you can stay awake long enough to play with me? Doubtful.]

[W01f: I have coffee. I'll be ready for you whenever you're prepared. Sounds like you don't think you'll be up to it.]

[R3d2: Coffee only does so much. You're lucky I'm too busy to play tonight or tomorrow.]

Too busy to play, hm?

So was I, but I couldn't help the nagging feeling I was going to miss something big if I didn't pay attention.

[W01f: watch your back. It might surprise you when I finally come out to play.]

[R3d2: I'm not scared of a nerd in wolf's clothing behind the screen.]

A tired hacker was a sloppy hacker. Red had been up working late into the night for the past five days. I wasn't sure about their location, but I imagined there was a life outside of the screens that they inhabited. I had one too, though not by much. I had my family. Did Red?

The Irish were grappling with the major blow we gave them last summer, already trying their hand at retaliation, though their reach was limited by distance. Our uncle, Romolo, had so far been on the receiving end of their wrath, which he dealt with easily enough. But they were planning something bigger.

I had put all sorts of alerts up for myself so I could try to mitigate any breaches but also be alert to physical threats. The O'Sheas weren't bold or strong enough yet to try coming into our territory, but they had R3d2 now. I was surprised O'Shea hadn't used them to break through to us that way yet. It would be easy enough for them to reroute or pull funds from our accounts, even to sully our online relationships with black market buyers and dealers. R3d2 was good enough to make it believable, even if it didn't come from me directly. But so far R3d2 had just been keeping me out and keeping the O'Sheas afloat.

And talking to me.

Did they know who I was?

Were they playing a long game that I was just now stumbling upon?

A foreboding feeling flooded me. It hadn't exactly been quiet all these months. My constant work was proof of that, but there wasn't enough from the Irish. Not enough activity to make me feel safe, and R3d2 was there, a taunting presence in our shared little dark world.

The footage was scrubbed, my algorithm going, funds being sent to the Cartel were queued for a virtu-ally trace-free transfer, and I was fading quickly with each tick of the clock closer to sunrise. I should have been looking up R3d2, trying to trace their location, to determine if there was a way to bring them away from the O'Sheas, but instead, I let my mind wander to the blue eyes of Ingrid, the deep tired circles around those bright orbs.

She set me on fire, even in my exhausted state. Right now, I didn't have a reason, not a real one at least, to ask why she was so tired, but I wanted to. I wanted to be the one for her to share everything with, not just the man she flirted with while she made coffee. I let my head fall, resting my cheek on the cool wood of the dining room table I sat at and letting my eyes drift closed with thoughts of Ingrid smiling, thoughts of the softness of her skin at inadvertent touches, of what it would be like to taste that intoxicating scent right from her lips, her skin.

My dreams happily, but also torturously, continued on that same path.

CHAPTER 8

ENZO

"**I** found you," I whispered, looking up from the computer screen I had been staring at. The words and numbers that should have made sense on the screen held no true meaning to me, but I knew what they indicated, especially when my eyes took in the silhouetted person just across the table from me. For some reason, I was in the coffee shop, though the lights were dimmed, and the place was empty as it usually was when it was closed. I was still there for some reason, when I was never there during closing normally. But that was because I was looking for R3d2.

I was looking for Red.

"Did you find me … nerd?"

The word "nerd" stood out as it was said. Something about it, the way it was spoken and annunciated, the structure of the sentence surrounding it, the teasing way it was used, pulled my thoughts from R3d2, the hacker, the mysterious virtual shadow image I had created in my mind for so long, to a red-headed beauty that I knew I had been thinking about.

I always thought about her.

Now the silhouetted form of R3d2 that was sitting in the chair just on the other side of the table from me was changing. Androgynous shoulders slimmed, shadows slowly lifting to reveal pale skin and red hair. Each passing moment where the shadows receded, Red transformed more and more into someone else.

In place of the faceless form of R3d2, was now Ingrid. And what an image she was in comparison to the anonymous thing that had been there before. Red hair like a vibrant flame, loose and curling around her head like a fiery mane, brilliant blue eyes almost glowing as they sparkled playfully at me. Just like they had earlier that day in this very shop.

"Did you find me, or did I find you?"

Her voice was heavier than normal, weighted while still playful, a tone I had never heard from her before.

In fact, everything was accentuated. The clothes she wore weren't hiding those delicious curves from me, as they usually did. There was no large apron or loose shirts, only her in a simple tank top and yoga pants. The table and my computer seemed to have disappeared at some point while I was looking her over, but I wasn't bothered by its sudden loss. Instead, I was far too focused on the way she looked and that cheeky little smirk on her face with daring eyes as she watched me.

I reached out, uninhibited by anything, not the table from before, or any of my normal hesitations with her boundaries, lightly touching her cheek, which just like her hand had felt earlier in the day, was so soft against my fingers, the fire in my veins only seemed to burn brighter.

"I just keep waiting, Ingrid. I'll always wait."

She smiled, her lips spreading over her teeth, eyes lighting even more with humor and desire as she reached her own hand up, caressing my cheek and causing every nerve ending within me to sizzle beneath my skin. Like an electric current was made, it felt like we were pulsing together, simply by touching one another.

She opened her mouth as I pulled her a little closer, a sharp intake of air, like she was about to say something to me, before her mouth quickly snapped shut and the harsh sound of high-pitched bells, or something like that seemed to take over any other sound around us.

And then the electricity, her touch, her scent, her breath was gone.

I opened my eyes, the bleary image of the dining room table I had fallen asleep at coming into view before I quickly snapped my eyes shut once more, the horrible sound of my alarm still going off loudly in my ear.

No!

Just a little bit longer and I would have kissed her. Even dream me seemed to have a hard time crossing the boundaries, but my awake imaginings didn't have that problem.

I sat up, turning the alarm off and rubbing my eyes lightly. I tried to remember the feel of her skin on mine and how it made my cheek and hand tingle as I tried to become awake. The image of the devious look in her eyes framed by her wild, unconfined hair kept my heart thumping in my chest as I pushed away from the table, making my way to the kitchen.

Coffee. Coffee would help me. If I was more awake, I'd be able to stop my thoughts.

Or so I thought.

The coffee gurgled, but images continued popping into my mind. That small distance between us finally closing; her lips would be even softer than her hands and cheek, her taste more delicious than her scent as it hit my tongue. My body felt hot, and I was getting hard just leaning over the counter as I thought about it; thought about the possibility of us.

"Enzo, look at this place!" my mother said, having come through the front door with no notice or knock, as usual. I nearly choked, quickly adjusting myself to hide the evidence of my musings before turning around to see my mother through the dining room to the front door. The look on her face was one of horror, but not because of what I had been thinking about.

Liliana Lupo liked to say she could read minds, but I had learned long ago she was only very good at reading people. I played into the tiredness I still hadn't shaken, pouring myself a cup of freshly brewed coffee and double-checking I had concealed my still half-hard erection, before turning around to her.

"I know," I grumbled, seeing now what she was looking at and realizing what a catastrophe the house had become.

It was Maria's old house that had now become "the kids' house," a place for any of the six of us to stay. I had moved in and given up my apartment to be closer to the moms in case something happened. The only request Maria had was that I wouldn't turn it into a "bachelor pad" as Ma had called it, and that's unfortunately what had happened.

Dishes and bottles sat on every surface, the shirt I had been wearing the day before as well as my shoes were discarded on a dining chair, and other clothes littered various other furnishings. I wasn't usually this messy, and I had been much better about cleaning up after myself at first, but I just hadn't had very much time these last few weeks. Maybe it had been months.

"This is…" She couldn't even finish the sentence, lips pursing tightly as she began picking up bottles. I didn't blame her. She was holding back what would have been her normal response had I still been a kid living in her home. Now that I was an adult, it was much harder for her to yell at me, but that didn't mean she didn't want to.

"I've been really busy," I said, hurrying to follow her lead and grabbing my dishes to put in the sink. She remained quiet, merely cleaning with a speed only a mother could master, before she finally stopped and looked up at me with her hands on her hips.

The clutter was gone, but I would have a lot more actual scrubbing, sweeping, and mopping to do before it would be considered good enough by either of the moms' standards.

"I expect better," she finally said in a very careful voice that was used only shortly before she usually exploded.

"I know. I'm sorry, Ma."

"Living like this is not helping you. Look at you, Enzo!" she said, coming closer now and taking my face in her little hands. She had to look up at me now, but the expression on her face was the same one she had throughout my childhood when I would look up at her loving face. Worry.

"I thought I was the most handsome of your sons. Are you taking that back now, Ma? I'm offended!" I said with mock seriousness that made her mouth turn up with a little smile before a scowl took its place just as quickly.

"Always the joker," she grumbled, pressing a little harder on my stubbly cheeks. "I'm not saying you aren't handsome, Enzo. You look tired. If there was something I could do—"

"There isn't," I said, pulling her hands away and holding them tightly. "You and Maria are as good as out. You can't do anything to change that status." She grimaced, but nodded. Having our mothers out of the Mafia life, or at least less in the forefront, was something all of us wanted to stay as it was. They were just to focus on the coffee shop and Maria's health. Nothing more.

"I'm glad I came to help get this place not looking like a sty, but that's not why I came over," she said, stepping back and glancing down at the dining room table that had become my main workspace.

"Should I ask why you came?" I asked, fake grimacing and hiding behind my coffee mug.

"You need to clean up for dinner and go pick up Ingrid and Nora."

Ah yes, the postponed family dinner. Family dinners usually happened on Wednesdays, but it had somewhat morphed into Thursdays over the last few months, having been further postponed to Friday this week.

It was harder to get all of us to come over now that Sal, Adrian, and Leo were not only busy but predominately living in Kansas City proper instead of Lee's Summit. Carmen was often too tired from pastry school that started at the wee hour of five in the morning, while Benny, Maria's younger son, still lived in Kansas City too, while he worked on trying to find another practice here to work for. His hours had been cut down significantly when he all but ghosted them last summer. No one blamed him when he decided getting Carmen back from the O'Sheas' clutches was far more important than his career.

I had been the most consistent, but lately, with everything that had been building up, I wasn't even sure what day it was anymore. Yesterday at the shop could have been days or hours ago and I wouldn't have recalled it completely.

"Why am I getting Ingrid and Nora?" I asked. Not that I minded, but she had a car of her own and I was fairly certain she didn't like help that wasn't asked for.

"She took her car in for an oil change and tire rotation after work and they're keeping it overnight. She tried to back out of dinner, but I'm not having it," my mother said, her face stern, warning me against any objections.

"Shower and pick up the girls. Easy," I said with a grin, bending over to give her a kiss on the cheek. She nodded, seemingly satisfied, before she went back to the front door.

"You might want to shave your face," she said, always needing to have the last word, before she disappeared from sight.

I glanced down at the screens, not sure if I should have been leaving them in such a state when I was so uncertain about R3d2 and when they might pop up and start pushing around. All six of us being at dinner with the moms made us, as an organization, a little less protected. I didn't want to leave us unprotected on this front too.

Fifteen minutes.

No, I didn't have time to do any more, not if Ingrid and Nora were counting on me being there on time.

If R3d2 pushed, I just had to hope my walls would hold long enough for me to come back to this.

Thirty minutes later, I was standing in front of Ingrid's front door. The apartment complex had open-air entrances, and hers was on the lowest level. Immediately the lack of safety set off alarm bells. Anyone could just walk up and break down her door. She and Nora would be sitting ducks. There were also far fewer security cameras than I would have preferred. This wasn't one of our properties, but I would be certain to install a few more cameras, especially ones that watched the perimeter of her home. I wouldn't watch the footage, but it should be recorded in case something was to happen. What kind of slumlord-run complex was this?

Not that I thought Ingrid would ever be someone specifically targeted, but thieves were thieves, and if someone wanted to break into an apartment here, hers would have been high on the list, simply with how easy it would be to get in and out undetected or unnoticed.

I listened for a moment, hearing the sweet sound of Nora's little voice singing as it floated through the thin door as well as what sounded like water running. It was strange being here. I had never come to her home before. We saw each other in more public settings, with only the occasional times she would be at my mother's house. I was eager to see what she lived like, how she decorated her space, what little nuances about her were missing from my mental image of her. Eager and nervous. This was new territory. I was good about keeping myself in check when we were at the shop or just generally in front of other people. Being in her intimate space, with no one around to see us other than Nora, was a whole different scenario.

With a nervous shake out of my hand, I reached up and knocked.

"Mommy! Someone's at the door!" Nora said, and the water shut off a moment later. I could see the shadow of Ingrid approaching the door cautiously before the light behind the peephole was eclipsed.

Good. At least she's vigilant.

The door finally opened, and I was greeted by Ingrid in a way I had never seen before. Her red locks tumbled over her shoulders, perhaps a little frazzled—it was oddly reminiscent of the dream I had woken from less than an hour before—she was wearing jeans, which she wore often to the shop, but instead of the T-shirt and apron that normally hid her figure, she was only wearing a tank top that fit tight to her ample curves, accentuating her body. She did look tired, but there was an ease in the set of her shoulders she didn't normally have. She was home, relaxed. That relaxed nature immediately was erased, shoulders tensing as she saw me.

"Enzo, what are you doing here?"

"Enzo!" Nora squealed, looking up and grinning.

"Hi, Nora! Are you missing a tooth?" I asked, noticing the gap between her top teeth that hadn't been there the last time I saw her.

"I lost it at school today," she said proudly, nodding her head before looking back down at what she was coloring. I glanced back at Ingrid, who was fighting a smile.

"It's a very big deal," Ingrid said to which Nora nodded again, though not looking up from her very important scribbles. "But why are you here?"

"My mom said you two needed a ride to family dinner," I said, grinning as her eyes widened a fraction.

"She did say something about that," Ingrid mumbled, looking at me a bit more appreciatively, as I leaned on the doorframe, her gaze lingering on the tattoos on my forearms before sliding back up to my face. Her cheeks turned a little pink when she saw the smirk I couldn't hide. I may have been wild for her from the moment I saw her, but it was clear she also liked what she saw when she looked at me. The way her breath seemed to quicken, making her chest rise and fall a little more rapidly, and her pupils dilated as they raked over me. The mutual attraction was there. It just wasn't something we had openly explored.

I glanced behind her at the apartment. It was small, the living room and kitchen one open room with a small two-person dining room table smooshed in one corner and covered in coffee mugs, little notes, and, of course, a laptop. Ingrid never talked about her other job. I only knew it was transcribing, but her set up seemed a lot more complex than that. Papers were scattered, notes were scribbled here and there with bits of code that I was familiar with, but nothing that I concerned myself with. Transcribing was not my area, and I had no need to understand what those notes meant.

"Are you ready?" I asked, though it was clear they weren't.

"So we *are* going to Liliana's for dinner?" Nora asked, pausing her coloring and looking up at her mom again.

"Well…"

"We have a little time. I can wait while you get ready," I said, grinning when Nora pumped her fist in the air with excitement, beginning to clear her art project from the coffee table.

"Do you want me to wait in the car?" I asked, watching as Ingrid's eyes started darting around as if she wasn't sure where to look, and a little blush started creeping up her neck.

"I'll show Enzo my pictures while you change, Mommy," Nora said, proudly prancing back to the coffee table and grabbing her notebook.

"You don't have to stay. It won't take long for me—"

"I'd love to," I said to Nora, taking the opportunity I was given, and stepping a little closer. Ingrid's eyes widened at our new closeness, but quickly stepped back, opening the door wider to let me in.

I breathed in her scent, sweet and a little spicy, like cinnamon and vanilla before I moved over to the couch, sitting down while Nora brought back out her drawings and Ingrid stood by the still open door, looking a little shocked that I was sitting in her apartment.

Ingrid closed the door, but I kept my attention firmly focused on the six-year-old who had eagerly plopped next to me, a small stack of drawings clutched in her hands.

"What have you been working on?" I asked, pulling the first one from her grasp and looking it over.

Children's drawings were usually somewhat of an effort for me to look at. The only drawings I ever really paid attention to anymore were artwork done by Rory and Daph. But Nora was surprisingly good for her age. Her proportions may have been off and the colors a little out of the lines, but she added details, like eyelashes and … tattoos?

"That's you," Nora said, pointing to the tall man in the center. There was something in his—my hands and beside me a little girl with red hair.

"And you?" I asked, pointing at the girl.

"Yep! It's my dream. You made me a flower I could keep forever because mommy wouldn't let me take a flower from a pretty garden."

Nora remembered that I dabbled a little in origami, which was interesting since that was two summers ago. She was four and spent the afternoons after camp in the shop. At the time, I would have made up any excuse to see Ingrid—I still did—but I decided to try to teach Nora some of it a few afternoons a week.

She was terrible, but it was fun, and Ingrid seemed to appreciate that I was keeping Nora busy while they closed everything down.

"Shoes, Nora," Ingrid said. I looked over at her, while Nora hopped off the couch and headed down the little hallway to her room, I suspected.

Ingrid had covered that delicious figure from view, but in a lacy top that elevated the jeans she was wearing to a nice casual look for a family dinner. Her hair was back up, but this time clipped, so her curls still framed her face in front, but exposed her neck.

I stood so quickly it was practically involuntary, stepping toward her and perhaps a little too close for casual acquaintances. But we were more than that now; weren't we? We were at least friends.

"You look lovely," I said, watching that beautiful pink color her chest and up to her cheeks.

"Nora was telling you about her dream?" Ingrid asked, taking a step back, which pressed her against the living room wall, right by her tiny dining table.

"She was. Mean Mommy didn't let her have a flower in the garden," I said, my hand moving to touch a curl just beside her cheek. Her breath hitched, pale blue eyes looking at me with desire in a way I was now going to crave with every fiber of my being. Whatever I told myself about staying away from her for her safety apparently went right out the window the moment we were alone.

"And you saved the day," she managed to whisper. Her breath was coming out a little faster, and I realized mine was too, as my face inched forward. I could feel her body heat against my front, my heartbeat pounding in my chest. With so little space between us, it was almost like a current or magnetic force was pulling us even closer.

"I'm not usually a good guy," I said, those words a little more honest than I would have liked to admit.

"No? You don't save the day by giving girls for-ever flowers often, Enzo?" she asked, her voice barely a whisper.

"I used to have girls bent over and begging me for things instead," I whispered, letting my nose get a little closer to hers, feeling her hot breath as it came out as pants against my lips.

"So you're usually naughty like this?" she asked, and the look she gave, as she sucked that thick bottom lip between her teeth, biting it and baiting me like a vixen right before my eyes had me struggling, desperate for her. Our lips were merely millimeters from one another, my hands trapping her against the wall, as my body fought the urge to press against hers. And it was good that I restrained myself—

"Enzo isn't naughty. He's the nicest," Nora said, from the doorway of her room, shoes on and hair in lop-sided pigtails that just accentuated her adorableness. Yes, there was a good reason why I couldn't cross that boundary. A very good reason why I was proud of how well I had held myself back.

I cleared my throat, stepping back away from Ingrid, and using my back being turned toward the door as I walked to it to adjust the growing issue in my pants.

"I think we're ready now," Ingrid said, her voice a mixture between breathless and amused.

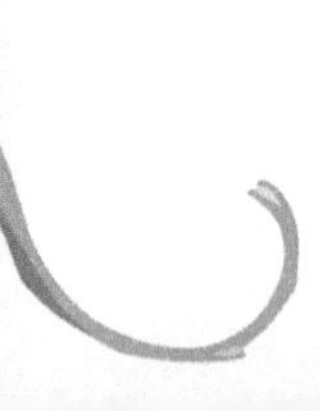

CHAPTER 9

INGRID

Driving to Liliana's house in Enzo's car felt both awkward and familiar. It was odd to know him so well, and yet not at all. What he wore, how he smelled, what each little facial expression meant were all thoroughly engrained in me, and yet I had never been in his car before. It was a nice car, a Lexus from what I knew about car logos. There were screens everywhere, and a place for him to put his phone that connected directly with the car without any wires.

My car was a beat-up twenty-something-year-old Ford that I had bought in cash from selling the car Joe purchased when I was running three years ago. I was surprised it hadn't broken down on me yet, and though I wasn't pleased that the oil change and tire rotation turned into an overnight to fully drain all the fluids and replace them as well as the brake pads, I felt like it was worth it. So many things could and probably would go wrong during this little trip and subsequent fleeing. I didn't need the car I would need to either abandon or sell to break down in the middle of it all.

Being in the car next to Enzo made the luxurious space within seem tight. I was intimately aware of the few inches between our arms on the console, and it was nearly impossible to ignore the way watching him drive did things to me. The only thing keeping me from being a panting mess, especially following whatever happened between us in my apartment, was Nora sitting in the back seat.

Any doubts I had about his flirting in the past had been extinguished. It was clear I affected him. He seemed like he was unable to hold himself back from approaching me, his pupils dilating with desire as he stepped closer. I didn't think I was very pretty. I hadn't thought myself a beauty before I had Nora, and now, my widened hips and additional pounds in my ass and tummy, as well as the stretch marks, didn't exactly make me feel desirable. It didn't help that my ex had made it seem like whatever little amount of looks I had before I got pregnant had disappeared with Nora's birth. A lovely abuse tactic to make me feel like no one else would ever want me.

Enzo looking at me with those gorgeous dark eyes, his body just inches away from touching mine, made me feel like the most beautiful woman in the world.

I had to shut these feelings down. It was easier thinking he had no real interest. I couldn't put myself and Nora in the position to have someone else to lose, someone else to leave behind. It didn't matter if my entire being craved him. It didn't matter if he acted like he couldn't resist me. I had to stay strong.

Enzo was peppering her with questions about other dreams she had, and she was telling him some slightly reimagined versions of the stories she told me over the course of the week. That was yet another thing about him that was breaking these carefully crafted walls around my heart. This man, who outwardly seemed like he could be dangerous, was nothing but gentle and kind with my daughter, so much so that Nora dreamed about him, like he was her knight in shining armor.

"Enzo, do you think you can show me the or-a-gummy again?" Nora asked as we pulled into the driveway of the house next door to Liliana's.

"Origami," he corrected, pausing and turning around to look at her.

"Or-eye-gum—"

"Or-i-gah-mi," he said slower this time, being sure she was watching his mouth as he spoke.

"Or-i-gah-mi," she said, mimicking him.

"Yes! You did it," he said, holding out his hand for a high five that Nora reciprocated happily. "And of course I will. That way you can make your own forever flowers." And with that, he turned back to me, winking and smiling so handsomely that I nearly choked, before he got out of the car.

Nora grabbed Enzo's hand as we made our way across the yards to Liliana's house. He opened the door with no knock or indication he was about to walk through. Like this was his home, although I supposed it had been. If I still had family, would I feel comfortable just walking into their house?

No. There had never been a time I had truly felt comfortable like that, except for the little apartment Nora and I had shared here in Lee's Summit. This was the only place that had ever really felt like home.

The scent of something delicious hit my nose as we made our way inside. A chorus of "Enzo!" rang out, but my view was still partially obstructed by Enzo's body.

I closed the door behind me, pausing at it as Enzo and Nora made their way farther into the living room, letting myself take in the scene so I knew how to behave.

All of them were there. Enzo's brothers, Sal and Leo, and of course the LaMartinas, Adrian, Benny, and Carmen. I assumed Liliana and Maria were in the kitchen making the final dinner preparations. Nora seemed so effortlessly comfortable waltzing in hand in hand with Enzo while he got round after round of hugs from the various Lupos and LaMartinas gathered there.

This was what family was. What it was supposed to be.

"Ingrid! I'm so glad you and Nora came!" Liliana said as she came through from the dining room, dish towel in her hands. She stopped to kiss Enzo on the cheek and gave Nora a hug before coming to me. I was still at the door, clearly set apart from the others, but she ushered me in for a hug.

"You kids sit, dinner will be ready in a few minutes," Maria said warmly from the doorway Liliana had come through. I knew this house fairly well from bringing Nora here nearly every day, but something about it being filled with people always put me off and made me feel a little less comfortable. Especially this particular gathering, since it was clearly strictly family attending this dinner. Family plus me and Nora.

"Red or white wine, Ingrid?" Carmen asked as the men all settled into spots on the couches, Nora squeezing in between Enzo and Benny.

"Oh, I shouldn't," I said with a smile, gesturing to Nora.

"I definitely understand," Carmen said with a little chuckle. "If you change your mind—which you might, having to deal with these heathens—let me know."

"Come sit," Sal said, gesturing to an open armchair. It faced the couch where Nora was poking at Enzo's forearm and asking about what his tattoo there meant.

"That one we all have," Enzo said about a six-pointed start on his wrist.

I had noticed it many times before but never thought to ask. I had never asked about any of his tattoos, even though there were plenty I had noticed and been intrigued about. I briefly wondered how many more tattoos he had that I hadn't seen, my mind wandering to the possibility of tattoos hidden from my view, especially with the new vision of him in that tight-knit shirt just a few days ago, his lean, muscled torso barely hidden behind that fabric.

"Why?" Nora asked, glancing around at the others now with a look of confusion as she tried to find the same one on them. I tore my eyes away from Enzo as his met mine, hoping he hadn't seen anything in my face in that split second. My cheeks felt hot, and I desperately wanted something to drink. Maybe a glass of wine wouldn't have been so bad after all.

"Because we promised to be here for each other always," Carmen said, standing and coming closer to Nora to offer her own wrist up for inspection. Carmen hadn't had any tattoos when she moved up to the city with Leo, so these must have been fairly recent.

One by one, they all pulled back their sleeves and showed their own six-pointed stars.

"Do I have to get a tattoo?" Nora asked, touching Carmen's wrist and then Enzo's.

"No one should be getting tattoos," Liliana said as she stepped back into the living room. Everyone grinned up at her, loving the way the moms thoroughly hated the tattoos.

"You could get matching ones too," Enzo said playfully as he stood.

"Enzo Salvatore Lupo! Don't even joke!" Liliana squealed. "Dinner is ready," she said almost indignantly, turning back toward the dining room.

We all moved together toward the large, round dining table. Nora and I had been at family dinners before, but mostly it had been when other non-family members had been there too, like Daph and Rory, Carmen's best friends, and one Christmas, Ash.

They all settled around the table, Carmen sitting beside her mother, Maria, with Leo right beside her, Benny next to him, followed by Adrian and then Sal, while Enzo sat beside his mother Liliana, leaving only space for me and Nora between him and his brother. I hesitated, unsure about sitting next to Enzo. I wasn't sure being so close in proximity to him, when I could barely hold it together in the car, was a good idea, but Nora made the decision for me, quickly sitting next to Enzo and smiling up at him.

"Minestrone," Adrian said, a delighted groan escaping as Maria pulled the ceramic lid off the giant crock in the center of the table. There was also salad, and a bread loaf laid out.

"I let it cook all day," Maria said with pride.

The soup was ladled out into bowls, salad passed around, which Nora wrinkled her nose at, and of course, the bread.

"Oh, Nora can't have butter," I said, realizing Enzo was preparing to pour some of the melted butter over the piece he had gotten her.

"It's olive oil and roasted crushed garlic, no cheese or butter. We know she's lactose intolerant," Enzo said, but still keeping the spoon paused, waiting for my go-ahead before he poured it over the waiting slice.

"If that's okay with you, Nora?" I asked, watching as her face scrutinized the contents of the spoon.

"Is it good?" Nora asked in a whisper, leaning a little closer to Enzo.

"I think it is," he whispered back, glancing up at me. "Maybe we try just a little and you decide. If you don't like it, I'll eat it, okay?"

She nodded, watching him slather a little of the mixture on the bread, before setting it on the small dish beside her bowl of soup.

I wasn't sure how to take this. Nora, though too young to remember anything about her father, hadn't really had any men in her life who actually took much of an interest in her, let alone treated her with such care. Hell, *I* hadn't ever been treated with such care as he was showing her. Something as innocent as Enzo being kind and patient with my little one had me feeling… Well, I wasn't sure, but I was getting unexpectedly aroused just by witnessing it.

Conversation started out normally, Adrian started talking about the gym and the slow in business over the winter.

"It will boom soon. Summer's coming," Sal said, trying to be reassuring, I assumed.

"I heard some women were scared to go back there after they heard about the shooting that almost happened last year," I said, immediately regretting letting the words out instead of just thinking them. A gun had been pulled on Carmen, and though it had been early morning, some of the ladies who normally jogged on the treadmills had apparently seen it from their cars in the parking lot. One thing about Lee's Summit being a small place was that people talked.

"Benny, how close are you to leaving that practice?" Sal asked, seeming to ignore my comment.

"A few weeks. They hired a new PT. I'm just waiting until his start date to talk him through my patients that I can't keep."

"Part of the slowness might be the construction," Carmen offered, also not addressing what I had said. I wasn't aware of any construction on the gym, but then again, I hadn't been going there as often to work out with Ash as I had been. I had been far too busy with my two jobs to do the one thing I felt was actually helping keep me and Nora safe.

"Benny is going to do physical therapy work out of the gym now," Enzo offered, his voice surprising me a little at its quiet closeness. So close I could feel his breath on my neck.

"Sasha said the shop was busy today," Liliana said to me, drawing everyone's attention back to my now blushing face.

"A normal Friday," I said with a nod, watching as Nora took a bite of the bread Enzo had given her tentatively, instead of the sea of Italian eyes that I was certain were scrutinizing every little move I made.

"Not normal, Mommy! You said Enzo didn't come in," Nora said, her mouth full of soup.

Why did I choose to share these things with her? It was only a matter of time before they bit me in the ass. I narrowed my eyes at her, and she gave me a questioning expression. "That's what you said when you picked me up and we were talking about our day."

"Yes," I said, a bit clipped, fighting with the instinct to look up and meet the gaze of the man, who I could feel was watching me. It was practically burning into my skin.

I failed miserably, looking up to see a heat in those brown irises like I saw in my apartment earlier. For the briefest of moments, we were in our own little bubble, the radiating heat of desire passing between us and through us. If Nora hadn't sat between us, if we had been able to touch, it may have been a massive problem. I couldn't afford problems like this.

"Who was at the shop then, Enzo?" Leo asked. I glanced at him, tearing my eyes from Enzo's. It should have felt safer to be looking away, but the mild anger simmering in Leo's face, as well as the concern, confused me more than anything.

"Travis. He was there yesterday too," Enzo said.

Something passed between the others. A strange silent communication I wasn't privy to was happening. Why was someone being sent to the shop if Enzo wasn't there?

Suddenly I wondered if the reason Enzo came into the shop every day wasn't for me, but for some other reason entirely.

"I brought some ciambella I thought we might try. If you like it, Liliana, I can come show Sasha and Ingrid how to make them this weekend," Carmen said suddenly, clearly trying to steer the topic to other subjects.

Both Liliana and Maria gasped in pleasure. I wasn't sure what was ciambella was, but I assumed it was some sort of pastry. Part of the reason Carmen had gone to pastry chef school was to help the shop. I wasn't sure if her plan was to move back to Lee's Summit following the program or not, but clearly, she was still wanting to help.

"Nora and I have to go somewhere this weekend, but I'm sure Sasha can give me the pointers if it's something we put on the menu regularly," I murmured. My discomfort at this dinner was mounting. It was hard enough coming into a family gathering, a family I was not a part of, then to have several awkward moments occur during the dinner conversation. I was ready to go and perhaps ready to not see most of them for several days, even if this trip wasn't going to be pleasant either.

"Where are you going?" Enzo asked, pausing from his soup to look over at me.

"It's none of our business," Liliana said, sending a warning glare toward her son. I appreciated that. I was far too much in the spotlight right now and preferred the idea of hiding back in shadowy silence for the remainder of the evening. That's honestly what I preferred always, which was why I was so much more confident behind a screen than I was in real life.

"We're going to St. Louis to see Uncle," Nora said, making me tense a little.

Joe was in St. Louis, and though he wasn't actually Nora's uncle, it was an easier way to explain him to her than anything else. I wasn't going to be visiting with him though. Nora would be staying with him, staying away from me and this meeting, to keep her safe. None of these things I could share with the people sitting around the table, though something deep within me wanted to. An urge, like I could truly trust them, ran through me with a force. It startled me a bit as I glanced over at Enzo, who was still watching me with a question in his eyes.

"Just a visit," I said quietly, forcing a tight-lipped smile at him, which only made his brow furrow all that much more.

"Boys, why don't you clear the table, and Carmen can break out that ciambella!" Maria said, thankfully pulling attention away from me once more.

I stayed silent, keeping myself out of the conversation and only uttering a word here and there to keep Nora from getting out of hand. The ciambella was delicious, of course, but it was Nora's large yawn and the way she leaned against Enzo's shoulder that finally got Liliana to put the evening to an end.

As we were saying our goodbyes, Nora in my arms and slumped, just about ready to sleep, Carmen came to give us a hug.

"I know something is wrong, Ingrid. We've been friends for too long for me not to notice. You know we're all here for you if you need help," Carmen whispered in my ear as she squeezed us tight.

"I know," I whispered back, clutching a little harder than I normally would have.

They all meant it. I knew the Lupos and LaMartinas would step up if I let them, but I knew, and it had been proven time and time again, that the only person I could really count on was myself. No matter how much it broke my heart to reiterate, I couldn't let these people in, not now.

CHAPTER 10

INGRID

Unsurprisingly, Nora fell asleep on the car ride home. She had been about asleep in my arms during the twenty minutes of saying goodbye to everyone, and it took little to no time to see her breathing even out as she slumped against the car door, limbs limp and head lulled. Nora's lack of consciousness made the air seem so thick once Enzo pulled up and parked close to where my building was. He turned the car off, looking over at me, but neither of us made a move to get out just yet.

I was on the cusp of overwhelming lust for this man, while simultaneously hoping he didn't notice my car had been brought back from the mechanic and was sitting just one hundred feet away from where he had parked. I had paid extra for the service to bring it so Nora and I could still leave tonight, but I didn't need him seeing it was returned. He had come over here to pick us up after all. And a single mother struggling to make ends meet for her daughter shouldn't have been paying extra for something as frivolous as having their car returned to them in the late evening.

"I can carry her in," he offered, his hand lifting like he was going to touch me, but instead his fingers curled into a fist, as if he resisted the urge.

"I can do it," I said, turning away from him and starting to gather our things. My bag and, of course, the leftovers that Liliana and Maria insisted we take were a bit more than I'd usually have to carry while hauling my six-year-old's dead weight, but I had managed worse before. As I climbed out of the car and started getting myself collected to grab Nora from the back seat, Enzo stepped out, opening the back seat and getting her unbuckled.

"It's fine, Enzo," I said, starting to come over to his side.

"Just go unlock the front door," he said, smoothly lifting Nora from the car, her head nestled in the crook of his neck, still soundly asleep.

I wanted to argue, of course, but I didn't want to wake Nora in the midst of it. I also had a lot that needed to be done before we left and, if I was being honest with myself, I wanted Enzo to come back into my apartment. I wanted him to be sweet to Nora, to lay her peacefully in her bed, so I could have another moment with him like we had before dinner.

I unlocked the apartment, quickly opening the door wide for Enzo to step through, closing the door as soon as he was. He strode toward the small hallway, pausing as he saw the three closed doors before him. I quickly set the bags on the coffee table, joining him in there.

"That one," I whispered, pointing to Nora's room on the left.

He pushed it open, and with such grace you would have suspected he had done this before, he laid her on her bed. I moved closer, planning to take off her shoes and tuck her in, but he kneeled beside the bed and began carefully untying the little tennis shoes from her feet, setting them on the floor, before pulling the covers over her still sleeping body.

We both froze for a moment when she stirred, but it was clear she was only snuggling into the warmth of her pillows, quickly falling still with even breathing a moment later.

The two of us crept out of the room and I closed the door soundlessly behind me, watching him as he walked back into the main living space.

"Thank you. You didn't have to do that," I murmured as I moved to grab the bag of leftovers.

"You didn't have to come to dinner," he said with a shrug. I let a little smile creep to my lips, turning and snatching the leftover containers to take to the kitchen so he hopefully didn't see how much his presence affected me.

No, I didn't have to come to dinner, and while there were moments I felt like an outsider, that was the sort of family I wished I had, the kind I wished I could give Nora. I had been silent for the last portion of the evening, but it gave me a glimpse into what a real family was like. Continuous conversation, inside jokes, and laughter filled Liliana's home and Nora was right in the thick of it, soaking it in with enthusiasm. I hadn't ever been privy to such a thing, but that didn't mean Nora didn't deserve it. It was just something I couldn't give her. I could only hope the new life we made after this she would be able to grow up and make that happen when she was an adult.

"And thank you for being so sweet to Nora."

"I'd say she's the best girl I know, but I'd be lying. There's one other that I like just a little more than her," he said. His voice was closer, and I turned in my small kitchen, container of soup in one hand, to see him leaning on the counter near the entrance, eyes burning as they scorched a path over my body before landing on my face.

"Whoever the other girl is must be lucky then, or cursed. I'm not sure what I'd do if I was the object of such a nerd's affections. Seems like he'd have his nose in a computer instead of paying any attention to me," I said, somehow unable to contain the words as they spilled from my mouth.

He stepped closer, pulling the container from my hands and setting it aside. He was so close now, his body heat radiating and warming me, even if he wasn't touching me. When he set his eyes back on mine, I saw every ounce of desire he felt. It was shocking. That raw need in him, a need he felt for *me*. I was a worn-out, stretched-thin mom with a body that wouldn't have been suitable for a bikini come summer, and yet he looked at me like I was the most beautiful and desirable woman on the planet.

"Why are you always so tired, Ingrid?" he asked, his hand that seemed to have a mind of its own going to my hair again, dangerously close to my cheek.

"Just a busy single mom," I whispered, unable to control the way my voice came out more as a pant. "Why are you?"

The question had him pausing, eyes searching mine as if he were debating telling me some big secret. I watched that war within him for a moment, my own hands moving to grasp his wrist. The electricity that flowed through us at the simple touch was amazing. A fire started low in my belly as my skin met his, one that was only mildly squelched by the concern that danced within his dark eyes.

"Oh, Ingrid," he whispered, that hand of his finally moving forward to cup my cheek. I let out a shaky breath. "I wish I could tell you… I wish it was safe," he murmured, his body inching its way to mine, his head dipping down to be tantalizingly near mine.

Suddenly my insecurities about why he was at the shop all the time and why Travis had been there in his stead reared its ugly head once more. Despite the fact that his attraction was now becoming obvious to me, that little mention at dinner had my instincts flaring.

"Nora," I said quietly, watching as his face grew even more solemn.

Enzo's head moved back, hand slipping from my face as he stepped away.

"Of course," he said with a nod, still looking at me, but it was with such a look of sadness and longing.

"I don't know what you mean by 'safe,' but I can't do anything to risk her," I said, watching as his fingers curled into fists and his forearms flexed with frustration.

"If my life was different, Ingrid, I'd—" He cut himself off, shaking his head and closing his eyes.

"Mine too," I whispered, watching as he opened his eyes and looked at me once more, though this time more thoughtfully and curious, but still with a hint of confusion. We were living such different lives, and he didn't even know all the factors that made me unable to be with him, let alone trust him.

"I'll see you at the shop," he said in barely a whisper before he turned and began walking toward the front door.

You won't.

My heart lurched in my chest as I watched him, his confident gait now a little stiff. He paused halfway, looking like he was going to turn and say something again. I both wanted him to stop, to stay, while simultaneously needing him to leave. I had to prepare. I had to finish doing everything so we could head to Joe. I needed him gone so I could cry while I did, release the pain that was building, and fully let myself feel the loss of something that never really was.

His brow furrowed, his face turned toward the little dining table that was really my desk, before he continued, opening and closing the door without another word.

I let out a shaky breath once I couldn't hear his footsteps anymore and grabbed the leftovers, placing them in the fridge as I had been before he took them from my hands. I had already begun packing our bags before Enzo got there. I just needed to do a few finishing touches. I wasn't even sure if we'd return here after I did whatever I needed to for Colin, but I knew there was a possibility we would never return.

My room looked like a bomb had gone off. It was a good thing Enzo hadn't pushed this door open instead of Nora's. Three large suitcases were lying out across the floor and two additional bags were on my bed. Clothes for all seasons were already in the suitcases, while toiletries and important documents were going in the duffels. I pulled Nora's clothes first, knowing once she was asleep, it would be far harder to take anything from her room. The final things were odds and ends essentials.

I'd have very little time to load the car up and get Nora in. Hopefully, she would sleep the whole way there. I was sliding my laptop into my bag when I realized I hadn't checked on my algorithm since Enzo came to the door, nor had I finished procuring all the contacts for the new documentation Nora and I would need following the job Colin wanted me to do.

It wasn't until I came outside for the first time, a suitcase in each hand as I rolled them down the sidewalk, that I realized Enzo was still there?

Odd that he would be here so much longer after he left, only to head right back to his car.

Odd, especially since it was so very late at night.

I didn't have time to postulate on that though. I would think about it more as I drove. Now, I hid in the shadow of the breezeway, watching until his headlights finally turned on with the turnover of his engine, before he backed out and left the parking lot. I stayed motionless for a few moments longer, not sure if I trusted that he was truly gone before I made my way to the car with the suitcases and loaded them in.

I took the next two loads of our things to the car, rushing back to the apartment to do a sweep. My mind was racing with thoughts. All the things I needed to do. All the things I might have forgotten.

Enzo.

Certainly, I would forget something, but it would be far too late by the time I remembered it. The last thing, the most important thing, was Nora.

Carefully, I scooped her up from her bed, slowly walking her to the car and buckling her in. She only sleepily groaned a time or two when I was doing so, but otherwise was fast asleep. Suddenly I was a little more grateful for being forced to come to family dinner. Between Maria and Liliana's dinner and Carmen's dessert, Nora was in a food coma that she likely wouldn't wake from until we were nearly at our destination.

I pulled out the burner phone from my pocket, quickly sending Joe a message that we were on our way, before starting the car and pulling away, unsure if we would ever step foot here again.

CHAPTER 11

ENZO

My heart lurched in my chest as I got back in my car. Breathing heavy, my body not sure how to deal with the varying emotions rolling through me. Desire that had been so potent my whole body was alight, wanting to touch her everywhere, not just on her soft cheek, had been nearly suffocated by fear and sadness. My life, especially right now, would put a target on her back. Nora wouldn't be safe, able to sleep peacefully in her bed, if any of our enemies caught wind of a relationship between us.

Ingrid and Nora deserved so much better than a mobster like me, even if every fiber of my being wanted her.

I sat in my car, looking out across the little walkway that led toward her front door. I didn't want to move. I didn't want to leave, but I had to.

I wanted to be able to check up on her, and the serious lack of security in this apartment complex was disturbing, to say the least. We only had two residential rental properties in Lee's Summit, the one I had lived in before and the one Adrian and Sal had apartments in. Neither saw much use these days, with both of them needing to be in Kansas City proper much more often. I had given up my apartment to move into Maria's house, but they kept theirs for when they came back into Lee's Summit from the Kansas City house that used to be our father's.

The energy that had been building up in my body with sadness, regret, and longing seemed to shift, turning into determination, as I started my car and whipped out of the parking lot.

One, this apartment complex was going to be purchased by us at some point soon. I wasn't going to allow people who lived in this area to have to deal with subpar property management and security. Two, I was going to make sure that until that time, Ingrid's apartment had appropriate imaging. It wouldn't be monitored all the time, but I would be able to check and make sure she was safe.

It was the only thing I could do to keep myself from going and knocking on her door again.

Fingers gripping the steering wheel, I headed over to Breakers, the bar we owned. For many years Breakers had been my workspace, the office above providing me with plenty of room for all my computers and monitors, but obviously, I had been spending all my time between the shop and Maria's old house, so this space went unused most of the time, and became more of a storage area.

I parked, and a moment later Sal pulled up beside me.

"I was going to text you. Wasn't sure if you'd make it back out of Ingrid's apartment tonight though," Sal said with a little smirk.

"Ingrid and I are just friends," I said, not even bothering to hide the frustration from my voice at the truth in that.

"Sounds like someone needs a drink," Sal said after a long sigh as he looked me over.

"No. Too much to do tonight," I said, thinking of what I planned to do before I even went back to the computer screens waiting for me at home. It would be an absolute disaster if I decided to do any drinking. I had too much to do, and now I had just decided I needed to do one more thing that had nothing to do with work, even if I was trying to convince myself it was for Ingrid's safety.

"Enzo, I don't want you getting too overwhelmed with all of this. Look at you," Sal said, taking my face in his hands and scrutinizing my exhausted features that probably looked worse due to the emotional torture I was putting myself through with Ingrid. "You look dead on your feet. We can wait another day. You should go home and go to sleep."

"Just one thing I need to grab, and I promise I'll head that way," I murmured, though that was far from the truth.

"Once we get through this arrangement with the Cartel, I want you actively searching for someone to take over some of these tasks. Salvatore shouldn't have had you running all of this on your own anyway, and then we were in the thick of it before we could even start thinking about the additional help," Sal said as we began our little walk to the doors of the bar that was already packed and booming with noise.

"I thought about reaching out to Kia for a little help with monitoring, just so I could catch up a bit," I admitted.

"On sleep?"

"On everything," I said with a chuckle, watching the genuine smile spread over Sal's face. That was something I was fairly good at, putting those around me at ease. I was a mediator, the middle child, the one who always fixed everything, but never got the credit. I was used to it, but it was rare that making something go smoothly for someone else made me as happy as it did them. Sal was just as stressed as I was, and here he was, trying to make sure I was okay. I was proud to get a real smile from him before we parted ways.

I waved toward the table that had become ours, the high top in the corner where we always seemed to gravitate ever since that first night out with all six of us when Leo came home last summer. All of them were there, now that Sal was settling onto the stool beside Adrian. They all waved back, Carmen looking concerned when I didn't join them, but Sal saying something that turned her concern to a deep pout, before I pushed behind the bar and up the back stairs to the office. I was there just a few days ago, grabbing new cameras to set up at the gym, so I knew how many we had and right where they were, but for some reason, my mind kept wondering about this whole life of Ingrid's that I didn't get to know about. It was an unsaid barrier, just like my involvement in the Mafia.

Not that I hadn't wondered for years, but I had decided to wait. I was waiting for us to be close enough, for her to trust me enough to tell me all about it herself, not for me to dive into her past and tear it all from the depths of the internet. That hadn't felt right to do, but now the urge, the need, especially with the impending feeling like there would never be a time where we were close enough or she trusted me enough to tell me herself… I was never going to get answers if I kept waiting.

That thought carried me and built within me as I took the camera, tucking it under my arm, and moving back down through the bar, completely not noticing if anyone was trying to get my attention as I did so, and back to my car. It stayed with me as I drove back to Ingrid's apartment and parked much farther away than I had before, so my engine wasn't noticeable to her if she was still awake. It stayed with me as I silently made my way toward her building, standing in various places until I found the perfect location for the camera to go with an angle toward her apartment that got most of the front door and exterior windows.

I couldn't get it out of my head, and more to that point, I was wondering who this "Uncle" was that Ingrid and Nora were going to see. She had never mentioned anyone or visited anyone from her life before coming here, and now suddenly she and Nora were going on a trip across the state to see someone Nora probably didn't even remember?

It made me nervous and jealous.

I knew it wasn't a healthy response, but I was too tired to be a decent man anymore. I needed to know.

I hooked up the camera, tapping into the building's public electrical source, which I hacked into on my phone to briefly turn off, quickly making my way back to my car and driving to the house.

At this point, my brain was working so fast and had already come up with so many possible conclusions to the answers I was burning to get that I wasn't sure where I would even begin. Every conversation Ingrid and I had ever had was replaying through my mind.

I didn't even remember how I got out of my car or into the dark house. I didn't remember sitting at my computer, but suddenly there I was, my fingers on the keyboard and all my screens alight.

The overwhelming need to check in on Ingrid and her life was pulling at me, tearing at my insides with insistence, while the other, more gentlemanly part of me was disgusted at what I was even considering.

But I wasn't a good guy. I had just told Ingrid that myself.

I was in the Mafia.

This is what we did.

We lied, stole, extorted, and blackmailed.

Looking up Ingrid's information was no different.

I pulled up a new window and began my search.

At first, it seemed like nothing. On the surface, Ingrid was exactly what she was on paper and before our eyes. A single mom who worked at the coffee shop, occasionally she had done small gigs to make a little more money, and she had been working as a medical transcriptionist online for some time, there were a few other jobs she had done, helping set up computers for people in the neighborhood on her days off, but nothing big. Everything about what I knew from the last few years was there and made sense.

I was about to dive into her life before she came to Lee's Summit when I realized that she had worked for the medical transcription job until late July of last year. The transcription work had always been to supplement her and Nora's income and make things a little more comfortable for them. She used that money predominantly for things for Nora and a savings account, from the looks of it, but when the shop closed last summer because we were all focusing on getting Carmen back, Ingrid left the transcriptionist job as well.

What was she doing on the computer to keep her up so late that she looked like she barely slept?

Thinking of the tasks that kept people from sleeping, I glanced at my other screens. One was monitoring the activity around us, there were a couple nudges, probably from smalltime hackers or smaller operations just seeing what I had up, but when I clicked around, looking for those telltale breadcrumbs that R3d2 usually left, the only things I found were old, from the night before.

Red wasn't logged on this evening either. They had boosted their firewalls at some point while I had been occupied, but it was odd that they weren't active, that I couldn't see their movements like I normally could. But if they were offline and I couldn't see anything they were up to, then they couldn't see mine. The last thing I needed was to have this hacker who worked for Colin O'Shea catching wind of Ingrid because I was looking deep into her life.

She'd become a target.

Target.

My mind flashed to the vision of Ingrid's desk. Sticky notes and loose papers scattered the surface, often like what my desk space looked like. Nothing on those papers was things that had to do with transcription work. It was code. Pieces of code, dates, locations, businesses.

What should have caught my attention immediately was the fact that Ultima Incorporated had been scribbled on something that had caught my eye for a moment before I had dismissed it at the time.

That was our business.

Ultima Incorporated was the family-owned company that fronted everything we did. It was started by our father, Salvatore Lupo, and was now taken over by my brother Sal. We had a dummy board of directors, which were essentially all influential people in the Kansas City metro area that would help us hide our true money-making, but that's all it really was.

Now, in all fairness, that was the umbrella company that held all our other assets. The coffee shop that my mother ran and Ingrid worked for was under this umbrella, the gym, Breakers, our rental company, and the others we had in Kansas City. Someone smart, like Ingrid, would have figured that out if she looked into it enough, but coupled with the rest of the notes and scribblings I had seen around her desk…

A lump had formed in my throat.

My fingers shook a little as I put them back up to my keyboard.

There was only one real way to solve this puzzle. I had to look at her bank accounts.

I had been itching to look at her monetary situation for a very long time. Originally, I wanted to try to figure out how to deposit additional money into her account each month in a way she wouldn't notice, but then I realized what a breach of privacy it would be, very nearly unforgivable if she ever found out. Now, I just needed to know what she was doing that was keeping her up so late. There was no way she was engaging in something that made her seem so exhausted all the time if she wasn't getting money from it in one form or another.

The first thing I noticed when I logged in was how many accounts she had. Most of them had little labels on them. "Bills," "Food," and "Emergency," were on display, but those weren't the only accounts listed there. Nora had her own separate savings account, but there was also another account. It was unnamed, just a checking account, but it had quite a bit of money in it.

There were more than a few thoughts going through my head, but all of them were telling me if I looked into this account, if I saw the activity there, I would not be happy with what I saw.

Deposits, not huge deposits, but decent-sized amounts were landing in that account each week. Some funds were transferred out to her other accounts, but all these deposits were coming from one source.

Stately Enterprises.

My lungs spasmed at the sight of those words. Heart squeezing and adrenaline flooding my system.

My first instinct was to believe she was innocent somehow. That the work she had been doing for Stately Enterprises had been sparing. Transcribing, as we had all been led to believe, but as I delved deeper, I saw this was not the case. The codes, dates, and times I had seen on her desk, they all lined up to attacks on our systems. Even the system going down just days ago, that was her.

No. It can't be true.

My mind was racing as I went back to the IP addresses I had traced for R3d2. I had always meant to dig deeper, knowing that if there was a time they were sloppy enough, I'd be able to follow the trail to their real location. They used the same one too many times in a row, but I had never dug into it enough. I should have. Oh, I should have.

The IP address in Washington state seemed to be R3d2's most used and recently they had used it quite a lot. Minutes, maybe hours, of peeling back layer by layer, all the while telling myself this was just a way to prove my own theory wrong, and I finally got to the final destination.

Lee's Summit.

Her apartment.

A VPN purchased from her accounts.

I could see the transactions lining up.

I could see it all now.

Each layer I slipped past showed me more. This girl was not only in deep, but she was in the trenches. Her call signs showed me everything I didn't want to know. Though a small part of me didn't want to believe it, there was another part of me that was utterly thrilled to be discovering this. Ingrid was R3d2. She was the White Hat hacker that I had revered for years, right under my nose and ornery to say the least. I was both thrilled, aroused, and horrified at the same time. This girl I had wanted for years was also the hacker I had been battling with. She was everything I wanted in a woman and more, but she was also my enemy.

My heart in my throat, I pulled up the feed to her apartment I had just installed. It had been hours since I left there, but if I was catching on to this news about her, I wouldn't be surprised if others were also on to her. I could have kept digging deeper instead of watching the feed from the time I left to the present, but I needed to know she was safe, at least for the night. Safe from me after tonight? That was uncertain for now.

But when I started from the moment the camera started recording, my face the only thing in view for a moment, before I quickly walked away to leave for the night, it was barely a moment later that Ingrid came out of her front door, two suitcases in hand. I watched with rapt attention, confused as to where she was taking these suitcases, but also intrigued. She made her way over to the parking lot and put the luggage into … her car.

Her car had been there?

My nostrils flared at the lies.

So. Many. Lies.

I had just been installing a camera for her safety, and she was packing her car that was supposed to be in the shop and—I stopped to watch again. Trip after trip, she was loading her car with more and more bags. This was far more than simply an over-the-weekend stay if she was taking nearly everything they owned except the furniture.

What was she doing?

What was she doing leaving the safe haven that was Lee's Summit and going to St. Louis? Why was she going there? Who was this "uncle" as Nora had called him?

I watched the feed, now completely fixated.

I knew this was hours ago now, but everything within me shook as I watched her carry the still-sleeping form of Nora to the car and buckle her in. My eyes glanced at the clock. It was nearly eleven. I had left her three or four hours ago. How far had she already gotten?

Without another moment to spare, I hacked into the GPS in her phone from mine as I stood, grabbing my keys from the table where I had thrown them, and heading right out the door. The moms had most likely been in bed for hours, not long after everyone left, but looking over at the darkened house where Ingrid kept up the charade just made me even more angry, slamming my car door unnecessarily as I pressed the start button and heard the engine rev to life.

I was certain there was a story about how she got involved with Colin O'Shea and had been actively working against us for months, and I was going to find out what it was.

CHAPTER 12

INGRID

The journey wasn't a long one from Lee's Summit to St. Louis. The four hours or so normally passed by in a blink, especially when you have a little one who chatters on about things, asks plenty of questions, or simply sings in the cutest way about everything she could see out the window. When that child is asleep and the world is dark and quiet, however, it's an entirely different story. I struggled to keep my focus, staring at the long stretches of dark highway, my mind racing with all the things I should have been doing as well as the ache of what we were leaving behind.

It was close to one in the morning when I turned off the exit, moving through the streets of downtown St. Louis toward the address Joe had given me. The neighborhood was pretty run down, not surprising for St. Louis, but still a little daunting when I was planning on leaving my daughter here for a few days. I pulled to the stop sign just before I arrived at his house, glancing in the rearview mirror at the still-sleeping face of Nora. The things I would do for that girl were limitless, but leaving her behind here, even for her safety, was going to be harder than any of the other things we've ever done so far.

With a deep breath, I pressed the accelerator, pulled up to the address, and turned off the car. Joe's house was a tiny thing that looked like it was a few square feet bigger than the garden shed that sat out in Liliana's backyard. The lights were on in the front windows, while most of the other houses on the street were dark. He was awake and waiting for us. I got out, going to Nora's door and crouching down so I could brush the hair from her face.

"Nora, baby," I whispered, watching as her face moved a little, rousing from her sleep.

"Mm?"

"We're at Uncle Joe's house," I said.

Her eyes fluttered open, landing on me, then moving to look around. She was excited to see her "uncle," having not met any family members before. I was hoping Joe had enough kindness in him to be sweet to her. Otherwise, this would be far more traumatic for her than I would have liked. Even if that was the case, it was the lesser of evils. I couldn't take her with me to this meeting and she couldn't come with me when I got the items we required to once again disappear.

"You think he'll like me?" she asked quietly, turning back to me as I unbuckled her and helped her out of the car.

"Everyone likes you, Nora," I said, kissing her red curls and moving to grab a bag from the trunk of the car.

"There she is!" came the gravelly voice of Joe as I closed the trunk.

He came wandering down the few porch steps, looking very much the same as he did three years ago. His hair was perhaps a little grayer, but his face was practically unchanged, except perhaps for the addition of a few worry lines. He was not a particularly tall man, perhaps short for normal, but when I knew him before, he was built and clearly formidable; that hadn't changed. Joe was intimidating, but the smile that spread over his face when he looked at Nora was genuine and showed a sweetness I had only seen once when we were running before.

"Uncle Joe?" she asked hesitantly, looking at me for confirmation. I nodded, and she immediately took off, closing the distance between them and jumping to give him a hug. He seemed a little startled, but scooped her up, hugging her back. His face seemed to melt into a sad one as he hugged her.

We silently went into his house. The furnishings were pretty bare, just a couch, a chair, and a few side tables scattered. A TV was mounted on the wall, but there was nothing else decorating the barren gray that they were painted. There was a two-seater dining table that sat against the wall just before the tiny kitchen. A small hall was on one side, where presumably the bedroom and bathroom were.

"I'll be sleeping on the couch, and Nora can have my bed until you get back," he said, watching me as I took everything in.

"I won't be long," I said as Nora slumped on the couch, eyes glued to the cooking show that was playing on the muted TV.

"I won't let harm come to her," Joe said, pulling my gaze from my dozing child to his face. It was sincere, but something about those words felt oddly specific.

"You better not," I said coldly, holding his attention for a moment to stress my seriousness, before moving to crouch by the couch in front of Nora. "I'll only be a day and a half. I promise I'll come back, and we won't be apart again."

"I can already tell I like Joe," Nora said sleepily, bringing her little hand up to my cheek as my own hand cupped her baby-soft forehead.

"Be good for him. I love you, Nora."

"Love you too, Mama," she said, yawning a bit before snuggling into the one pillow on the couch.

I stood, watching her for a moment, then giving Joe a final warning look, before turning and heading back out to my car. Each step away from my daughter was like a painful stab in my heart that made it hard to breathe.

The room was dark, but I wanted it that way. Somehow, the dark was comforting at that moment. I needed a little extra peace as I tried to get my body to calm. I had panicked most of the ride to Chicago from St. Louis, feeling the ever-growing distance between me and Nora as well as the mounting anxiety of doing one final job for Stately Enterprises. It didn't help that I was driving right back into the city I had fled from three years ago. I had no idea if Elliot was still living there, let alone alive, but if he was, I felt like he'd have some sort of sixth sense as soon as I breached the barrier of the city limits.

I had gotten to the Airbnb I rented, went in, and then sat in the complete and utter darkness, for I wasn't sure how long. I knew I had plenty to do. For one, I needed to solidify some of the documents I had arranged, making sure to plan pickups of these items before I returned to Nora. I also wanted to do a little digging into Stately. It seemed weird that they would have one big task for

me now and that would be the end of it. I had never peeked into their files or questioned what they were doing as an organization to have uses and ties to the black market, but when people are rich, it's not that questionable the things they buy in undisclosed or even unscrupulous ways.

I just wanted to know what I might have been facing. If I knew, I could plan. If I planned, I'd execute it better. If I did it better and faster, then I would get back to Nora that much more quickly.

With that thought, I stood, turned on the light, and pulled out my laptop. As soon as I got a secure IP, I moved to the system I had spent the last eight months protecting, and dove in like I was entitled to know. I could have done this at any point. I could have known more about the information I had been protecting, but I hadn't. What I saw made me wish I had looked so much sooner. I should have looked when I approached them before I officially worked for them.

I should have considered why I was watching another hacker break into their system.

What I saw hidden here were some of the worst, most depraved things I had ever witnessed. Stately Enterprises was far more than just a corporation dealing in large sums of money… it was the front for organized crime. Based solely on the clover insignia I saw here and there; I knew exactly which group I had been working for.

The O'Sheas. The Irish Mob. I had been working for the very people I had refused, had fled from, was still probably fleeing from now.

Like a punch to the gut, I sifted through months of my work, seeing how many things I had been pro-tecting. Drug hauls, money transfers for blackmail, video footage of tortures, photos of dead bodies, and trafficking… so much human trafficking. I had been helping these people hide all their dirty dealings and had been none the wiser.

My head was spinning. I felt sick.

What had I done?

What was I going to have to do for Colin now?

Colin had to be Colin O'Shea. I had never dealt with his full name before, and the only O'Shea I had ever met in person had been his son, Freddy.

Colin wouldn't know my face, but Freddy would, and even if that held any protection for me, I had no idea what they were going to ask me to do.

Who could I turn to for help?

What could I do to remedy this? To prevent whatever heinous act was going to occur when I completed whatever task he had set aside for me?

W01f.

W01f had been my enemy but also sort of my friend over these months. We had been actively fighting against one another, each trying to break into the other's securities. They had to be from an enemy organization, which was concerning, because would I want to get further entrenched in organized crime? But maybe they would help me.

Whatever task I was about to do for the O'Sheas could be completed, I could go free with money in hand, and then I would let W01f take whatever it was they wanted, gaining access to everything I had tried so hard to keep them out of. I wouldn't get anything in return out of it except for peace of mind that I didn't help that Irish monster any more than I already had.

I pulled up the chat we usually conversed in, but instead of the blank screen or a snide quip about me being later than usual tonight, what I saw there was far different.

[W01f: This has got to be some sort of sick joke. Ingrid? This is Ingrid, isn't it? Are you fucking kidding me?]

My heart about leaped out of my chest.

Something about that message made me think I might really know who W01f was. That I knew them in real life, not just the online versions of ourselves.

[W01f: Who are you? You aren't who I thought you were. Both of the you aren't who I thought they were.]

Each message I read pulled at something deep within me.

[W01f: And I thought keeping away from you was protecting you. How silly of me. You don't need my protection, do you?]

Yep. I knew him outside of this world. We probably knew each other quite well, based on the way they were reacting to realizing I was also living a double life.

Protecting me by staying away? Who would be staying away from me?

I never had enough time to truly dig into who W01f was, using the few hours I had to get the work done for Stately as fast as possible, but now I knew I had to look. It wasn't easy, but since W01f was clearly offline, nothing was as protected as it usually was. In fact, there was a clearly unfinished code I found immediately. It wasn't protecting much, just a small window into what looked like real estate investments, but once I weaseled my way in there, it was so much easier slip right into the system they had been trying to keep me out of for so many months.

It was immediate, instantaneous.

It made so much sense I should have been struck by lightning for not realizing this sooner, especially for how obvious so many little things had been before that I could only see now that the filter of normal had been pulled away from my eyes.

The Lupos were an organized crime family. They owned and operated a plethora of businesses, including the shop I worked at. What were they known for? Weapons, timber, medicine that can't be accessed easily in the Americas, as well as blackmail and extortion of wealthier companies, mostly centered around the Kansas City Metro area. They did do the protection racket, but only for places within the metro that fell on bordering territories of smaller gangs. These businesses were left alone by the Bloods, Crips, and smaller gang groups, because the Lupos were backing them.

The Lupos hadn't gotten too much press or public attention since their father, Salvatore Lupo died, but enough. I had known that Salvatore was connected to the Mafia when I had begun working there, but I had no idea that this wasn't simply them being backed by the Mafia. No, they *were* the Mafia. My eyes skimmed more and more of the information before me, my heart thudding loudly as my breath quickened in panic.

I had White Hatted my way into being the enemy of my own boss and hadn't even realized it until the pieces fell together in my head. Enzo Lupo was the wolf behind the screen, always there, always watching. He couldn't have known everything about me until now, otherwise his reactions via these messages he left here would have either happened a lot longer ago, or I'd be dead.

It was like a gun was being pressed to my forehead. I realized how incredibly screwed I was in this moment and how immeasurably happy I was that I had placed Nora in Joe's care. Enzo being offline at a time like this could only mean he was coming for me, possibly with others who would help him dispose of my body afterward. I had nowhere I could run to, not really, because though I could reach out to Colin and hide there, I was just as unsafe in that situation as this one.

My vision blurred with tears as I closed the laptop, unable to keep looking even though so much of me wanted desperately to dig even deeper and see all the things Stately Enterprises had asked me to collect for them. I wouldn't dig for Colin though. If I could keep the tears from rolling down my cheeks, I would have been looking for me.

CHAPTER 13

ENZO

It was a miracle I was driving straight and not swerving all over the road. My mind kept drifting somewhere between enraged and confused, heartbroken and worried. I had definitely white-knuckled it from Lee's Summit to St. Louis, where I was now sitting in my car just down the block from a tiny house, having traced her movements to this very location. She had been here hours before and stopped longer than any other time, so I stopped for a bit too.

At first, I just observed. It was pretty late in the night by this point for any normal person to be up. Most of the houses on this street were dark and quiet with sleeping people, but not the one she had been in. No, there was still a light on in that house, the front room's curtains glowing with it. When I pulled up the information about the property, it was registered to a Joe Smith. Too generic of a name to mean anything to me or anyone else looking into it.

I should have just kept looking up who this man might have been, or maybe dug a little to determine how Ingrid may have known him, but instead, I suddenly found myself stepping out of my car and heading toward the house. She wasn't there. I knew that, but I had a funny feeling if this part of the story was correct, perhaps other parts that had been mentioned were as well. Lo-and-behold, as I went to the window, I saw exactly what I feared had been the case. Nora was slumped, sleeping peacefully on the couch in the living room. She was all alone in the small space, but that didn't mean Joe wouldn't come back from wherever he was hiding in that house and spot me staring through the pane of glass.

Nora's red hair, which looked so much like her mother's, was fanned out around her against the dingy, brown couch cushion where her head rested. She seemed unperturbed by the circumstance, but then again, she was excited when she was telling us about their little trip at family dinner. Some strange, deep-seated part of me wanted to go in there and take her with me. Something about this situation didn't feel right. Even though she was there, wrapped in her own blanket and sleeping soundly, the pit of my stomach told me something was wrong about this. She shouldn't have been there.

It didn't matter though. I couldn't go in there. Her own mother left her in this man's hands, and I would be kidnaping her if I brought her with me.

And there was still the question of what I was facing when I did find Ingrid. How far was she really in the Irish mob? Would she care enough to listen to me? Would she shoot me?

Would I shoot her?

The very thought of it made a cold shiver run down my spine.

A shadow moved from the little hallway just off the living space Nora was in and I stepped back into the shadows a little farther so I wouldn't be spotted. The man I presumed to be Joe entered the room, phone in hand. He glanced at Nora, then moved to the kitchen.

He was a little less than average height, his body a bit weathered, but still clearly fit as he walked gracefully. His hair had been cut short, wrinkles adorning his features and faded tattoos littered his arms. I had seen many men like this from other groups we worked or were rivals with, but for some reason, he seemed very familiar to me. I didn't know who he had been before, because Joe Smith had clearly not been his name in whatever life he had previously led, but I was going to find out.

For now, I could only hope that Nora would be safe long enough for me to catch up to Ingrid. What happened from there was still unknown. I would never, enemy or otherwise, take a child from their mother, but I wouldn't let my family be damaged because of someone like Ingrid tearing at our systems and giving our information to our enemies to use against us.

I quickly made my way back to my car, getting in with one final glance at the window, before I was both pulling up Ingrid's newest location and dialing Sal. I should have called him sooner. I should have called him the moment I found out before I went racing into the night after her. I should have, but I didn't, and now I couldn't stop. No one would be able to pull me back from this ledge.

"Where are you?" Sal asked, clearly hearing my engine rev as I drove through St. Louis, hopping back on the highway quickly to continue on toward—I checked the location again—Chicago. Of course, she

was in Chicago, where the O'Sheas called home. Why wouldn't she be?

"Ingrid works for O'Shea."

There was a long pause on the other end of the phone.

"What the fuck?" Sal had clearly gotten up out of bed and was pacing now, his voice harsh and the panic only the six of us Lupos and LaMartinas could hear there in his voice. Sal was the calm one, the levelheaded one, but this news was just as shocking to him as it was to me.

"Something clicked in my head tonight and I dug around," I said, the words feeling more like a dirty thing I had done instead of my job of protecting our family.

"What do we do?" Sal asked.

There were a lot of solutions that Sal and Adrian would normally employ in a situation like this, in fact, they had just had to do something of this nature to some of our father's old guards who had been caught giving information about drops and shipments coming into the Cartel. They had been swiftly dealt with, and we all assumed the catfish had gotten their fill of them in the Missouri River. And the Cartel were now our allies after what Leo and Adrian had just done.

But in this instance, Sal was deferring to me, because I—

Love her.

No.

"I'm tracing her now. I'm confronting her about it," I told Sal, quickly cutting off my train of thought before it could go any further, though my heart had heard it, and it ached in my chest.

"Confronting? What do you think she's going to say to you?"

"I just want the truth," I said, my voice much shakier than I intended.

"And what if it's not the truth you want to hear?"

"Not now, Sal," I hissed, choosing anger, which was fueling me to keep going instead of the gut-wrenching despair every part of me was hurtling toward.

"This is crazy, Enzo," Sal grumbled as my foot hit the accelerator, eyes flashing as I passed a sign for Chicago.

"I'm going to confront her. I'm going to find out why," I said, my voice rougher than I would have liked as the words left me. He could see right through me. He knew what my voice sounding like this meant. He sighed deeply, the sound resonating through the speaker on my phone and almost cocooning me in the power of my brother like a blanket of safety. I had chosen to do this on my own, but he wasn't going to abandon me.

"Either she's been a spy the whole time, or they've had something on her. There's really no other explanation," Sal said, and I knew he was also struggling with the very real possibility that she may need to be taken out of the equation. Not in a witness protection type of situation, but in a, "she would never speak or do anything against us or O'Shea because she'd be dead" situation.

I must have made some sort of noise, because Sal sighed again.

"Didn't you check up on her when she first came around?" he asked.

I had, but not thoroughly. I didn't want to pry because I wanted to get to know her the real way. It seemed almost laughable now that I was in this position, driving in the dead of night toward Chicago and our number one enemy's territory to confront her and find out her reasoning, the why behind her actions, and deception. There was some missing piece of the puzzle there that connected her old life to this one and, therefore, her current situation, but I hadn't seen it. That was probably partially because of my haste to keep digging, and the visceral feeling of betrayal I felt about a woman that was in no way mine.

I almost laughed at myself for admitting that in my own head. How ridiculous that I was angry and jealous when thinking about a woman who owed me nothing in this life.

"I'll take care of this myself if it comes to it, Sal. I just need some time."

"What can I do to help you, Enzo?" That ache in my heart was really trying to push its way to the surface.

"See if Kia can keep an eye on things and don't do anything stupid while I'm gone. I won't be able to clean up your messes and mine at the same time."

"Anything else?"

"I'm sending you the address of where Ingrid left Nora. I don't feel good about the man she's with. Have Kia investigate that for me and let me know." And with that, I hung up the phone, because if I kept talking to him, I would break down, and I needed my anger to fuel me now, or I would never get to Chicago.

About thirty minutes later, the phone was ringing again. I felt like I had barely made a dent in the many miles between me and the location that Ingrid was still at, according to the trace in her phone I was still following. I glanced at the screen to see who was calling me.

Kia.

"Hi Kia," I said after angrily swiping to answer.

"Enzo. I wasn't really expecting to be playing the role of you so soon." Her deep smooth voice slid out from the phone speaker with such ease and sass I couldn't help but smile. It was probably not the usual grin that came over my face, but no one was here to witness what had become of my normal demeanor. I wasn't sure anyone had ever witnessed me the way Ingrid was about to.

This feeling, my behavior, was so out of my own character I didn't even recognize myself.

"Something came up," I said, my voice sharp, even to my ears.

"I heard. I did a little bit of my own digging. I figure if you're driving, you aren't doing a thorough job getting all the facts on the woman you're about to ambush."

She wasn't wrong. Kia was so good at finding information about people. That was part of the work she did with Leo when they worked for a black ops division of the military, working on tracking down human traffickers and taking down some of those operations. Her focus within that team had been searching for people, which was why she had been such a help in tracking down Carmen last year, and now that she was stepping into my shoes at the last minute, she was offering to look into Ingrid while I drove.

"What did you find?"

CHAPTER 14

INGRID

I paced. The small one-bedroom townhouse I was renting was getting worn down just a little more with each pass of my feet. I couldn't leave. I had to meet Colin O'Shea in the morning. Since I now knew he was Irish Mob, it seemed unlikely he wasn't aware of my presence in the city already, especially since he knew to expect me. I had certainly known I wasn't the only person working on security measures for Stately Enterprises. I was just the only one who was keeping people out. I was never asked to track or trace anyone or anything, probably to keep me away from their illicit activities. I was only to retaliate and try to find holes for the others to get through for Ultima, which I realized must have been the Lupos' umbrella corporation.

I also couldn't leave because I was certain, deep down in my bones, that Enzo was on his way here. The fact that he hadn't been online since he sent me those messages, which was hours ago at this point, told me he was coming. And again, I wasn't sure what would happen when he got here. Would he have a team of other Mafia men with him, ready to drag me away or kill me on the spot?

I shivered at the thought.

I sat back down at the computer, eyes immediately landing on the messages he had sent me to reread them and perhaps gain a better idea of what I was about to face. They didn't give me the answers I wanted, but they did give me the smallest amount of comfort. His reaction seemed emotional. It shouldn't have mattered, not with how disastrous it was that he found me out, but it somehow made it better that he knew. If he was having a reaction like this on the screen, who knows what his reaction in person was going to be? The emotions, the fact that he cared for me and Nora, might have been more than just fleeting flirtatiousness.

Regardless, I needed to try to do something. If he somehow didn't come, and I managed to meet with Colin, get the job done, and have enough money to disappear again, I would probably need to be prepared for that. I went back to what I had been doing off and on, checking to see if I had any messages from the contacts I reached out to for the creation of new identities for me and Nora. This time we would head somewhere much farther, to another country, to start a new life.

The phone rang as I got confirmation from the contact I had for new identity creation. All I needed to do was put in the parameters and give them photos and we'd be getting those new documents within a day. "Comp Boss" was what I had Stately Enterprise's number named in my phone, partially because it never seemed to be the same person who called me from this number, and partially because I really didn't want to have to come up with covers for who I was speaking to on the rare occasions that I got a call in the middle of working at the shop. It made sense I'd get calls occasionally if I worked for a medical transcription company. Right?

"Ingrid," I said, somehow keeping my voice from shaking as I put the call on speaker to continue trying to quickly find the next innocuous location that Nora and I would move to.

"You arrived in town and are staying at an Airbnb instead of the hotel room arranged for you."

That wasn't a question, but often I found the people calling me from this number didn't care to ask questions, always assuming the worst about a situation before it even occurred. Unfortunately, this man was right in this instance, not that I had planned it that way. Staying at an Airbnb instead of the hotel was more about my comfort. I didn't want a company—even if it had been unbeknownst to me that they were the mob— knowing my every move.

"I need my own space and quiet to do what I need to do," I said without even pausing.

"Tomorrow I expect you to be ready at the designated time."

Again, no question, not even the hint of it in his voice. Normally I would have probably found it funny, but for whatever reason, knowing that Enzo Lupo knew everything and was out for blood searching for me right this very moment, made me want to lash out instead of remaining agreeable. Agreeable was a lot less likely to cause me to end up dead.

"With bells on," I said, my tone biting, and he quickly hung up the phone.

This should have been the moment when I was scrambling to finish everything up, to call Joe to clue him into the plans once this job was through, but as I turned, standing to pace again as I clutched my phone in my hand, the door to the Airbnb flew open, slamming against the wall loudly. In the doorway to the house, now seeming so incredibly small, having been filled with an imposing figure, was Enzo Lupo.

Those dark eyes seemed to gleam with malice as he looked at me. I was frozen in place, unable to even fully grasp that this was occurring honestly. I'm sure I looked ridiculous, mouth agape, as I took him in. His hair was mussed, eyes burning with anger as the muscles in his cheek seemed to twitch with his clenching jaw, his breathing was rough, and he simply just stood there, staring at me while I stared right back at him for several very long seconds.

"Enzo—"

"The fuck, Ingrid?" he roared, stepping into the house now, and reaching to slam the door closed behind him. I was certain Enzo knew that I was being monitored by the O'Sheas, just how closely wasn't known, but he had clearly been working diligently to keep the Lupos in the know about how O'Shea operated. I had to assume he came in the front door, knowing no one was watching.

"About which part?" I asked, because honestly, I hadn't known where to begin. There were too many facets to this entire strange mess that I wasn't sure what part he was most angry about. Well, I was fairly certain it was the part where I was working for an enemy of theirs while my daughter ate breakfast with his mother every morning.

Enzo stormed forward, bending his head down so our noses touched, and his hot, labored breathing fanned out across my face.

"From the fucking beginning, Ingrid," he practically growled, tearing himself away from me to pace back toward the door.

"That's going to be a really long story," I said quietly, though my voice wasn't shaking, which was odd, considering I was certain I was going to die.

Wasn't I?

If Enzo Lupo had come here to kill me, yes, he may have asked a few questions and better understood what kind of negativity this might bring them in the future, but I wouldn't have been alive for much longer. Enzo seemed angry, itching for a fight, maybe, but he wasn't going to kill me. I could tell that in the way he held himself back from even touching me when he finally entered the Airbnb. He had come alone, and he was letting his emotions take the lead. If he were just going to murder me, he would probably just as soon kill me and go through my devices than question me and kill me later.

It gave me a little solace, but didn't shake the fear that still coursed through me.

"How long until your meeting with O'Shea?" he asked, his voice still rough.

I glanced at the digital clock on my computer screen. It was already nearly two in the morning.

"About nine hours," I said.

"Great. That's plenty of time," Enzo said, his voice now calming and his tone cold as he moved to sit at the large couch that was against the wall adjacent to the front door.

I couldn't help but stare at him. I'm sure my face let on the amount of shock I felt at not only seeing him there, but everything that was transpiring since he violently opened the door.

"I—" I had no idea where to even start. How much did he know?

"Why don't we start with why you've been lying to all of us saying you were doing medical transcribing while you were working for the Irish, directly thwarting everything I've been doing for months?"

Shit.

"What was I supposed to say? 'Hey, I know you guys are in the Mafia, but I kind of stumbled into working for another Mafia group on accident and now I'm stuck?' Also, I had no idea W0lf was you until I saw the little messages you sent before you left," I said, gesturing to my still-open laptop.

"On accident?" Enzo scoffed, putting his elbows on his thighs and leaning forward on the couch from the leisurely position he had been in. "One doesn't simply become cyber security for an organized crime syndicate on accident."

"I did," I said, laughing a little manically as I realized how strange all of this was. "Last summer, the shop closed down. I *had* been doing medical transcribing on the side. I wanted a little cushion for us, just in case." I didn't feel like I needed to explain what the "just in case" was. Enzo knew.

"And you quit because?"

"Because the shop closed, and I needed to make more money than the dregs that the transcribing gave me. I looked and looked, but we had bled through all that I had saved when I realized I wasn't going to find any-thing suitable. Not with the amount of money I needed to keep us afloat and replenish my now meager savings."

"So, what? You decided to put that White Hat on again?"

Somehow, the way Enzo said it was as if he had been watching my online persona for years. The strange little bubble of pleasure that gave me was only damp-ened by the continued hard look on his handsome face.

"Yes. I decided to do one job. *One* time I would find something big, some huge leak I could point out.

Perhaps threaten to give that away to legitimate hackers if they didn't give me the money I wanted or even offer my services to help fix it for an additional fee."

"How did that turn into you becoming O'Shea's main cyber security person?"

"I'm not. I just handle breach prevention and fire-walls. I make them and break them. Deals, transactions, negotiations, video monitoring, and actually retrieving the data I break into; someone else handles all that. I just ensure the code is good, that there aren't any breaches or weak points, and, of course, I spend an exhausting amount of time keeping *you* at bay."

That was true. The biggest contender for my time as far as working for O'Shea was keeping a certain hacker from breaching the walls like he had last summer.

"And you didn't know who you were working for?" he asked incredulously.

"Not until recently," I admitted, finally letting my hands fall from where I had been nervously twisting them together in front of me.

"How is that? Didn't you see everything they were pursuing online? The deals they were making? What the files they were working so hard for you to keep protected?"

"I just told you, Enzo! I didn't look in deep, I just saw what I needed to, superficial only, so I could keep their stuff safe. I was mostly playing defense against you and occasionally building up firewalls and making encryptions for them, but that doesn't mean I looked at what I was protecting!"

"So what clued you in then?"

I gulped.

"I just dug deeper trying to see what this different job might be that I'm supposed to do for them," I said, my voice barely above a whisper. His muscles tensed, hands clenching into fists at that admission.

"Why are you here, Ingrid?"

"I was told if I did one big job, I'd be given a significant payout and be released from employment. I wanted to get out of this for a while. I didn't want this to become a long-term thing, but they kind of forced me into it."

"And you thought that a normal company would do that? Would find a way to force you to remain in their employ?" Enzo asked, his voice condescending and face incredulous. It had my temper flaring immediately.

"You don't know the kinds of things you'll do and go along with when someone you love is depending on you to survive!" I yelled.

As soon as I said it, I knew it was wrong. *I* was wrong. Enzo *did* know about that; he lived it every day. His brothers and the LaMartinas were involved in far darker and scarier things than I had ever been witness to, and it was confirmed by the sinister look that came over his face.

"I actually do, Ingrid," he said, his eyes flashing with pain for a moment before he sighed, running his hands over his face like he was resetting, before opening them once more and pinning me with another dark look. "So what is this job?"

"They haven't told me yet. That's what the meeting tomorrow is about, but I decided to dig into their business since I had been keeping myself separate from them, so I could try to gauge what I was in for." I paused, my stomach knotting as I thought about everything I saw when I finally pulled back that curtain just perhaps an hour before. "That's when I realized who I had been working for… and then I saw your messages." When our gazes met, his eyes narrowed, scrutinizing my face, clearly trying to pull apart what I had said to make sense of it for a moment.

"You expect me to believe that you didn't know you were thwarting me and my brothers, working for our enemy this whole time?"

"I had suspicions about you all for a while, but I didn't know who I was working for, and then your messages—" My eyes flashed up to meet his, the dark look in his eyes shimmered with a strange, unreadable expression, but somehow, I felt safe enough having seen it. "I knew it was you."

Enzo stood now, moving back through the small space and pausing only a few feet from me, his height still overwhelmingly tall in the small space of the Airbnb.

"How can I believe you, Ingrid?" he asked, his voice hard as he looked down at me, breaking the tense silence that had overtaken the room with his movements.

"You know me," I said, realizing it was true. I may have tried my hardest to become someone different, to do something different, but I hadn't been allowed to be myself, not until I felt safe, and that's what the Lupos and LaMartinas had done for me. They made me feel like Nora and I were safe.

"I don't know you at all. You've had this whole secret life. You aren't even Ingrid Jacobs. That woman, I quickly realized, does not really exist," Enzo practically growled. I winced. He wasn't wrong. The name and the person I had told them I was when I showed up there was mostly a lie. There was plenty of truth to the story I told them. The details were just not exactly right. My name was certainly one of those.

"My name is Mary Ingrid Michelson. I always went by Ingrid when I was growing up, or Ri for short. I was raised by my addict mother, no father, until she died when I was still a teenager. I am a self-taught hacker and I used to be a White Hat exclusively until I had Nora. I escaped my abusive ex, changed our identities to keep us protected, and now I *am* Ingrid Jacobs," I told him, holding his gaze firmly with mine.

"And what about Nora?"

"Nora was Elenora. We had already given her the nickname. I'd be surprised if she even knows what her old name was."

"And her father?" The way the word "father" came out of Enzo's mouth made me look more closely at his features. He was worried about her, that much I could tell, but his anger was still there, simmering and ready to explode with any new catalyst to the equation.

"He—"

"Elliot Berns. A low-life criminal, used by every syndication for odd jobs with high stakes they don't want to use too many of their actual men for. He's worked for Irish, Russian, Polish, and even worked for the Italians on occasion in Chicago. He has been doing it for years and it's a wonder he isn't dead yet."

I held my breath as Enzo spit the words from his lips, hatred so potent I could almost smell its foul stench.

"*Him*, Ingrid?"

"He's who I escaped," I said as an answer, nodding slightly in defeat. My eyes dropped to the floor. The idea of Enzo looking at me and seeing the poor choices of my past, knowing what an absolute mess I had made of everything, was just too much. He stepped a bit closer, and I could see his hand twitch as if he wanted to reach out and touch me, but thought better of it.

"But somehow you didn't know he was connected to this world? That it wouldn't follow you, no matter where you ran?" he asked, his voice having softened quite a bit, so it was now just barely above a whisper. I managed to force my eyes from the floor to look back up at him, seeing the struggle of pity, anger, and pain in his eyes.

"I thought Nora and I had escaped. I never would have dreamed that the company I had been working for was the Irish, or that they were your rivals. I had no idea, Enzo."

"It doesn't matter. I can't trust you."

That sick feeling in my gut returned, my previous certainty that he wouldn't kill me now faltering a bit as I watched the different emotions play out within his eyes.

"You can, Enzo! Had I known, I would have—"

"What? Told me? Worked with us?" he asked, letting out a strange bark-like laugh at the notion.

"I might have," I whispered, still watching his face, even if I wanted to turn away, to curl into a ball of shame and hide. I had been stupid. I should have done better, if not for my own safety, at least for Nora's. "If there was a choice between loyalty, I'd always choose you and your family. No one else could have made me feel like a person again after what Nora and I went through, except for all of you. It really doesn't matter what you do differently than O'Shea. I'll take the monsters I know, the ones I care about," I whispered, watching as the hard look in his eyes seemed to melt at my words.

CHAPTER 15

ENZO

I had driven across the state, pushing the limits on what speed my car should have been going at. Thankfully the night traffic was much lighter, and I could weave in and out of the other cars, passing them by before they even noticed I was there. Kia had gotten quite a bit of information in her short time looking into Ingrid. I was glad for it. I wanted to go into this knowing who I was dealing with, not just what Ingrid told us about herself.

Ingrid Jacobs had been inserted into quite a few documents, but she didn't really exist, at least not the one we knew, and Nora Jacobs was a completely brand-new creation only three years earlier. Nora's identity had been easier. Being a three-year-old when the new name had been created, meant there was a lot less history that had to be generated for her, but Ingrid was a different story.

I knew she had been a White Hat before, but Kia had gone so much deeper than that. Mary Michelson was who Ingrid had been before. She had lived in Chicago. Nora's father had been Elliot Berns. That man, by all accounts, was scum. The con artist, scammer, and want-to-be mobster spent all his time in the dregs of society, only to continue to maintain a bottom-feeder status. Why had Ingrid stooped so low?

She deserved so much better than this pathetic low life that aspired to nothing greater than drugs, money, and thwarting the law. It was astonishing he'd managed to live that way so long and kept himself out of prison.

Kia's research only came up with information about Mary Michelson's dead mother, no father mentioned. While it didn't reduce my anger, knowing all this had been a sort of comfort. Ingrid didn't grow up in a good situation, and she had, in fact, escaped a very bad one, getting away from Elliot and the Chicago mob scene.

Knowing more felt good, but I had to keep myself from feeling too sympathetic. Ingrid could very well have been doing this purposefully. Had she worked for O'Shea the whole time? Did she know who we were? Did she help with the kidnapping of Carmen last summer? How far did this go?

I wouldn't get any answers until I saw her, until I confronted her. Maybe fear of death at my hands would be enough for her to admit how deep the deception had gone.

I pulled up in front of the Airbnb a few hours later. Part of me wanted to check my phone and dig a little on a few things, but the other, larger part of me wanted to hear what she had to say before I proved her story to be true or false.

It was then, as I walked up to the front door of the small house, that I heard her voice. She was on the phone with someone, I could tell, but through the wall, I could only hear her side of the conversation. She sounded odd, different from her normal tone. Her words were forced in a way that made me know she was both uncomfortable and on edge. As soon as she uttered the words, "With bells on," and I heard the phone getting set back down, I knew the conversation was over, and there was no further reason to wait. I kicked open the door, letting my eyes take in the sight of her.

Something about the fact that we were truly alone for the first time set a different fire blazing within me, as well as the flames of anger. I wasn't sure if she was the enemy yet, so I couldn't let that feeling take over, even if the sight of her red locks falling over her exposed shoulder made me want to curl around her and bury my nose in her scent.

But despite my abrupt appearance there and the obvious anger radiating from me, she didn't cower. She stood her ground, talked to me, fielded my questions, and I found that I believed her. I believed each and every thing she said to me. The truth in her eyes, the fact that her voice didn't shake, the way she looked me in the eye. Even when she was wringing her hands together with nervousness, I understood. I certainly hadn't made it easy for her to be comfortable.

But it was what she said about loyalty, and how she felt about me and my family, that sent me over the edge.

"If there was a choice between loyalty, I'd always choose you—" Though I heard the rest of her words, these words were circling in my mind as she continued to speak.

She chose me.

The tiny thread of control I had over my actions and feelings for her snapped. Her words had barely finished leaving her mouth before my hands gently, but firmly grasped the soft skin of her face, tilting her face up to mine for me to fully look into her blue eyes.

"Right now," I said, sucking in a breath as she grappled with the suddenness of my hands on her once more. "You choose right now if you are going to let me help you fix this," I said, watching as her pupils dilated and her breathing picked up.

"Fix it?" she questioned in a whisper, brows scrunching together just slightly with confusion.

This was a tricky situation, as someone with an analytical mind, the idea of me fixing this situation, was probably baffling. I didn't need her to know how I would fix it. Hell, I didn't even know all the pieces to the puzzle yet, but it didn't matter. What mattered was if she wanted me to help her find a way out of this.

"If you want me to help you, if you want me and my family to fold you in fully and give you and Nora protection, I will do that. If you choose to go it alone, I will leave. I will leave right now, but that means you never come back."

"You'd help me? Even though I —"

"Ingrid, if you want me, if you need me, I am at your disposal. I would do far more than help you, but only if you want me to," I whispered, my head dipping closer, unable to stand the distance there. I could feel her breath on my lips, the warmth of her body so close to mine yet not touching. I wanted her to accept this. I wanted her to say she would let me help her. That she wanted me. My whole body was tense, waiting for the response.

Because truthfully, no matter how gruesome of a monster I was, I would wait forever for what I truly wanted. That much was clear to me from the moment I laid eyes on her and solidified by the fact that I hadn't come here to kill her. No, even if she had turned out to be my enemy, had done this on purpose, I couldn't have killed her. She would have just had to leave once more and never return. Somehow, the idea of Ingrid Jacobs or Mary Michelson not living anymore was absolutely unnatural and abhorrent to me.

"I want you, Enzo," she whispered.

The reality of her words didn't fully register immediately. The way her eyes flashed with desire, as well as fear and vulnerability, told me this had a dual meaning. If I could have controlled myself a moment longer, I would have reassured her first, made sure she understood I would do everything in my power to keep Colin O'Shea and the rest of his men from harming her, but I couldn't hold back any longer.

My lips closed the distance, touching hers and igniting a fire within me that had been smoldering since the first day I had laid eyes upon her. Now that I had a taste of her, I wasn't sure I'd ever be able to let her go. The guttural moan that broke from my throat at just the way her lips felt against mine as she started to move them, and how, as my hands traveled to wrap around her back, I felt her muscles tense and then relax at the feeling. I wanted to kiss this woman every day. Every single day for the rest of my life, I wanted to be able to kiss her, to touch her, to press her against my chest, and to feel the swell of her breasts and stomach against the hard plains of my body.

I broke from the kiss, pulling back to look at the beautiful blush that had blossomed over her chest and cheeks, the way her lips were slightly swollen from my attention.

"You're so beautiful," I said in awe, brushing a curl that had fallen over her face back with the rest of them.

"That's ridiculous," she said, that blush becoming more embarrassed as she tried to pull away from me, but I didn't let her.

"Nothing ridiculous about it. You are beautiful. Fucking stunning in every way. So much so that I have been like some sort of lost, lovesick puppy, waiting until you showed me even the vaguest notion I wasn't hideous to you."

She did pull farther from me, giving me a look of such confusion, eyebrows stitching together on her forehead and lips pursing slightly as she studied me. I was, admittedly not in my best-looking form, looking frazzled, my hair unruly from running my hands through it repeatedly and my clothes wrinkled from sitting in a car for hours driving.

"No one would ever really want me. I'm damaged goods, Enzo. My body is used and scarred. How could someone as beautiful as you think *I'm* attractive?" she asked, gesturing down at her body. Those full hips with enough soft flesh for my large hands to grab onto made my mouth water. There was nothing that I could imagine was hiding under those clothes that would deter me from the overall beauty that was her.

"I have wanted you from the moment you stepped foot in the coffee shop. I have wanted you every time I've seen you, with the messy hair or the oversized clothes, even those little bitty clothes you were wearing the other day at your apartment," I told her, stepping back into her personal space and placing one hand on her chin to tilt her head back to me, and the other at her hip, fanning my fingers out before tightening my grip there just slightly. "But I cannot wait to see how beautiful you are when I take all the clothes off you and get to see how magical your skin feels against mine."

Her breath hitched, and she watched as I moved my hand at her chin down her throat, touching the skin of her chest and hovering just over the edge of her shirt. My other hand, the fingers that dug in there, found the top of the leggings she wore. Those damn things left so little to the imagination I couldn't wait to uncover it all, to taste her skin. It was going to be mine. Every inch of flesh would be for my consumption. The intoxicating sound she made when my whole hand slipped under the waistband of her leggings, fingers fanning out to grasp her hip while my mouth descended onto her chest, licking the edge of her shirt and waiting for permission to press farther. Because, oh, how much I wanted to press. I wanted to pull down that shirt and see those breasts I had only fantasized about. I wanted to encase her ass in my hands, squeezing the tender flesh there and spreading them apart. I wanted to feel the heat I could tell was coming from her center, to touch that rich wetness with my fingers and my tongue. She was wet for me.

"Enzo," she whispered in a moan as her hands came up to grasp the hair at the back of my head. It was all the permission I needed. I dragged her top down, exposing her bra, which quickly was pushed aside so I could see those beautiful pink nipples, hard and ready for attention. My mouth wasted no time, tongue swirling over the bud and eliciting a groan from her, her hips bucking forward. I used that opportunity to slide my hand farther around to her ass, feeling the luxurious globe under my fingers made my erection throb. I couldn't wait to have both cheeks in my hands as I slipped into her from behind. So many ways I wanted to fuck this beautiful woman. But only if she was pleased first.

My hand moved around to the front, toward that undeniable heat, and I smiled against her nipples I was still relentlessly sucking and licking as her breath caught.

Oh, she was wet.

"Fucking dripping for me, Ingrid," I said, pulling away to look at her face, which was so flushed and aroused I almost came just from the sight of it.

"I want you," she whispered, her own hands reaching forward to grasp at my belt. I let her, watching those little hands move precisely to undo my belt and pants, her hand quickly slipping in and wrapping around my hardened cock. The feel of her firm little grip there was amazing. My body wanted to cum from that simple touch alone, but I had waited years for this. I wouldn't be cuming until I made her cum at least twice.

With no warning, I pulled her hand from my pants, scooping her up bridal style and glancing around this little Airbnb for the bed. I wanted space to spread her out so I could feast on her properly.

Across the room was a small hallway, and I moved quickly toward that, the bed coming into view. It wasn't extremely large, maybe a double or a queen, but it would do for our purposes.

"I'm placing you in this bed, and I'm stripping you naked," I whispered in her ear before I set her down. She immediately scrambled away from me.

"The light first," she hissed as I looked at her, confused.

"The light?"

"Turn it off first."

I paused, watching the nervous way her hands had gone to cover her chest with her bra once more, still clutching the fabric there a little. Her breath was a bit erratic now, and she was avoiding my gaze.

"You don't want me to see?"

She scoffed.

"You think I want you to see how disgusting my body is?" she asked, her voice incredulous.

I took a deep breath to keep myself from yelling. How was I supposed to tell her that it didn't matter what was under those clothes, that I would want her anyway? That the level of desire I had for her went beyond any odd physical insecurities she had?

"We can start with the lights off. But I want you to know, someday I'll look at you with all the lights on, maybe even in the daylight, and see nothing but the object of my desires."

Before she could say another word, I moved to switch off the light. Only the faint glow from the other rooms and the vague lights from the darkness outside cast into the room, giving only our silhouettes to one another.

As I approached the bed once more, the tension somehow grew stronger. She leaned back against the pillows, her hands falling away from her shirt now that darkness was encasing us, and I could see the way she relaxed a little. This lack of confidence in her body was going to be corrected as soon as possible. It would be work, I was sure, but she would need to know that every little thing I had ever seen about her body was something that made me pine for her. Never the opposite.

Instead of getting back into the bed with her, I stood at the foot of it. I was certain if I could see the silhouette of her, she could see mine. I used that to slowly take my shirt off, pulling it over my head and letting it fall to the floor. My pants were already unbuttoned and unzipped, so all I needed to do was kick off my shoes and slip them from my hips.

Her breath hitched as I did so, legs squirming a little and hands grasping at the comforter below her. I smiled, though I didn't think she could see it, not sure if this was something I was dreaming up or reality, but wanting to make the best of it either way. I moved to crawl on the bed. Bracing myself with one arm, I used the other to trail up her arm slowly, loving the smooth softness of her skin while it made its way to her shirt.

"I hope this shirt isn't one of your favorites," I murmured as my fingers ran down the front of it, moving to touch her stomach.

"Why?" she whispered in response, but I didn't give her an answer. I couldn't keep my lips from hers anymore. Words were done for now as I kissed her once more, groaning as I tasted her sweet mouth, and she kissed me back with fervor.

Her little hands moved to grasp my shoulders, before sliding up my neck and nestling in my hair. The feel of her nails raking over my scalp as she moaned against my mouth was intoxicating, but coupled with my own hands slipping beneath her shirt and touching the bare skin of her side? Perfection.

I hated to break the kiss, but my tongue was eager to taste the skin that my fingers had just touched. I parted the kiss, unable to hold back my smile as I saw the little hint of a pout come over Ingrid's face in the small bit of light we were getting through the bedroom curtains from the exterior lights. But that pout soon turned into a little gasp as my lips descended her neck, traveling down with small sweeps of my tongue along the way, toward the top of her shirt. I hated this shirt for being in my way while also loving how the thin material showed me the prominent, hard nipples just begging for attention beneath it.

With one swift movement, my hands at her sides grasped the fabric, pulling so quickly, the thin material tore away at the seams. The suddenness of my actions caused another surprised sound to come from her. I tossed the scrap of fabric away, leaving her bare to me, even if still covered in a fraction of the light I would have liked to see her in.

"Oh Ingrid," I said, my voice barely more than an incoherent groan at the sight of her splayed out for me, under me. I wanted to savor this moment, while also fucking her to oblivion right now.

"What?" she whispered, her hands going to cover herself instinctually, but I snatched her wrists.

"You are more beautiful than I imagined," I said as I leaned over her, her wrists still trapped, and pressed my lips to hers. She broke the kiss with a scoff, and I looked down at her incredulous face.

"You can't even see it, but you know that's a lie, Enzo. My body is covered in stretch marks, loose skin, and an extra layer of fa—Where are you going?"

I had released her, hopping off the bed and taking the two steps to the light switch.

"Then I'll just have to see it in the light," I said, flipping it before she could protest, the room coming to life with color, and especially with *her.*

She immediately tried to cover up. Her arms moved to conceal her supposed flaws, but it was everything I had dreamed, and more. My cock hardened further, bobbing at the mere sight of her half-naked form. There she lay, her breasts out, but now partially hidden by one hand while the other snaked across to hide her stomach from me. These places where she was insecure were not at all unattractive.

She was beautiful. The curves of her body were luscious. I knew my hands would fit perfectly in the divot between her ribs and her hips. My hands ached to take over the handfuls of breasts she was trying and failing to keep from me. The silver stretches of skin were like war paint, shimmering in the light, accentuating one of the most beautiful aspects of her. Motherhood. She wasn't marred by these flaws; she was perfected by them. I was eager to get the leggings off her, to see those legs and have her fully at my mercy.

"Turn it off, Enzo," she hissed, and I finally looked up at her horrified face. No longer did her eyes hold the burning desire they had before. It was now changed to fear and anger.

CHAPTER 16

INGRID

My heart rate soared as I watched him take off his clothes in the darkness. Even the silhouette of his body was something I couldn't take my eyes from. The mild light coming in from the curtains was enough to see the hard lines of his body, the cut of his muscles. That body was going to touch mine. This man wanted *me*, and he crawled over the bed once more, hovering over me and letting his lips trail over my skin before finally meeting my waiting lips again. I could have died.

I wanted this.

I wanted him.

But apparently not enough to keep my mind from the self-deprecating thoughts that couldn't help but creep in.

When he groaned and said, "You are more beautiful than I imagined," I couldn't hold back the words that spilled from my mouth. I couldn't take a compliment from him and just let this fantasy come to life. I had to ruin it somehow.

When he got up abruptly, I didn't think he'd actually do it, but the light flooded the room, and horror and fear washed over me as his eyes took me in. Somehow, the fact that seeing his body in the full light didn't take over the terror I felt at the likelihood of his rejection. Because that was the only possible conclusion in my mind. This body was not that of a beautiful young woman. It was used, stretched, and scarred from the life I had created.

"Turn it off, Enzo," I hissed, my arms tightening over my breasts and stomach as I watched his erection grow harder from where he stood across the room.

"Take off your pants," he said, his hand dropping from the light switch and moving to grasp his cock, like he had to touch it to relieve a need in him.

"The light."

I didn't want to take my hands away and show him the marred skin that was my stomach, especially not to bend and bulge and show even more disgusting features of my body to this god of a man.

"Pants," he said, his voice little better than a growl. That sound hit me straight in my already soaking core, heating me again from within in a way I hadn't anticipated. His eyes burned into mine like fiery embers of pure want. And those eyes were looking at *me. My* body.

His muscles flexed with each slow stroke of his hand on his cock, lean, hard body tensing, and I felt my arms falling away, exposing the parts of me I had been trying so hard to keep from him. If this man, even in the light, wanted me with the beauty of his body, I couldn't ruin this. Not after years of wanting him.

I hooked my thumbs under the waistband of my pants, pushing them down to my knees, before sitting up to pull them the rest of the way off. I quickly fell back to lay on the bed once more, looking at his body, but not capable of seeing the rejection I was certain would be present on his face.

"Look at me, Ingrid," Enzo said, making my eyes snap back to his face, the hunger there evident and his hand moving a little faster over his cock. "Do I look like a man who is disappointed in what he sees?"

My breath stuttered in my chest as he took a few steps forward, climbing back on the bed to kneel between my legs. His eyes roamed over my form, taking in every inch of my skin, but somehow never touching me.

"You don't like your body?" he asked, his gaze moving back to my face.

"No," I whispered, unable to make my voice any louder or more confident.

"Do you know what I see?" he asked, his hand falling away from his erection, before slowly moving to touch my calf. The feel of his hands on me again was electric, causing a pleasurable shiver to move over my body. I shook my head after a long moment of watching his fingers trail up my calf, heading past my knee and splaying over my thigh. His fingers were so long that half the surface was covered with his hand. "A warrior, a goddess. These marks—" He paused to trace the silvery lines of stretch marks that reached down the tops of my thighs, tracing them over my hip bone and to my stomach. "They are the result of you creating a life within you. Nora, who is a wonder in and of herself. *You* did that."

I felt the blush that had come over my face throughout all this deepen as I averted my eyes from his face and hands to look at the wall. He didn't let me do that for long though, taking his other hand and gently touching my chin, bringing my face back to look at him as he loomed over me.

"You're beautiful. I want to look, touch, and taste every part of your wonderful body if you'll let me, Ingrid."

So sincere was the look in his eyes as he said it. And I believed him.

For most of my life, I had been disappointed and thoroughly lied to, so I had always assumed that no one was truly honest. There was always a glimmer of dishonesty in everyone's eyes, always something they held back from me, even if it wasn't malicious. But the words Enzo just said to me held none of that. Every word he had just told me was completely true. He wanted me. He thought I was beautiful, and all I had to do was let go to have him.

"Kiss me," I whispered, craning my neck up against his fingers on my chin to put my face just a fraction closer to his. The way his eyes lit up with excitement and need set that fire in my core blazing. He leaned down, his lips pressing to mine once more, and the feeling was just as intense as before, if not more. There was no hesitation on my part this time. I wanted him, and I was going to have him.

His hands roamed over my skin as mine threaded through his hair and skimmed down the muscles of his back. He broke the kiss with a pant, lips trailing down my neck to my chest, while his hands set scorching trails down my sides, pressing beneath me until he was grasping my ass. The feel of his fingers pressing into my cheeks while his tongue swirled over my nipples had incoherent sounds tearing from my throat.

"Enzo!" I gasped out as he latched onto the nipple he had been licking, sucking, and lightly nibbling. The feeling was explosive. Never had I experienced such pleasure from my breasts. The only sexual attention I had received had always been very one-sided, my pleasure coming second to the person I was with. I only had orgasms when I was alone. But with Enzo, I hadn't even touched his cock yet, and I was getting very close, the tension coiling in my belly, the little bursts of tingly pleasure telling me that if he just touched my clit one time I'd cascade over the edge.

As if he read my mind, one of his hands released a cheek, swiftly moving around, still caressing as it went, to touch the little bundle of nerves that was practically vibrating on its own, needing attention. That was all it took. His fingers dipped into the dripping wetness at my center before making a few tight circles over my clit sent me over the edge. Stars exploded behind my eyelids, the rush of the wave of pleasure crashing over me. I wasn't sure what sounds I was making, but I knew as I came back down to Earth, I was panting, nails digging into his shoulders.

My eyes fluttered open and his were right there, watching me as he brought his fingers to his lips.

"That was the most perfect thing I've ever seen," he said, rubbing his glistening fingers to his lips and taking in a deep breath from his nose. He popped his fingers into his mouth and closed his eyes. Almost like he couldn't help himself, he drove his hips forward. His cock throbbed as it pressed against my wet folds and clit and a moan burst from his chest, fingers still in his mouth. "I have to taste you," he said, his eyes flashing open once more before he crawled away from me.

He looked down at my dripping center, then up at my face. The absolute awed expression there had me enraptured, but that soon fell away with the first swipe of his tongue. He went slowly at first, groaning as he tasted me, laving at my clit, my lips, my entrance, like he couldn't get enough of the taste. Then his tongue pressed against my entrance, slowly, methodically, deeper and deeper. I was crazed. Everything felt like heaven, the most distinct and drawn-out pleasure, so shortly after the best orgasm I had ever had, and now I could feel a second one building within me with these gentle, reverent movements at my center.

As if he could tell I was getting close, and perhaps he could, my stomach was visibly clenching as his tongue drove deeper within me, his nose pressing against my clit, he exchanged his tongue for his fingers, driving two into me and making a cry burst from my lips.

"Are you getting close, Ingrid?" he asked, his voice like rich dark chocolate, just dripping with sex.

"Yes!" I managed, my hips moving on their own, grinding against his face as his tongue went back to its relentless swirls on my clit.

His fingers curled as they drove into me, hitting some spot inside me that was nearly impossible. At least the pleasure of it felt impossible. The pressure was at a point I had never felt before, the need for release so close and at the forefront that I was grunting and crying out for more.

Orgasm two washed over me with his machine-gun-like drive into my pussy with those fingers and a nip with his teeth at my clit, this one was a different kind of cascade, like a gushing and release of pressure so pleasurable I thought I might die. But it was nothing compared to the needy croak that came from his throat as he lapped at me, my pussy clenching around his fingers as my hips slowed.

"I need you," I whispered, hands releasing the covers that they had been clenching to run through his hair.

"Hm?" he asked, not taking his head up from where he was devouring my climax.

"Enzo! I need you now!" I snapped, causing his head to pop up and fingers to still. He looked at me, pure need and passion there on his face.

He sat up straight, now towering over me as he kneeled between my legs. His eyes scanned over my body, face glistening with my juices, abs tightening and cock bobbing. It seemed like he was savoring this view, as if this might be the one and only time he would be able to see me this way, before he backed up, slipping his feet back onto the floor so he stood at the foot of the bed.

"What are you—" But I didn't get a moment to finish my sentence as he was grasping my ankles, pulling me down toward the end of the bed.

"I could have simply feasted on you for hours, but then you had to go and say *that*," he grunted once he stopped pulling me, my core now flush against his throbbing erection. He bent over, caging my face between his arms, his head ducking down so his nose nearly touched mine. I could smell the delicious scent of him and my climax on his face. "What do you want, Ingrid?" he whispered hoarsely, looking into my eyes, lips hovering mere inches from mine.

"I want you, Enzo," I managed to whisper back.

That was all it took for him. His mouth crashed into mine, one hand bracing his body weight while the other grasped my hip, tilting me so the head of his penis brushed at my entrance. I gasped into his mouth as his tongue danced with mine and he slowly pressed.

Yes.

It was perfect.

It was everything.

With each slow thrust into me, he went deeper and deeper. My body was opening to him, the little high from my previous orgasms building as I felt him stretch my walls. It felt so wonderful, and then he pulled his face from mine, standing tall once more.

Both of his hands grasped my hips, his eyes boring into mine as his hips snapped forward. The new angle hit something within me, like when his fingers curled into me previously, but this time, it was so much more. I screamed as he picked up the pace. The only sounds in the room were my cries, his groans, and sharp breaths, and the slap of our skin together with each brutal thrust.

"You're so beautiful," Enzo managed to grunt out between thrusts, and I opened my eyes again, seeing the complete truth behind his words coupled with the undeniable pleasure written all over his face, and it was enough to set off my third climax. This time, it coiled in my belly, sending shocks of pleasurable tingles throughout my limbs. My legs shook of their own accord, muscles tightening. Enzo deftly took one of his hands from my hips, fingers moving quickly to rub on my clit and causing the final straw to break within me.

I screamed, my body convulsing with the power of the pleasure I felt. The white-hot feeling of ecstasy washed over me. As I came down from it, becoming more aware of my surroundings, I felt his cock harden within me, his own cry bursting from his lips and his muscles strained, his eyes rolling back as he thrust once, twice, and a third time firmly against me, filling me.

We stayed there like that for a moment, him panting, having collapsed back over me, his arms caging my head in, as our breathing returned to normal.

And then reality came crashing back over me.

Enzo came here to what? Kill me?

I was his enemy. Or I had been unknowingly. Did he come here to get this fantasy out of his head before he did away with me?

I know what he had said before we had sex, but that didn't mean that wasn't a ploy to get me to bed before doing away with me. I squirmed under him, managing to get unattached, making it clear I wanted to move away. He looked at me strangely, but stood back up, watching as I rolled off the bed to where my clothes had been discarded, pulling on my torn shirt and then pants and folding my arms over my chest to cover myself.

"Are you okay? Did you not want…" he trailed off, clear hurt on his face as he watched me pull my clothes on.

"I…"

What should I have said?

That I wanted to be dressed before he shot me?

He must have seen some fear on my face because that hurt look transformed into compassion. He quickly took the two steps he needed to be in front of me, his hand reaching to grasp my chin and tilt my face up to his, effectively halting my frenzied movements.

"I promised you my family would take care of you, Ingrid. That didn't change because of this," he whispered, his thumb rubbing soothing circles over my lip.

He *did* say that, didn't he?

"But—"

"No buts. If you want me, if you want my protection, I'm yours," he said, watching my eyes with an intensity I had never seen before. He wanted this, but the hardened part of him, the part that didn't really want me to see his pain, was trying to put up walls. I had seen some of that pain in his rage earlier.

He wants me.

The realization that this wasn't what my brain had immediately jumped to as the logical, tried-and-true reaction I was used to, but that he actually was hurt that I potentially betrayed him, that he had always wanted me, truly wanted me, and I had been the fool.

Did I want him?

Absolutely.

"I want you," I whispered, watching the magic as his face seemed to transform with those three simple words, the hidden fear being replaced by the twinkle of joy. His fingers became firmer, now cupping my face as he brought his head down to mine, his lips and mine finding one another again in a breathtaking kiss.

CHAPTER 17

INGRID

It was shortly after another round of amazing sex—the kind where I was astonished I could feel so good, I wasn't sure if I was more alive than I had been in years, or if I had passed on and was actually in heaven, especially because of who I was having sex with—that I heard the faint sound of a ping on my computer. The sound was like a Pavlovian response. I sat bolt up in bed from where we had been dozing.

"What's wrong?" Enzo asked, sitting up to look at me.

"Computer," I grunted, rolling off the bed.

"What?" he asked, clearly confused and sitting up as well, watching me.

"I was looking into some things about O'Shea, trying to figure out what the job he was going to ask me to do tomorrow was," I said, moving and getting my clothes on once more, perhaps minus a few things that I no longer found necessary, like my bra, before I bolted from the room and headed toward my laptop. Enzo followed a moment later, only having pulled his jeans back on.

"What did you find?" he asked, now hesitating to come closer as I sat at the tiny table.

It was an unwritten rule that you didn't stand behind a hacker while they worked. We are all paranoid creatures, and with the work Enzo and I did, it made sense that we would be paranoid about it. But for some reason, the idea of Enzo standing behind me, watching and catching things I may not have, set me at ease. W01f had been quite a contender, someone I would have trusted in the capacity of the dark web where we had dwelled, to find something I hadn't, even if we had been actively working against each other for so long. Knowing W01f had always been Enzo somehow made the trust even more than it had been.

I gestured for him to come see, and he smiled a little as he sauntered closer, placing his hands on the back of my chair to lean toward the screen.

What had pinged was current assignments. I had dug into older things, finding information that led me to the truth, but I wanted to know what the current assignments were. What information was Colin O'Shea so bound and determined to get that he needed me for?

That's when I saw the pictures.

Current pictures of Carmen. Ones of her from just a few days ago when she and Leo were in town for family dinner. She was there on Liliana's porch, holding Nora's hand as they came back in from putting the food scraps in the compost after dinner.

Nora.

They had pictures of my child.

My heart nearly leaped from my chest.

"He's not going to let it go," Enzo practically growled from behind me, pulling his phone from his pocket.

"Nora's in this picture," I said quietly, not noticing that he had gone completely still, his thumb the only thing in motion as he began scrolling through notifications on his phone.

"Shit," Enzo let out on a hiss. "Shit. Shit, shit, shit, SHIT!" he said, turning to pace, his phone still his predominant focus.

"What?" I asked, now partially annoyed and still feeling extremely uncomfortable with Nora being in these pictures. Part of me wanted to dig through even more, create a quick facial recognition tracker to sort through O'Shea's files for me and to make sure Nora wasn't in any other documents he had; anymore "current jobs."

"Do you know the man you left Nora with?" Enzo asked. I knew it was in response to my inquiry about what he'd seen on his phone, but somehow it didn't fully register what he was asking. Why wouldn't I know Joe? Why would I leave Nora with someone I didn't know?

"Excuse me?"

"Joe, do you realize who that man is? Who he works for?" Enzo asked, now looking up at my irritated face.

"Joe *used* to work for one of the mobs in Chicago, but he left when I did. We got out together. He's the only reason I could have escaped with Nora," I said, crossing my arms and planning on defending Joe, no matter the cost. Joe had saved us.

"Joe Smith, or should I say Joel Smythwick, works for O'Shea," Enzo said, turning his phone and putting it in my reach so I could see what was on the screen.

Still fuming at the suggestion I would hand Nora over to anyone I didn't explicitly trust, I snatched the phone from Enzo's fingers. It took a few moments for my brain to fully comprehend the fact that Enzo said a name that I was vaguely familiar with, but not in association with the Joe Smith I knew, and the fact that he had just said that Joe worked for O'Shea.

"Worked. He *worked* for O'Shea… he doesn't anymore," I murmured, my voice small as I saw the words, documents, and photo evidence that Joe Smith hadn't left the organized crime life when we ran three years ago, as he led me to believe. No, Joe had been continuing to work for O'Shea, and not only that, but he was Colin O'Shea's cousin. There was no way that Joe—or I supposed Joel—had done anything, but let me think I had escaped the watchful eyes of the Irish Mob.

"He certainly looks like he still works for O'Shea, Ingrid," Enzo said, his voice rough with the tension I could feel radiating from him. Or maybe it was mine. My whole body, which had only moments ago felt the most relaxed it had in maybe my whole life, was suddenly as taunt as a bowstring. My heart hammered in my chest, breath coming out as harsh pants as I realized I left my daughter, my baby, in the hands of a mobster.

Without another word, I rushed back to the bedroom, tearing through my bag to pull on clothes. Enzo was hot on my heels.

"What are you doing?" he asked, grabbing his shirt from the floor to pull it on as I frantically got dressed.

"Going to get Nora," I hissed as I wobbled trying to put my socks on, balancing on one foot. I was shaking, adrenaline pumping through my veins and inhibiting my rationality.

"You are not getting Nora," he said firmly, coming up to me and taking the sock from my hand.

"The fuck I'm not!" I screamed, reaching for the sock again, which he held out of my reach.

"One, you are in no way capable of going to get Nora in the state you're in," he started, a calmness taking over his previously tense demeanor.

"But I—"

"Two, if you don't go to this meeting with O'Shea tomorrow, if you go and confront Joe right now, it will only make things worse. You need to proceed as normal, as if nothing is amiss."

"I can't leave her there and pretend that everything is fine, Enzo! She's my daughter!" I yelled, but this time my voice cracked, my heart aching as tears began flooding my vision.

"We aren't leaving her there," he said, his voice only slightly shaking as he pulled me close, pressing my face to his chest as a sob ripped from my lips.

I don't know how long he held me there like that, but at some point, he dialed a number on his phone, my body still encased in his.

"I need people at the address. Eyes on Nora and Joe. I want someone there and ready to get Nora if anything goes wrong," Enzo said, his voice sure and strong. Muffled talking came over the line, a male voice. I assumed it was Sal because it made sense for Enzo to be calling his brother, to have him sending dependable men to keep watch.

"She didn't know, not until tonight," Enzo continued, answering a question Sal must have asked him about me, no doubt.

"I can't leave her. She has to meet with O'Shea in a few hours."

A few hours.

Yes, in just a few short hours I would need to be appearing back to myself, normal and ready to perform this job that would have taken me out of this forever … but would it have?

It seemed so strange that O'Shea would have just offered to let me go after everything I had done for him over the past few months and how much it seemed he depended on me to keep Enzo out. It dawned on me then. This was clearly just a ploy. Perhaps to get me physically back here in Chicago, or something else entirely, but I was certain there was no other reason for him to have played such a long game if it wasn't for a reason. He wasn't going to let me go either way.

"Does Carmen really have to get involved?" Enzo asked; the conversation had progressed as I pondered.

"Fine. Just see to it. I'll update you when I know something," Enzo said, irritation clear, before ending the call.

There was a moment when he brought his other arm around me, holding me close, pressing a kiss to the top of my head, and breathing in my scent. I pulled away first, looking up at him and seeing the determination set in his eyes, the way the darkness swirled and shimmered with purpose. I had seen that same look there a time or two when he was working on something in the coffee shop, but never had it been directed at me. Never had he looked into my eyes the way he was now.

"How am I supposed to go to this meeting with O'Shea?" I asked, my voice watery and shaking as I pulled my hand from his back to wipe away the freshest of the tears from my cheeks. His hands took over the job, gently brushing the tears away, smoothing over the skin on my face, before leaning down to kiss my lips.

"We are going to do it together," he whispered against my mouth.

Something about the confidence he was bestowing on me seemed to be a lifeline. Like a rope, I grasped it, pulling myself up from the pit of uncertainty and fear, a pit I had dragged myself out of before, but this time, it wasn't only me that had to take the weight, Enzo was right there, pulling me up on that rope too.

"Okay," I let out with a breath, straightening my spine and taking another few deep breaths, before I opened my eyes once more and looked up into his face. "Together."

"There she is," he whispered, bending down again to give me a kiss, a faint smile on his lips, before he straightened himself once more. "We are going to find out as much as we can about O'Shea's plans and use it to our advantage," Enzo said, holding onto me and turning to head back into the living room. "What information did you pull up earlier?" he asked, steering me toward my computer.

I rushed past him, sitting down to pull up the photos I had seen that set this whole spiral in motion.

"He's been watching Carmen, but it looks like he's been keeping tabs on Ash too?" I said, a question in my voice and more photos came up, these of Ash at the gym and her apartment, and then more of Nora and me. All women. Only women in the Lupo's lives.

"Damn human trafficking pieces of shit," Enzo growled, pulling out his phone again. "Can you discreetly let someone else in on this?"

"You?" I asked, wondering why he wouldn't just look at my computer himself if he was so interested.

"No. Kia is taking over for me right now. I want someone watching his cameras and she is about as skilled a hacker as we are and can go undetected if we give her the path," he said, pulling out his phone from his pocket once more.

"Yes," I said, continuing to look through the photos, while I pulled up files on offers and arranged transactions that Colin had been making to sell new girls off.

Two women and a child. "One is a fighter!" a description said I assumed in reference to Ash, but they could have very well been talking about Carmen.

"Kia, we're getting you access to feeds. Ingrid will be meeting with O'Shea tomorrow, and I want your eyes

on it while it happens. We don't need missteps," Enzo said, glancing over at my screen. "She's going to walk you through how to get in."

The rest of the early morning hours were spent making calls to various people. Enzo reached out to his uncle, who was the Italian Capo here in Chicago, as well as a Russian. They were both willing to lend tech and potential support, but only if it wasn't traceable, at least until after our meeting. Enzo had snuck out of the house and gotten back with comms for us, a tracker that would nestle undetectably under my clothes and a weapon. The knife was small, not something that would go too deep or do too much damage, but it would be surprising, and hopefully, that surprise would last long enough for me to get away or for Enzo to step in.

"Only use it if absolutely necessary. I will never be too far that I wouldn't be able to get to you," he said as he helped me get all my gear on. I had never used a weapon before, which was odd, honestly, with the type of people I used to be around before and a little after Nora was born. Elliot surrounded me with bad people, but I only stumbled into the relationship with Elliot because I was also mingling in dark crowds.

It was 8:00 a.m. I stood in the mirror of the Airbnb's bedroom, my eyes looking over my appearance. I was put together, looking every bit the part of a professional, from my dressed curls that were pinned in just the right ways to look elegant, to my navy pantsuit that complemented my coloring, and the subtle makeup I had put on. There was no way to know that I was wired and armed.

"We have to drive separately. I will follow shortly," Enzo murmured, coming around to my front and blocking the view of my reflection in the mirror.

"I'm not sure—I don't think I can do thi—"

"You can. Ingrid Jacobs can do anything she puts her mind to. Mary Michelson died three years ago. That woman was put to rest so that Ingrid could soar. *You* are capable. You can do this," Enzo said, his hands firm as they grasped my upper arms, eyes showing a sureness I was starting to believe.

We both knew that the pieces of O'Shea's plan that we had were not everything. We knew I was walking into this situation partially blind, but I tried to take solace in knowing that what I was facing, I wasn't alone.

CHAPTER 18

ENZO

My heart had left my body. It walked out the front door in the kitten heels that matched her leather laptop bag. It got in the beat-up car that I had spent the last three years looking out for around the neighborhood, slamming the door to make sure it closed fully before starting it up. It drove down the street and out of sight, only the little dot on my phone indicating where it was as it drove away from the Airbnb and into the main part of the city of Chicago.

Ingrid was brave. Too brave. I hated sending her there, into the clutches of Colin O'Shea, our biggest rival—or proclaimed enemy—but there was no other way. Nora's safety hinged on Ingrid showing up at this meeting. The hope was that O'Shea wasn't lying, that he had a job that he needed her for, and that she would begin to work on as we set the rest of the plan in motion.

The plan.

It wasn't fully thought out, because there were too many factors that could send this whole thing up in smoke. If all went right, Nora would be safely in

Lee's Summit before Ingrid and I even made it back to Missouri, and we would have yet another knot to untangle with O'Shea to add to the mess we already had with them. But it would be worth it. Just like Carmen was worth everything we went through since she had been taken. Ingrid and Nora were just as worthy of the trouble.

We had to get Nora out of Joe's hands. Sal said he had sent people to St. Louis and the shabby house in Joe Smith's name to watch and be ready for extraction. I wasn't sure who Sal had sent, but I hoped it was someone we trusted implicitly, because if it was one of the fuckups that regularly dropped the ball, like Joey, I would lose my mind. Nora needed to be protected, especially if it came to violence. Every one of us loved Nora, so it would have been shocking if Sal sent someone who would botch the whole thing.

We also needed more protection around Ash and Carmen. Carmen wasn't surprising. The fact that O'Shea's sons, Freddy and Jeremy, were killed last year while we got her back was not something the Irish brute would let go. It was truly an eye for an eye. They took Carmen. We killed Freddy and Jeremy. But Ash... pictures of Ash and her history and habits being in his files made me uncomfortable. Sal and Adrian hadn't taken that news well either.

"We don't have enough men!" Adrian had hissed in the background of my phone call with Sal in the wee hours of the morning, as this plan was being put together.

"We'll be fine," Sal grunted at him, though his tone was just as angry as Adrian's. "We have things here, Enzo, and eyes heading to Nora, but we don't have anyone for backup to send to you."

That much made sense. We were building up our numbers, many of the people under us when our father was Capo had left or we had to take them out, but the manpower wasn't nearly where we needed to be. Uncle Romolo wasn't going to lend any of his men to me on this mission, this wasn't Italian business, or not enough for him to get involved more than he already had been, and Gregor Stepanov, the head of the Russians here in Chicago, wasn't going to do anything to jeopardize his own plans for O'Shea. As long as we didn't kill the bastard, Gregor was out.

This was a rescue mission, a mission to make sure Ingrid and Nora came out of this and back to our home alive, nothing more.

"I've got eyes on Nora," came a far too familiar voice on my phone. I had the comm directly to Ingrid in my ear, listening to her breathing and the sounds of the traffic she was driving through, but the line for Kia and the team that was in place in St. Louis for Nora was on a sat walkie that I had on my dash.

"Leo? What the fuck are you doing?" I hissed. Hearing my younger brother's voice on the other end of that walkie was the last thing I expected right now.

"Sal sent in the big guns. You said no fuckups, right?" came Carmen's voice.

"Carmen? What the fuck?"

Carmen! Carmen, of all people!

"Nora needs someone she is comfortable with here," Leo said, as I gunned the engine on the car, trying to get closer to Ingrid, so I'd be parked before she got out. The Saturday morning traffic in downtown Chicago was not going to make that possible, I was realizing, only increasing my frustration.

"It's not safe for Carmen. I can't believe you're letting her do this, Leo!" After everything we went through to get Carmen back, the fact that Leo was fine with Carmen being in the mix of this potentially lethal chaos was astounding.

"I'm not some delicate flower, Enzo! I know how to defend myself!" Carmen practically growled back.

"One man, Enzo. It's one man against me," Leo grumbled.

"And Nora will be more likely to trust me than this man named Joe she's only met a few times," Carmen said, though her voice was still stiff with irritation.

"Fuck!" I yelled, hitting my palm on the steering wheel. They were right, but that didn't mean I wasn't pissed that I had to rope them into this. This was the worst part of being in this life. The people you trusted the most were also the people you would be most heartbroken if you lost.

"Where's Ingrid?" Carmen asked. Only Kia and I had access to the feed of Ingrid's tracker. My eyes darted to the little dot, stopped at a light a few blocks ahead of me, but only minutes away from arriving at the hotel where O'Shea said to meet.

"Nearly there," Kia said, her deep voice coming through the walkie in a strangely calming way.

"She's got this," Carmen let out on a breath.

I knew she did. Ingrid would be able to handle anything thrown at her, and I would be right there to keep her standing if she needed me to be.

I pulled up to a red light a block away and watched as Ingrid's dot stopped in front of The LeSalle Chicago, a luxury hotel that had a five-star restaurant inside. It was a bit early on a Saturday for the restaurant to be open, but I supposed this was one of those places that O'Shea had his hands in, letting him come and go as he pleased.

A few minutes later I was parking at a nearby hotel's free lot, somehow miraculously getting a vacant spot, something very hard to come by in downtown Chicago, when the comm in my ear made sounds.

"I'm here to see Colin O'Shea," Ingrid said. There was a pause on the other end for a brief moment. I imagined they were looking her over.

"May luck be your friend," came a gruff voice with a faint Irish accent. This must have been a code phrase, a way of identifying who she was. She had shown me the emails between her and O'Shea, the only communications she got directly from him.

"And may trouble be a stranger to you," she said back. Only I heard the quake in her voice. It would have barely been audible to someone in her presence.

"This way," the man said after a beat, and the distinct sound of her heels on the tiled floor of the lobby echoed in my ear.

Pulling the walkie from the dash, I made my way up to the top of the parking garage, where I knew the vantage point would be better. I wasn't as good a sniper as Leo, but we had all been trained to use weapons from an early age. I couldn't be right beside Ingrid, so the next best thing was being her guardian angel through the scope.

I wasn't surprised after I got the rifle I borrowed from my uncle set up in record time, the motions coming to me faster than I thought they would, and saw that they sat her in a dark back corner booth in the restaurant, farthest from the windows. No O'Shea in sight yet, but his decision to seat her in that spot in the restaurant was something all of us would have done. Far from the windows and in a more shadowed area, good to protect from snipers, like me. That didn't matter though. If I made a shot, it would only be in desperation or distraction. I wouldn't dare try to take out O'Shea with everything else going on. Who knows who would rise up to take his place and retaliate? And Gregor would consider that an insult. We didn't need our slight alliance with the Russians tainted because I decided to shoot him before Gregor could exact his revenge.

"Kia. When we're done with this, I want your help with the hierarchy. We have a way in now, so we should be able to see who he most communicates with," I murmured, realizing that if we were going to stop them from coming after us again, we would have to take out everyone who would be meaningful, everyone who would care that O'Shea or his sons were dead and gone.

I was certain Gregor Stepanov would love to help us with that.

"Already backing up everything I can get my hands on," she said, a smile in her voice that echoed over my own lips.

"Ah, Ingrid! So glad you came. I wasn't sure you would when I heard you were staying at a dirty Airbnb instead of this lovely hotel," came the voice of Colin O'Shea.

Like other mob bosses, Colin had an edge to his voice, a way he said things that kept your senses on alert. His words may have been pretty, but his insincere tone and the over-exaggerated gestures were what made them feel off.

"I like my space," she said back, standing from the booth to greet him with an outstretched hand.

Through the scope, I watched O'Shea walk from a back entrance, his frame lean in the well-tailored suit, his hair more gray now, but matching the sandy blond that once adorned the heads of his dead sons. For a man who just lost both children, he seemed at ease, but there wasn't any other way to be in the position he was in. We dealt in illicit and illegal activities, death and pain were part of our jobs. It made sense he could muster a jovial mask in the presence of someone who shouldn't know what darkness he had hidden under the surface.

My gaze moved to look at Ingrid. I could see the look on her face. There wasn't an ounce of trepidation there. She looked confident, her eyes bright, a little smile on her lips, but it was when he reached his hand to hers after crossing the room to approach the booth, grasping her fingers in his and shaking, that I saw her other hand curl into a tight fist.

"Sit, sit!" O'Shea said, finally releasing her and moving to sit opposite of where she had been. That was just fine. I still had a decent shot of his shoulder through my scope, and hopefully, it wouldn't be necessary. "Well, Miss Jacobs, I wanted to first thank you for working with us for these last few months. It has made a difference. So little breaches since you were signed on to be part of the team," O'Shea said as a server came to their table, ice bucket in hand.

"Oh, yes. Thank you for the work. It's been both challenging and helpful," she said, watching as the server set the bucket on the white linen tablecloth, pulling out the bottle of wine that had been hidden in its depths.

"Californian rosé. That's your favorite, yes?" Colin asked, gesturing to the bottle.

"It's a bit early in the day for wine," she said, smiling nervously, her cool and calm mask slipping ever so slightly.

"Never too early for a glass of something this delicious," he said, gesturing for the server to uncork the bottle. They did, pouring first a small portion into his glass to taste, before meeting his approving nods and filling both glasses before them.

"Would you like to order a starter?" the server asked after setting Ingrid's glass before her and stepping back a pace from the end of the table.

"No," Colin said, finally letting his eyes fall on the server fully. The way the server recoiled from the table, and Ingrid stiffened, told me he set the full force of his heavy glare their way. That look may as well have been a threat.

Without another word, the server scurried from the dining room and into the back, leaving Ingrid and Colin in the empty room.

"Guards posted at all entry points, but none in the room with them. He must think she's harmless or help-less," Kia piped up. I was glad to have her eyes on the places I couldn't see.

"Better for us," I said.

"Anyway," Colin said, bringing his focus back to Ingrid. "Where was I?"

"Not sure, Sir, but I was curious what the job was? You asked for the meeting to discuss a job you want done," Ingrid offered. Her little anxious pants wouldn't have been noticeable normally, but it was right in my ear, and I swear I could feel the way she was on the verge of spiraling with fear, barely keeping that mask in place.

"I'm right here, Ingrid," I said quietly into the comm. Her breathing slowed slightly.

"Ah yes, the job," Colin said, plucking the glass from the table and taking a nice big swallow of the pink liquid inside. "You are rather work-focused, aren't you? Coming to us, offering your services to fix the holes in our security, then only maintaining strict work com-munications. This is our first time meeting in person. I thought you'd like us to at least get to know one another before I put you onto the biggest and most important job I've asked of you yet."

Something about the way he said it, I could hear the grin in his voice. I watched her posture stiffen once more; hands clamped closed in her lap.

"Of course. I'm sorry. I'm a bit of a workaholic," she said, her voice light as if the self-deprecating joke was easy banter between the two of them. She seemed to fool him though, his laugh radiating out from his end of the table to her.

"Workaholic, you are! *That* I definitely already know about you," he said once his laughter waned down to a chuckle. "Let's see if I can dig anything else out of that interesting little wall you've got built up."

She swallowed loudly in the comm but smiled across the table at him.

"What would you like to know?" she asked.

He took another sip of the wine, clearly watching her for a moment, trying to find any tells that might show him her true intentions. Like any good boss, he could read body language well.

"So you live in Lee's Summit, Missouri. What brought you there?"

"What do you mean?" she asked, her voice a little less charismatic now, almost tentative.

"You moved there three years ago. I've wondered why that place, in particular, was where you and your daughter landed."

It was like the air was sucked out of my lungs. We were hoping that Joe reaching out to Ingrid, that he was watching Nora while she was here, was simply a coincidence, but now it was starting to feel like a deliberate plot. Ingrid had said that Joe told her someone was coming for *him*, and that she needed to be careful, but now, knowing that Joe had still been working for O'Shea, it seemed like this was all part of some plan. Offering her a job with a large sum of money, enough for her to run with Nora when they were threatened once more. Too coincidental. The timing was too perfect.

But the plan didn't make complete sense. Why would O'Shea care so much about one woman and her child who got away, when the person she was running from wasn't even someone in his employ at the time? And it couldn't have been her connection to us. Three years ago, we hadn't done anything to offend O'Shea, nor had they to us. We were only baseline rivals, vying for goods and connections, not actively trying to thwart one another. If O'Shea had been plotting this, tracking Ingrid for this long, it had to be for some other reason than her ties to us.

"I wanted a good neighborhood for my child. That area just seemed to fit the bill for now," Ingrid said, clearly being careful with her words. She seemed just as unsure about O'Shea as I did.

"Someone found me," came Kia's voice over the walkie.

"Found you?" I asked, only taking my finger off the trigger to talk for a moment, my eyes never straying from Ingrid as she fought, squirming under Colin's gaze.

"Men are moving through the hotel and my attention was split. I'm being attacked. Pushed out. I'm going to lose access," Kia said, her cool, calm tones now transitioned to a bit more frantic.

"Where are they coming from?"

"All sides. Guards coming toward the restaurant," she said, though it seemed far away and the sound of her fingers hitting the keyboard the most prevalent sound in the background.

"I just wonder why you'd reach out to me, back in your home state, when you had your own little crime lords to take care of in your new city."

The silence that persisted after he said those words seemed to stretch for an uncomfortably long time.

"Crime lords?" Ingrid asked. Her voice and her face managed to come off with a sort of strange nonchalance, like she thought he was joking.

"Ingrid Jacobs. Or should I say Mary Ingrid Michelson," he said with a tsk. "You think I don't know you work for the Lupos?"

"I'm locked out, Enzo! I can't see the feeds anymore," Kia said through the walkie, just as O'Shea leaned forward on the table, the glass of rose dangling as it was pressed between his thumb and middle finger.

"Don't play dumb, Ingrid. I am not a fool," Colin said, his voice far darker now than it had been mere moments earlier.

CHAPTER 19

INGRID

My pulse hammered. The beat of my heart pounding in my ears was so loud I was surprised I could even hear the words Colin O'Shea said to me as I sat across from him. I wasn't sure what expression I was making. I no longer was in control of my own reactions, because it was clear there was no part of this interaction I *could* control. Things were clicking into place in my head quickly. There was no threat to Joe. That should have been obvious once we knew he was still working for O'Shea. There *was* someone coming after me, but instead of turning tail and running right when I got the warning, I allowed myself to get swept right into his trap.

My lifeline, the only hope that I would make it out of this at all was the fact that Enzo was watching, waiting, somewhere nearby. But how much of a comfort his presence was, was now up for debate, seeing as I was very much alone in this restaurant. Alone and only protected by the rifle Enzo had pointed this way and the tiny knife hidden in my clothes.

"Ah, I think our guests have arrived. We'll wait until they've joined us before you answer that question. Even if I'm burning to know," Colin said, standing from the table and turning to the doors he had strode through a few minutes before.

I stood too on shaky legs, turning to face the same direction as O'Shea. Two men came through the doors, one man had a cane, limping as he moved slowly closer through the vacant room toward us, the other was right beside him, walking just as slowly, but not in an effort to remain at the man's side, more to keep the appearance of unity. They were a team, or at least that's what they were trying to exude.

"Ingrid, I believe you know Elliot," Colin chimed in, gesturing to the uninjured man. From the distance, I couldn't quite make out his features, but now that it was pointed out to me, the resemblance to the man I had run away from three years ago, the man I had shared a bed with for six years prior, was undeniable.

Elliot smiled, but it didn't reach his eyes. Instead, there was malice there in its dark blue depths. Panic flowed through me in a way I hadn't felt in years. A fear so visceral it felt like it grasped directly at my heart, making my body run cold.

Images flashed through my mind, the drunken fury coursing through him as I shielded my infant from his hands and fists. Every word from his vial, spitting lips was hatred, pushing the ideas that had already had little roots inside my mind deeper.

"You're trash!"

"You deserve this!"

"You've ruined everything!"

"All this? This pain? It's because of you!"

But I wouldn't let Nora feel that way. Nora would never know the pain I had felt. Never know the sort of life I grew up with. She wouldn't know Elliot. That's why I left.

"Of course you do. He's the father of Nora, isn't he?" Colin continued, as if unaware or unconcerned with my clear distress, as I tried desperately to hold myself back from flinching away and cowering from my nightmare. Elliot was my own personal demon, and he had just stepped into this room, back into my life, as if it were nothing.

"Ingrid! It's okay. I'm right here," Enzo said in my ear, though I could hear his own fear in his voice. What I wouldn't have given to have him beside me right then. Having him watch and talk to me wasn't enough. I needed his presence in this room. How was I going to face all these monsters on my own and make it out alive?

"And this is my son. I believe you met him before," Colin said, now turning my attention to the other man beside Elliot. They were close enough now that I could see the details of his features.

It was as if someone had pulled off pieces of his face and tried to sew what remained. Large, deep silvery scars ran over his skin, his sandy blond hair, blue eyes, and the shape of his shoulders were the only indications of his relation to Colin O'Shea, but I still saw the familiarity to the man I had met briefly in my apartment years ago now that I was looking. His foot was turned in a strange way, as if his leg was broken and had healed incorrectly, and the scars didn't end at his face, I could see them on his hands, snaking up his wrists and under his own tailored suit, where I was certain more were hidden.

"I don't recall—"

"We most certainly have met," the scarred man said, blue eyes gleaming as his face twisted into an eerie smile. The smile was frightening, not just because of the way the scars pulled as his mouth widened, but because of the devious way he was looking at me. "Freddy," he offered, passing his cane to his other hand before holding it out for me to shake.

Freddy O'Shea.

"But—"

"But what? I'm supposed to be dead?" he asked, chuckling as if it was all just a big joke as his marred fingers curled around mine.

"Ingrid, listen to me. I'm going to get you out of this. I won't be watching, but I'm listening. I'm coming for you," Enzo said in the comm, his voice a panicked pant, and I could tell he was running now.

"Those Lupos of yours should have shot him in the head to make sure he was dead," Colin said smugly, wrapping an arm around my shoulders. "Let's sit back down and get reacquainted, shall we?"

He turned me, which was probably necessary because I was grappling with what was happening and was very uncertain of what my next steps should be. Enzo shouldn't have been coming here. He should be trying to get far away since this was going far worse than anything we had imagined. Sure, we went through plenty of scenarios where things didn't go to the ideal plan, but none of them could have come close to this.

I sat in the booth, hands gripped together tightly as the other men sat, Elliot pulling up two chairs to sit on the end instead of sliding in after Colin. Once everyone was settled, Elliot pulled the bottle of rosé from the chiller and took a long swig of it straight from the bottle.

"Now, back to your question, Ingrid," Colin said, after giving Elliot a disgusted look and turning back to me.

I couldn't remember any questions I had asked; I couldn't remember much of anything at all between seeing Elliot and fighting through the terror it evoked within me and then seeing the scarred and mangled version of Freddy O'Shea, back from the dead.

"You wanted to know about the job I mentioned, yes?"

I nodded woodenly. Yes. The job.

That seemed like so far away, nonexistent at this point, because everything about this was different than I had thought it would be. I was used to predictability, numbers and code were predictable. I could see the patterns, find the flaws, but this was way out of my depth. This was something I had never, and thought I never would, come to have to deal with.

"You're a smart girl, so I won't beat around the bush. Freddy came to you, wanting your help with something six years ago and you refused him," Colin said, pausing only to take a sip of his own wine and glancing at me as if to make sure I was following.

"Y-yes," I stuttered. The memory of that day etched in my mind. It was the same day I decided to leave hacking behind, to try to be a better person for the child I was growing within me, and also the day that Elliot turned from the verbally abusive, but generally harmless and worthless excuse for a man, into a nightmare I had to escape from.

"Did you know there were several attempts made to procure that particular girl in the years since? All of them thwarted?"

Girl? What girl? My brows furrowed together, not at all aware of what Colin was talking about.

"We never made it too far in the talks, did we *Ri*?" Freddy asked.

"Ah," Colin said, leaning back against the booth and gesturing for Freddy to take over.

"When I came to that apartment, the idea was that you'd help me track down a girl. She had been put up for sale and then it was taken down, the offer withdrawn.

But I had seen her and the potential such a woman in my custody would give us, and I had to get her in my grasp," Freddy said. A cold chill moved down my body.

Enzo had said the Irish dealt in human trafficking, and I had seen it in the information I had been avoiding looking at for all these months. I was glad I said no to him, even more proud of my stubbornness all those years ago, because even if I had loved Elliot fully and deeply, I still wouldn't have helped these monsters steal a woman, even if it was for Elliot's benefit.

"Do you know who put her up for sale in the first place?" he asked me. I shook my head, unable to speak as I absorbed all these pieces that had been missing; the image of the puzzle finally coming into view. "It was by none other than the Lupos you work for."

"It was by my father, Salvatore. Not us," came Enzo's voice in my ear. "It was Carmen. Salvatore was trying to sell Carmen off years ago. Adrian joined to keep that from happening."

Somehow, that knowledge was like a lightning bolt through my veins. Fury poured through me at an alarming rate.

Carmen.

The woman who had been nothing but a friend to me since I came into their lives was what they wanted to buy. Enzo told me about what really happened when the shop closed last summer, how Carmen was taken and they had pooled all their efforts into not only getting her back, but also ridding us all of their father, Salvatore, so that it wouldn't happen again.

"This is some sick game to you?" I asked, unable to make myself stop speaking.

"Excuse me?"

"A carrot was dangled in front of you and snatched away, so now you've spent years trying to get it back? What value does one girl have for you?"

That must have struck a nerve, because the venomous looks I was now getting from the three men sitting there were nothing short of horrifying. They didn't need to tell me; that was clear. I didn't need to know the details of any of their plans, and the fact that I asked for them was an insult.

"What does this have to do with Elliot?" I asked when the deadly silence stretched a little longer.

"Shut your fucking mouth," Elliot yelled, slapping his hand down on the table and making the place settings and the wine rattle.

"Elliot provided information. He was present for something in helping the Italians and when he wasn't fairly compensated, he decided to turn to us," Colin said, giving a sharp look to Elliot, who was breathing harshly as he glared at me.

"Just do your fucking job, you bitch. I deserve my seat at the table," Elliot growled. If I was as I appeared, completely alone with no one else listening or coming to help, I might have been more fearful, more willing to go along with this, if only to save Nora from some sort of horrific fate. As it was, I felt much more emboldened. The fear that pained me earlier had washed away for the adrenaline and fury, and now all I wanted to do was use the knife stashed in my clothes to rid the world of Elliot's existence.

"Enough, Elliot!" Colin yelled, making Elliot still, but the hatred his in eyes for me didn't wane.

"What is it that you expect me to do about this? You want Carmen, but I don't have any way to help you get to her," I said, gaining a laugh from Colin and Freddy.

"You know, it was strangely easy to convince you to go to Lee's Summit. Joel just had to say a few things about it once or twice to have it stuck in your mind while you were planning your pathetic little escape from Chicago," Colin said, making my blood run cold. "It worked better than if I had sent you there myself. Off you went, trusting implicitly that this would be a safe place for you, and right into the lap of the Lupos."

I felt sick.

"You befriended the very girl we wanted. We could watch you and her. If things fell through with our negotiations with Salvatore, as they did," Colin said, pausing momentarily as the beast behind his eyes flashed to the surface at the mention of Enzo's father's name. "Well, we had a backup plan in place. One that's gone swimmingly so far."

I couldn't quite comprehend what I was hearing. It was an elaborate long game plan from the beginning. All of it.

"What do you want?" I managed to grit out, my teeth pressed together tightly, my fingernails cutting into my palms with how tightly I was clenching my fists.

"You are going to help us do exactly what I asked of you six years ago, Ri," Freddy said, and I turned my gaze back to look at him. "Help us get Carmen, or you never see Nora again."

CHAPTER 20

ENZO

*F*uck!

I was taking stairs two at a time in the service stairwell of the hotel. Now that Kia was kicked out of the video feeds, I had no idea where the guards were stationed, but that didn't matter to me in the slightest. The addition of Elliot and—*Jesus fucking Christ! He's supposed to be dead*—Freddy added a layer to this fucking catastrophe of a meeting that none of us expected and I wasn't going to leave Ingrid alone to deal with it, even if it meant I went down in a shower of bullets.

But it was the admission of why all this was happening that made me freeze as I made it to the door on the level of the restaurant and main lobby.

They were still coming after Carmen.

My brain was trying to make sense of it. We had thought she was only valuable for being the link between the families and now, it should have been that they wanted her dead for all the trouble taking her had caused, but it didn't sound like revenge was their reason. No, it hadn't been simply taking her and creating a bridge and an alliance as their main reason for wanting her in the first place. Freddy's brother Jeremy had been obsessed with her, that much we had gathered, but he was definitely dead by Carmen's own hands. There was something more about why they needed Carmen that we didn't know about.

"Joe is on the move," came Carmen's voice over the walkie in my back pocket as I reached my hand to the door handle.

"Leave Nora out of this," Ingrid's voice came from my ear just a moment later.

"No can do. You clearly need motivation and thus far, the only thing that seems to get you moving is that little girl," Colin said. "Let me just give Joel a quick call and—"

"She's just a child!" Ingrid cried out, her voice sounding so much more desperate than I had ever heard it. They had her exactly where they wanted her.

"Enzo! What's happening? Do we move in? What's going on with Ingrid?" Leo said over the walkie, his voice too loud, the sound of his yell reverberating over the steel and concrete of the stairwell. Someone definitely heard that. I pulled the walkie from my pocket, taking in a deep breath as I heard a door from the level above creak open.

"Be safe, but get Nora," I said into it, before setting it on the ground near the door.

"Enzo, what's happening?" Carmen asked this time.

"I'm almost into the public CCTV," Kia said, but it was too late.

Footsteps descended on the stairs as I turned my back to the door, waiting with my handgun drawn to see who was coming down to investigate. It could have been a maid or some other hotel worker, but the likelihood that they weren't kept far away from the restaurant at this moment was low. This had to be one of O'Shea's men.

As soon as I saw the dress shoe and the burgundy dress pants of a man who was clearly not in a hotel uniform, I shot at it. The bullet was silenced, but the quieted sound still rang out around the echoey chamber of the stairs. The toe of the shoe exploded, blood and small bones splattered everywhere, and the scream of the man as he tumbled down the remaining stairs was all that could be heard for a deafening moment.

His gun which he had been drawn clattered away and out of his reach, and I approached quickly, kicking it farther into the corner of the landing, before I was standing over him.

"How many of you are in this building?" I asked.

"Enzo? Enzo!" came Carmen's voice. The reminder that this was all because O'Shea wanted her just heated me further. Carmen was like a sister to me, one we all sacrificed a lot for, but would do it again in a heartbeat, and this man, like all the others before, wouldn't think twice about taking her from us once more. I kicked the downed man, who was still wailing as he weakly reached toward his obliterated foot.

"Answer the fucking question!" I snapped, kicking him again.

"Fifteen!" he screamed, and the sound of the same metal door opening could be heard.

"Roland?" a man hollered, quick steps coming down as Roland continued to cry loudly.

"Wait!" Roland seemed to choke out at the last second, but it was too late. The man who followed him down had just long enough to see me standing over his friend, his eyes widening with surprise, before I raised my gun and shot him right between his eyes.

"Fuck!" Roland cried, but that was the last thing he said before I did the same to him.

These weren't the first people I had killed, nor would they be my last I was certain, but watching the life leave Roland's eyes, to see the breath escape his lungs and his body go still, was not something I was used to. Seeing dead bodies after my brothers and Adrian were through with them? Sure. But it was usually in the context of being the man behind the screen, directing them to safety or the best way to get rid of the body.

Oddly, though this was new and strange territory, my need to ensure Ingrid's safety outweighed any hesitation and fear about what I had just done within me. Two dead Irish were two less we'd have to deal with later. And there most certainly would be a later.

I wasn't sure how many people were now alerted to my presence. They didn't know it was me, necessarily, but clearly, a threat was in their midst. If I was going to get Ingrid and get out, I had to be fast before the room she was in became full of O'Shea's armed goons.

I turned back to the metal door as Kia's voice came back through the walkie. "I can see into the windows from a camera across the street. Go through the kitchens, hug the left. No one has made it to the dining room yet, but they're holding close to the exit points. From what I saw before I was booted, it looks like the kitchen entrance is your best path."

This stairwell led right out onto the back alley. I just had to get Ingrid out of there and back here. We'd figure out how to get back to one of our cars from there.

"You can't do that," Ingrid said, her voice shaking as it came through the earpiece.

"Oh, I can," Colin said back, his voice like a snake, a greedy smile in his eyes.

I wasn't sure what was happening with Carmen and Leo, and I certainly had no control over whether they were successful in getting Nora out, but I couldn't leave Ingrid, not with that monster.

I pulled the door open, my gun at the ready, and found myself in a tile hallway, used for dry storage for the restaurant. Not a soul was there, but I could hear the quiet whispers of a few people on the right. To my left was a server station, drink mats lined with stacked glasses sat amongst pitchers of water beside the soda fountain and ice dispenser. Beyond that was a set of swinging doors that led to the dining room.

I didn't know until I got close to those doors that there was another opening to the kitchen just before the doors. Peering around, I could tell there were several restaurant staff that were huddled behind the expeditor line, whispering with fear. This wasn't a normal occasion by any means, and I couldn't blame this staff for being frightened, especially after what they had probably overheard, what little they had been told, and who they were dealing with.

"I don't know what you expect me to do," Ingrid said, her voice coming out like a gasp, the pain in her voice like a vice to my heart.

"You're going to tell us everything you know, and then find anything else we want with those lovely computer skills of yours. Track her, find her habits, tell us when she's alone, vulnerable. We already have some of that knowledge, but clearly, we need a better picture," Freddy said.

"And if I can't get any more information for you?" It was like Ingrid knew the answer before she asked it. I could almost hear the tears streaming down her cheeks.

"Then we'll try to make as much money as we can from the sweet little red-haired angel that Joel is bringing to me later today."

Fury so potent I could feel it radiating from my skin burned within me. I glanced one last time at the staff and the door to the stairwell before reaching the swinging doors and looking out the small window. There they were, barely a hundred feet from me, past these doors. Ingrid was mostly sheltered by the side of the booth she was sitting at, but the other three were well in my sight.

"I—"

I didn't want to hear what Ingrid was going to say. I knew what her choice would ultimately be, especially when faced with a choice between anyone else and Nora. She didn't have to make the decision. I would do that for her.

I burst from the kitchen; my gun trained on the men across from her. The first bullet exploded from my gun without anyone even turning their head. It flew through the air almost in slow motion, lodging straight into Elliot's shoulder. The second bullet was aimed at Colin, but his eyes and reflexes were fast for a man of his age, moving just enough that the bullet intended for his shoulder hit the upholstered booth behind him.

"Fuck!" Elliot screamed, scrambling from the chair with one limp arm and turning to face me. Freddy slipped from his chair and the weasel slipped beneath the table at Ingrid's feet.

Colin pulled out a gun from his waist, slipping from the booth and aiming it my way, but I was faster, running and upturning a table that took the brunt of the shots he fired my way.

"A fucking Lupo. Of course," Colin snarled, raining a few more bullets into the table I hid behind. "Freddy, get the fuck up and go with Ingrid to the car," Colin shouted as I checked the bullets left in the clip. I had shot four thus far, eight more left, and another clip in my pocket, but I wasn't sure it would be enough.

It would have to be.

"Enzo?" came Ingrid's voice, pain and concern there. I couldn't respond, no matter how much I wanted to. They might think they hurt me or killed me if I stayed silent, and I would take a new element of surprise if possible.

I knew the layout of the restaurant, the tables I could get behind if I needed to. And what I needed was to get Ingrid in my grasp so we could book it out of there, but I wasn't sure she'd leave with me until we had confirmation that Nora was in safe hands.

Just then the comm at my ear crackled. It could have been Ingrid removing the device from her ear, but then I heard the sound of Kia's voice.

"Hacked into this so I could make sure you knew. Leo and Carmen got Nora. Heading to Columbia as quick as they can. More men came, and it got … complicated," she said. But if I heard Kia, so did Ingrid.

"Where the fuck do you think you're going?" Freddy's voice sounded behind me and I risked moving closer to the edge of the table to look around.

There, in all her magnificent, glorious strength, I saw something I never thought I would. All three men's attention had been diverted from my table, Ingrid having moved to get out of the booth. From where Freddy dove under the table to hide, he had grasped her leg. In a move that I would have missed if I had blinked, Ingrid deftly pulled the short blade from the liner of the jacket she wore, quickly bending down to slice at the outside of his already marred fingers.

The scream that came from his lips was nothing short of satisfying, as he released his hold, allowing her to break free and race toward me, shoving over a table only a short distance from where I was holed up as the gunfire from Colin's gun renewed.

I shot at him in return, but he merely backed quickly away, narrowly avoiding getting hit.

Two of the other doors burst open and a flurry of armed men started filling the restaurant.

"With me," I hissed at Ingrid, watching with so much fear as she raced the last small space to hunch with me behind the table. "Now or never," I said, gripping her hand and looking into her eyes for confirmation. She briefly closed her tear-filled blues before nodding once, and I immediately stood, pulling her behind my back and taking in our enemies.

Colin looked shocked for a moment, but it didn't take long for him to train his gun, hollering at his men to shoot us. Somehow, we were fast enough. A bullet grazed my arm, but I didn't slow, adrenaline keeping me moving toward our goal. With our fingers laced together, I rocketed us through the kitchen doors, earning screams from the staff who undoubtedly heard the gunfire, and back to the stairwell. Roland and the other goon's body lay where I left them, the stairwell eerily quiet once the heavy metal door closed soundly behind us.

"Down one flight and out to the alley," Kia said in our ears.

"Which car?" I asked as I pulled Ingrid behind me down the stairs.

"Ingrid's is compromised."

"Mine then," I said as the other door opened to a back alley that was lined with dumpsters, crates, and linen carts. There were several blacked-out vehicles parked at one entrance to the alley, but at the other entrance, a delivery truck was just pulling in. Even more convenient, it was at an awkward angle.

I started running toward it, my fingers still laced with Ingrid's, before I risked a glance behind me. First, my eyes focused on her face; she was keeping pace with me, her skin flushed with the exertion of running, but determination written all over her expression. Freddy's blood coated her fingers where the small blade was still clutched. Then my eyes moved to the door we had just exited just as it burst open. O'Shea's men flooded out, weapons drawn, but their bullets missed us as we rushed past the truck, taking a right and immediately being out of their line of sight.

"We need to be sure we've lost them before we double back to the car," I said through rough breaths.

"Take the next left. There's an empty storefront with boarded windows. Shouldn't be too hard to get into," came Kia, our guardian angel from the earpiece.

"Nora?" Ingrid asked, panting as she miraculously kept pace with me in those kitten heels and her much shorter legs.

"Leo and Carmen have her, Ingrid. It's okay," Kia said, her voice much softer than when she had been speaking to me.

We turned the corner, finding the abandoned storefront. With a quick glance behind us to make sure no one had spotted where we turned, I bent down to inspect the lock. It wasn't even dead-bolted, just a knob lock. Ingrid offered the little knife before I had to ask for it, and I snatched the bloody instrument from her fingers, sliding it between the door and the jam. The door opened.

Without another moment to spare, we slipped in, closing it behind us with a definitive snap, and pushed through the small space, finding a counter we could hide behind until Kia let us know it was clear to move to the car.

The small space was so quiet in comparison to what we had just come from, save for our breathing and the rapid beats of our hearts. As the adrenaline started to wane, Ingrid finally took her eyes from the small sliver of light peeking out from a crack in the boards over the windows to look at me. I hadn't taken my eyes off her since we sat down. I wasn't sure I'd ever be able to again.

She was a glorious mess. Warrior goddess indeed.

CHAPTER 21

INGRID

My heart was still pounding. I could feel it in every inch of my body, like I was pulsing with each contraction of the muscle in my chest. I wasn't sure how we made it out of there relatively unscathed. I was certain my fate was sealed the moment Elliot and Freddy walked out of those doors and into the dining room. Certain that no matter what I had expected and intended when I went into that hotel restaurant, it was all thrown to the wayside, especially since Enzo and I were an island unto ourselves here in enemy territory.

But Enzo never ceased to surprise me. The moment I saw him burst through the kitchen doors, gun aimed and face set with ferocity and determination, I was awed. It also helped that Kia had confirmed Nora was no longer in Joe's—or Joel's, I supposed—hands anymore, and with Leo and Carmen. I wasn't going to leave thinking they had access to my daughter. I would die before I left her to the fate they had in mind for her.

Enzo wasn't going to let that happen.

I saw it in each move he made through that room, each shot he took, the way his fingers grasped mine and pulled me through the building and out onto the streets of Chicago.

Enzo wouldn't leave me to any of the harrowing fates I thought I had in store for me. He meant what he said when he promised to protect me.

The way Enzo was looking at me now didn't help my heart rate either. Those dark eyes were looking at me like I was somehow the most desirable thing he'd ever seen. He looked at me like he would fuck me to oblivion right now if we weren't in the middle of a dirty, abandoned shop, hiding from the Irish mob.

Somehow that sobering fact made the adrenaline plummet further in my system, and I gasped at the suddenness and chill I felt come over my body.

"How long do we wait?" I asked quietly, turning to look at the sliver of the window we could see out like he had been off and on.

"They're about to come by your location. Hang tight. I'll give you the signal to leave," Kia said over the comm.

The fact that she was still there, in our ears, was a comfort, but only so much of one. I wouldn't feel comfortable until I had Nora safely in my arms and we were back in Lee's Summit or Kansas City with the whole of the Lupo's forces at our disposal.

Our eyes parted, focus narrowing to that sliver of the outside world that we could see. Car screeching and rough, running footfalls came, as well as shadows passing by quickly. They were trying to chase us, but as they kept going, assuming we had rounded another corner, we had slipped in here.

"I've got the rear!" came a very familiar yell as the last of the footfalls came past. Elliot was the last. Not that I was surprised. Part of the reason his ambitions hadn't gotten him a place with any of the organized crime groups the years before was that he was lazy. But beyond that, he had been injured. His shoulder had been limp and bleeding rather profusely after Enzo put a bullet there.

I tensed, waiting intently as I listened to his footsteps slow even more as he got closer to where we were. Enzo's hand tightened on the gun, his own breathing quickening as we watched the shadow that was Elliot slow and stop before the boarded window. If he tried the door, it would open. We didn't do anything to secure it, because that would have been too obvious.

The moments seemed to linger, seconds feeling like minutes stretched as we waited to see what he would do, but it passed eventually. The shadow of Elliot set back off and disappeared from our view.

"Wait about five more minutes and then I'll have you take a right back toward the garage you parked in, Enzo," Kia said.

I relaxed at her words and the way Enzo set his hand with the gun down on his thigh. It wasn't at the ready; he wasn't worried. I shouldn't have been worried still.

Silently we continued our wait and just a minute before we were going to leave, the seconds zooming past each time Enzo checked the watch on his wrist; we stood from where we sat behind the counter and made our way back to the front door.

"No, Leo! Left! Shit!" came Kia's voice, just as the sound of a door swinging open and banging on a wall could be heard from some back area in this small shop.

"Where are you, you bitch?" Elliot called. I moved to go out the door, but the hand in Enzo's tightened and held me there.

"I'm ending this with him," Enzo said, his voice low, more like the harbinger of death than the man I knew.

Elliot's loud and clattering movement from the back of the building to the front where we were echoed around me, but I could barely hear it with the way my heart thudded in my ears. It was less than a second before Elliot's presence came into the front room from the back. Without hesitation, he lifted his hand with a gun, aiming right at Enzo, not me. A shot rang out, and I felt the hand that held mine slip from my grasp.

A small sob tore from my throat. My hand Enzo had just been holding, balled into a fist. The danger here wasn't over, or I'd been dropping to the floor beside Enzo, checking to see if he was at least still breathing. But I couldn't do that, not yet, not with Elliot standing before me.

"You thought you could get away from me, huh?"

"I did," I said coldly as my eyes turned to where Enzo had been standing. Now he was on the ground. The room was too dark to see where Elliot's bullet landed, and I knew if I made any sudden moves to Enzo's gun I would be shot easily.

"He knew where you were!" Elliot yelled, and I shook my head.

"Colin O'Shea knew where I was. *You* didn't," I said, not sure how my voice was coming out so evenly and calm, when I was internally screaming. Was Enzo dead? It was too dark. I didn't see any blood, but that meant nothing. He was still. Too still.

"You're so fucking stupid, Leo! What the fuck was that?" Kia's voice said through my ear, but I couldn't be too concerned about what was happening with them. Hoping that my Nora was okay and still in Leo's hands was about as good as I could do while Elliot stood mere feet from me, gun raised, his other arm lifeless at his side, as he looked at me with the most hatred I had ever seen there before.

"You ruined everything! I should have known you'd ruin it all. I only let you keep that baby because I wasn't done with you yet. I should have just killed you both when I found out you were knocked up and saved myself some trouble."

Elliot's ramblings were nothing he hadn't said to me before. Especially after that first time I had met Freddy, he very blatantly blamed me for all the misfortunes that had come since then. Nothing bad was ever his fault, his inaction, his failings. It was always my fault when things went wrong, not that this had been the life he chose. But I also knew I had chosen him as well, which was why I chose to leave him too.

"You aren't going to do what he wants, and he might kill me either way, but this time," he stepped even closer, the gun now close enough that he pressed it to my forehead. "I'm taking you with me first."

It wasn't going to happen though. I wasn't going to simply let him kill me. I may have laid down my own life to protect Nora if it came to it, but that wasn't what was happening here.

Several things happened all at once. Enzo had given me the knife back, and it was in my hand, still caked in Freddy O'Shea's blood. I moved the knife up, easily piercing into the flesh of Elliot's tender throat, while Enzo sat up, kicking out his knees and causing him to fall deeper onto to blade. As I ripped my arm away, blood shot out from the wound like a pressurized hose, coating me and the walls in its spray.

Elliot fell to the ground, the gun completely discarded as he tried to staunch the wound with the only hand he had use of. His mouth opened and closed, small, strange sounds coming out like gurgling moans instead of the screams I was certain he would have been making.

I had never killed anyone before. I never thought I would. If I had thought myself capable of that sort of thing, Elliot would have died years before. Somehow, though, as I stared down at him, his blood pooling around him as he writhed and struggled, the fact that he was dying before me, at my own hand, was not as horrifying as it probably should have been. It was satisfying. This scum had walked the earth for too long, had taken up air, had made my life far more miserable than it ever should have been, and now he would walk it no more.

Now he would be nothing more than a ghost, a memory, and one that I would happily forget. Because even Nora wouldn't need to remember him, not if he was dead and gone. He wouldn't be a feature in her nightmares, because he would never return.

I turned to Enzo as soon as Elliot stopped moving; the light dulling into his widened eyes. Enzo stood, the shot he had received from Elliot a small bleeding cut at the side of his head. He had been knocked out by the force, but no damage had been done.

"Are you two okay? You haven't left. I heard some strange things. It's past five minutes," Kia said into our ears.

"Elliot found a back entrance. We're fine," Enzo said, reaching out to take my hand.

"Is Nora okay?" I asked Kia, because I couldn't pretend I didn't hear some commotion. I knew something wasn't going right with them, otherwise Kia wouldn't have been reacting the way she had to Leo.

"She's fine. They had a hiccup but are on the right track. I've got an address for you to meet up with them once you get back in Missouri," she said, as Enzo pulled me through the front door of the abandoned shop and back out onto the sidewalk.

I was certain we both looked very strange. I was covered in someone else's blood and Enzo had a bleeding shoulder and now blood running down the side of his pretty face. Enzo didn't seem fazed by the idea that someone might spot us, pulling me through the streets, watching anyone he spotted along the way closely. Occasionally he would stop me, press me into a little indented doorway, the length of his body pressed to mine, so I was shielded from view as someone passed, but then he would silently take my hand once more and pull me along.

We reached the parking garage that was across the street from the hotel in a very roundabout way that kept us out of sight of the hotel itself. Enzo brought me to his car, a familiar thing that sent a rush of relief through my body at seeing it.

"I have to get something. You just get in the car," he said, before running off. When he came back, he had a large black case in one hand, his gun still gripped in the other, and before I knew it, we were speeding through the parking garage and getting on the first exit to get on the highway and head back to Kansas City.

CHAPTER 22

ENZO

We barely spoke the whole drive to the safe house. It wasn't the traditional sense of the word, but it was a house unassociated with us where Leo, Carmen, and Nora went following whatever took place in St. Louis with Joe. The safety was that no one could connect it with us or our companies, but it wasn't completely isolated like the safe houses Leo had when he had been on missions in the military.

We were going to meet them there and head back toward Lee's Summit together. It was better to be in those sorts of numbers, and it would give Ingrid the opportunity to see and hold on to Nora, something I was sure she was dying to do.

We stopped a few times for gas, and I managed to pull some clothes from the various shops for her to change into, while I changed my shirt and bandaged my head and shoulder. Both wounds were nothing more than grazes; the fact was not lost on me how lucky I was. I wasn't sure what Sal would do when he heard about my near misses, but I was certain he would have a hard time keeping from killing me himself for this entire thing.

Thankfully, I had news to distract them all from what I had chosen to do, going after Ingrid myself. The news that Freddy was actually alive would be something of a revelation to all of us who had been operating under the assumption he was dead for nearly a year now.

The adrenaline having worn off meant that Ingrid, who had been through quite a hell of a lot of shit the last twenty-four or more hours, was sleeping against the car door as I pulled up to the house several hours after our last stop. It was dark now, the sun having set. As I shut off the car in front of the strange-looking little cabin, the large frame of my younger brother Leo came into view at the front door.

When I stepped out, I saw his shoulders visibly relax, and he leaned over, presumably to put away the weapon he had grabbed just in case he had to fight someone else off.

"Glad to see you're alive," I said, trying for my normal cheer and humor, but the tone was off.

"You too, I guess," Leo said, stepping closer to me as I reached the little porch.

We stopped in front of each other for a moment, Leo scrutinizing my face, glancing over the bandage at my temple and seeing the exhaustion and concern I was certain too, before he reached his arms out, pulling me into a tight hug.

"That was so incredibly stupid. You should have had me come with you," Leo said, still holding onto me.

"If I had, then something else wouldn't have happened. And I very much wanted it to," I said, pulling back and looking through the windshield of the car to Ingrid's still sleeping form.

Leo's brow furrowed for a moment, before he followed my line of sight. A grin spread over his face, and he clapped me on the shoulder rather forcefully in excitement.

"Finally!" he said with a chuckle, turning as Carmen came to the door.

"Nora?" I asked her.

"Sleeping," she said with her own tired smile. It had been a long day for everyone, but then I noticed the little bit of blood on her clothes, and then Leo's. It was hard to tell in the evening's darkness taking over everything, but it certainly looked like blood splatter.

"What happened with *you*? Kia didn't say," I said, narrowing my eyes at them.

"Let's get Ingrid inside first," Carmen said, causing me to turn back to the car where Ingrid was rousing.

I rounded the car, opening it for her as she unbuckled her seat belt. Her sleepy eyes seemed to shoot open when they landed on the house and then the two people standing together at the door.

"Nora?" she said, almost desperately.

"She's sleeping," I said, trying to soothe her, but there was no way I could keep her from storming into that house.

"She's in that first bedroom," Carmen said, coming behind her as she burst through the door and took in the layout. Ingrid immediately went to the first closed door she saw, pushing the door open and stopping dead in the doorway. I was hot on her heels, stopping right behind her.

Ingrid's breath was heavy as she looked at the little twin bed where Nora was lying. She was breathing deeply, her little hand flung out of the covers and over her head, so it was lying in the pile of frazzled curls that framed her head. We stood like that, silently watching her peaceful sleep for a long time, before Ingrid stepped back, pressing her back into my chest and letting me wrap my arms around her.

"Let's find out what happened getting Nora out, then get some sleep," I said, and she nodded. I closed the door as she moved toward the small kitchen and living area where Carmen and Leo had settled on one of the couches.

"Why do you have blood on you?" was the first thing Ingrid said as I got closer to where she was standing.

"Let's just get the story from the beginning," I said, pulling her to sit with me on the unoccupied couch. She did, letting me wrap an arm around her, but she didn't relax against me, watching Leo and Carmen exchange a look and waiting intently.

"There must have been some sort of ulterior plan. Other men started showing up and looked like they were planning on moving her with guards. Enzo gave me the go-ahead to go in to get Nora. Carmen went around the back and managed to get her out of the way and to the car while I had them all distracted in the front," Leo said, smirking as the word "distracted" left his lips.

"The blood isn't yours?" Ingrid asked, her voice a little relieved.

"Oh, some of it's his," Carmen grumbled, poking very lightly at his side.

"Just a little knife wound," he murmured through a grimace.

"And the commotion when you were driving?" I asked, having remembered Kia's exasperation while we were hiding in the abandoned shop. Leo's face faltered a little and Carmen was fuming.

"Car chase. One of them followed us. Unfortunately, Nora did have to witness a few things during that ride.

I tried to shield her from it when we were getting her out of the house, but it was unavoidable in the car," Carmen admitted. "She might have some questions for you, Ingrid."

I stiffened beside Ingrid, but she merely nodded, resignation coming over her features.

"Did Kia scrub the footage?" I asked, suddenly very aware of what an exposure this was.

"I'm not sure," Carmen said, glancing at Leo, who shrugged.

"Shit," I pulled away from Ingrid, heading straight back out to the car where Ingrid's laptop lay. Somehow, she had kept hold of her bag the entire time we were running. Much better than having to remotely destroy that before one of O'Shea's other hackers got their grubby hands on it. And I was able to be certain footage was scrubbed when my laptop was still hours away at home.

When I came back inside, Ingrid was now at the little dining table, Leo clearing off the decor to give me space for the computer, while Carmen looked around for food. I handed the laptop to Ingrid, letting her get it started up, and logged in before she passed it back to me.

"You'll be much faster at scrubbing us from the record than me," she said with a little smile. "I don't have as much practice."

I got to work as Leo's phone rang from his pocket.

"They're here. When is it clear to come home?" Leo asked once he put it on speaker.

"So rude, my brothers," Sal said as if he didn't answer the phone similarly. "It should be clear. Kia said she'd keep eyes on their CCTV around our frequent locations, but there's no good way to watch the highways. I'd say hunker down until morning. Head home once the roads have a bit more traffic."

"Nothing amiss there?" Leo asked.

"Adrian is out talking to the Cartel and negotiating with the little motorcycle gang that's popped up in the metro," Sal said, his voice a little strained as he said it.

"Now?"

"Well, Carmen texted him something about O'Shea still going after her?"

Ingrid sat up from where she had been hunched watching as I quickly sifted through various feeds, finding the ones that were most likely to feature any of us and pulling up the timeframes we were passing through.

"What exactly did O'Shea say to you, Ingrid?" Leo asked, his hands curling into fists against the tabletop.

"Just that he wanted her. They need her for something, and it goes back as far as when Salvatore offered her up years ago," Ingrid said.

"What do they what with Carmen?" Sal sounded as exasperated as the rest of us felt. "Carmen? Do you have any idea of why they would want you? It just doesn't make sense."

"Why would she know?" Leo snapped, glaring at the phone in front of him like he would ring Sal's neck if he were in front of him here.

"It's just a—"

"We can speculate on it when we're all together," I said, glaring up at Leo, then glancing at Carmen who had frozen with her back to us holding a loaf that had been stashed in the freezer.

"I wonder…" she mumbled, turning around, her eyes lost in thought.

"Carmen?" Leo asked, standing now and moving to hold her face in his hands. The tenderness my little brother showed her never ceased to amaze me,

especially when he was still spattered with blood from the men he had torn down just hours before.

"Papa took me somewhere not long before he died," Carmen said, her eyes focusing now on Leo's face.

"Save it for when you're home. Too many ears," Sal said abruptly. "Adrian just texted me. We have more bodies and eyes at our disposal now. Rest. Get home. Family meeting as soon as you're in town."

"Where?" I asked.

"Maria's," Sal said, before he disconnected the phone, and an eerie silence took the place of his voice.

"Carmen?" Leo asked, still looking into her face with concern as tears started streaming down her cheeks.

I refocused on the CCTV Footage, pushing to get through it as quickly as possible. One or two small blips that were missed wouldn't be a big deal as long as the more incriminating ones were taken care of, and those were the ones I had gone after first. Ingrid was clearly stuck between shock and exhaustion. I, too, was worn very thin, not sure how much sleep I had in the last forty-eight hours or more, and Leo and Carmen clearly needed some time alone.

I closed the laptop a few minutes later, causing Ingrid to startle slightly from where she had been staring off in thought.

"We are taking the room next to Nora," I said, gaining a dismissive nod from Leo, before I took Ingrid's hand and led her back to the four doors that were closed to us.

We knew the first one held Nora, opening it to take a look at her still sleeping form, before closing it and trying the door directly next to it. There was a bathroom there, which was good to know, and then beside that was another bedroom.

I pulled Ingrid in with me, closed the door, and just stayed still as she slowly walked forward toward the bed. Her curls were in disarray, the gas station clothes were ill-fitting and too big for her, but still, she was beautiful to me. Then she shocked me by unbuttoning the bedazzled jeans, pushing them over her lush hips, and letting them fall in a heap at her feet. Her shirt was pulled over her head a moment later.

Remnants of the day still marred her skin, which was almost completely exposed to me. A rough bruise was forming where Freddy had grabbed her, blood stains from Elliot's blood spraying over her that had seeped through her now discarded dress clothes and into the strap of her bra, and even some other scrapes and bruises I wasn't sure where exactly they had come from littered other parts of her skin.

I was sure she was in shock, her body and mind had to have been reeling from everything she had been through, not just today, but the last forty-eight hours. Especially everything that revolved around Nora. I had half expected her to crawl into bed beside the little sleeping munchkin, but instead, she had chosen to come into this room with me. She chose to fully undress with the light on.

I stepped up behind her, my hands gently resting on her waist, loving the way they filled that dip between her ribs and her hips and pressed into her soft flesh there. She shuddered, leaning back against me and putting her hands over mine as I let them snake to rest against her belly.

"You'll protect us."

It wasn't a question. There was no hesitation in her tone. She said it as a statement, like something she knew to be a truth so solid, nothing could shake it.

"With my life," I said as I brushed my lips over her ear.

She pulled away from me again, and honestly, I was glad for it. I wanted to see her face.

Ingrid turned around to me, tilting her head up to look into my eyes. That same conviction from her words was shown in her eyes. I couldn't help my hands as they moved to cup her face between them, but then she didn't seem to mind as her little hands moved to touch my neck and gently tug. I granted her request, bending to press my lips to hers.

This kiss wasn't some divine moment of inspiration or thunderbolt as the first time our lips touched, but it was volcanic. We may have been worn from no sleep for days and our systems having been flooded and then purged of adrenaline, but we needed the comfort, the contact of one another.

Without breaking the kiss, Ingrid slipped her hands from my neck and moved them to the buttons of my shirt. Languid kisses were punctuated as each button released through its hole until her hands reached the end, the last button released, and those fingers pressed against my stomach, gliding over the hard plains of my muscles for a moment or two, making me groan at the soft but tempting sensation, before they traveled farther down, grasping at my belt.

I may have been lost in the euphoria of the fact that she was undressing me, but it seemed like only a second passed, before my belt was fully undone and those fingers had already opened my pants, slipping around my hips to the sides of my jeans and pushing them down to the floor. I wasn't sure I could wait any longer, mine having wandered over her cheeks to her neck, down to her still-covered breasts where they had been kneading softly, gaining little gasps and mewls into my eager mouth, but now I wanted to be fully naked with her. I pulled back, breaking the kiss, and toed off my shoes to release my feet from the pants fully. Then I let my shirt fall to the floor a moment later, before I strode back to her, naked and in need.

She readily slipped her remaining garments off, looking at me with blue eyes that danced with desire and a little desperation; she needed this as much as I did after everything that happened. I wasted no time picking her up and easily bringing us down on the bed, softly laying her there beneath me. The first few times we did this were hard and fast, even her own orgasms coming quickly and brutally with my fingers and tongue. This time I wanted to go slow, to savor it, to really feel everything, to fold myself into her. And that was what I told her in the softness of my next kiss to her lips, the gentle way I pressed my tongue to enter her mouth. Her panting moans told me she wanted this too.

CHAPTER 23

INGRID

Something about the way Enzo was so eager, yet patient, protective, yet willing to let me make my own choices, made me crave him in a way I had never felt pulled to someone before. This man would either be my undoing or my completion. Apparently, I had decided he was the latter because I was the one who chose to stay in this room with him, to take off my clothes and present myself before him despite how exhausted we both were.

But I couldn't regret that decision, because the way he kissed me as we lay against that bed, his weight against my body, but not completely, one arm bracing over my head while his hand threaded through my curls and the other traveled down my body with such a soft touch it made me shiver with anticipation. I already knew what those hands could do, and it was far more than anyone else had ever done for me.

By the time his fingers reached the apex of my thighs, I was more than ready, my center dripping with the evidence of what he did to me, my clit swollen and presenting, ready to be touched. I wasn't sure it would take much to even get me to orgasm with the way he had already built me up. But it wasn't the first touch of his fingers to my slick entrance that had me already clenching my abs, it was the moan that came from his mouth into mine that had me quivering before he had even started moving those fingers.

"I wanted to go slow, but you're already so wet for me," he whispered against my lips, those fingers dipping into my entrance, before pulling back out and moving slowly up to my clit.

"I don't want anything but you," I whispered back, my hands threading in his dark hair to pull his lips down to mine. He groaned again, and I could feel his hardened length get even harder against my thigh, his hips pressing forward just a little more, as if he could barely hold himself back.

I wished I could reach down and touch him while he touched me, but his additional height made that impossible, maybe only if we had been in a different position, but with him on top of me like this, I was powerless to reach where I wanted, but that didn't matter for long. His tongue became more vigorous as my moans grew more frequent. His fingers alternated between pumping in and out of me, deeper and deeper as they curled, hitting me in exactly the spot that made me see stars, before pulling those slicked digits back out and making tight circles on my clit that left me breathless, panting in his mouth.

My fingers raked at his hair and across his back. The building, burning pleasure something I was still awed by. Last night could have been a figment of my imagination. After years of being alone and all the years before that not finding pleasure, to have this man not only help me get to the peak I had only found myself but make it a priority was astounding.

His lips and tongue moved messily, but seamlessly over mine, a guttural groan coming from his throat when I arched my back as he added another finger within me, my walls contracting around them as the pressure mounted at my core.

But after this day, after living through what we had, after killing Elliot, after Enzo made sure Nora and I were safe and protected, I wanted us to fall into that bliss together. I pulled my lips from his, my chest heaving as his fingers slowed and his brown eyes opened, a question within them.

But there weren't words I wanted to use for this, only action. I pushed my hips up, turning them as my hand simultaneously pushed on his shoulder. He caught the hint, rolling onto his back, but bringing me with him, my legs on either side, straddling him, and my heat pressed right against his hard cock. I felt powerful in a way I wasn't sure I had ever felt before.

Without question or even a word to contradict, Enzo had relinquished control of this situation, now looking at me with eager eyes.

As my hips began moving, slicking his cock with each grind of my pussy. I leaned over, kissing his lips, before bringing my mouth to his ear.

"I want you to cum with me," I whispered, gaining a squeeze to my thighs where his hands had landed.

The only response I got was a moan when my lips met his again as I lined his cock up, pressing the head at my entrance. It was a wholly different experience to feel him slowly fill me and for me to be in charge. I had to sit back up, leaning into it, my stomach clenching and my breath hitching in my chest as I felt him go all the way in, impossibly, hitting deliciously deep within me.

It seemed like he could have been happy to just watch me sit on him like this, breathing shakily, filled to the brim, while his hands moved over my skin, grasping at my thighs, my ass, ghosting gently over my hips and up to my breasts. His cock throbbed within me at each little sound I made. With each intake of air, I knew it wouldn't take either of us long when I did finally move.

I opened my eyes, looking down at him, and what I saw there was awe. I didn't see disgust or doubt in that expression. I saw *love*.

I started moving then, rocking my hips slowly at first, loving the way it felt to have him within me at this angle, but it quickly built up to a much faster pace. I fell on top of him, my hands bracing on his shoulders as my hips moved in a relentless motion. My slick channel grew tighter as the orgasm he had already built up started to cascade.

Our breathing was ragged, filling the room, and I knew the moment when I had pushed us past the point of no return, his cock getting harder within me, his hands at my hips becoming a vice grip as he began thrusting up to meet me.

"Look at me," he managed to get out, his voice harsh, more like a growl, and I opened my eyes to look into his.

Complete and utter love was in those eyes. Need and desire, and the amazingness of watching him let go to me completely, his love pouring into me, causing the explosion of my own pleasure, spreading out from my core and tingling through my whole body.

I fell against him, the feel of his skin on mine, now slick with our sweat, his arms coming up and around me, holding me to him, I had never felt more desired, more loved, or safer than I did in that moment.

CHAPTER 24

ENZO

I dozed for maybe an hour, Ingrid's head resting against my chest as she slept peacefully, breathing even and body relaxed, but I couldn't quite get my over-tired mind to turn off. Never mind that I had spent who knew how many hours at this point awake, I couldn't rest, not really, not until I knew we were all truly safe and back in Lee's Summit.

Would we ever be safe?

The thoughts swirled in my head, the things I could have done better. There were areas I should have checked beyond scrubbing us from most of the record. I slowly began slipping my arm out from under Ingrid when I heard the ring of Leo's phone. It stopped as I began pulling my pants on, but then rang again. Then another ringtone went off. I assumed Carmen's phone, just as I went to the bedroom door and slipped out into the hall. Leo was also coming from the bedroom he and Carmen had gone to at some point hours ago. I was otherwise occupied and didn't care in the slightest what they had been up to, but clearly, the soldier in my bother remained, keeping him a light sleeper and ready for action at a moment's notice.

Silently, we nodded to one another and went to the main room to see what the calls were about. Both of their phones sat beside the laptop on the small table, but before Leo even had a chance to unlock the Home Screen on his, my phone began ringing in my back pocket.

"Kia? Wh—"

"They traced your location," she snapped, yelling over me.

"How the fuck did they do that?" Leo asked, immediately going to the door where his boots were placed and getting them laced in record time.

"They must have put a tracker on her, but didn't ping it until now," Kia said, as I put to call on speaker.

"How is that possible?" Leo repeated, standing once again and moving to shove his phone in his pocket. I didn't wait for Kia's response, making my way back to the bedroom, only to see Ingrid already sitting up in bed, a strange, nearly imperceptible tone resounding in the room.

"They put a trace on you," I said, moving closer to her.

"I changed my clothes," she said, almost to herself, eyes darting around as if she were trying to comprehend how that was possible. As I crouched near her, the tone was a little louder. It didn't make sense. How and when would they have been able to put anything on her during that commotion at the hotel restaurant? And beyond that she was right. We had changed clothes at one of the gas stations. The only things that hadn't been removed and disposed of had been her undergarments.

"What's that sound?" she asked, her voice barely more than a pained groan as her fingers reached up to rake into her thick curls, brow furrowed.

It was louder for her, I realized. The whining electronic sound was much more intense for her than it was for me, even if I was less than a foot from her. Suddenly, she straightened, her hands stilling in her hair and her eyes snapping to mine.

"Freddy," she said, her left hand moving to join her right on the side of her head and digging into her red strands there.

"What about him?" I asked, arching an eyebrow at her fingers as they moved almost violently in her hair.

"He must have—"

But she didn't need to finish her sentence. Her fingers came away from her hair, and with them was a tiny piece of metal. It was about the size of a watch battery and had a little adhesive on one side that still had pieces of her hair stuck to it. He must have buried it in her hair when he grabbed her, just in case she got away.

"Oh my fucking god," Ingrid hissed as I held out my hand for her to drop the offensive object into.

The sound had intensified as soon as it was out of her hair. A potent fury flooded me as I looked at it and the sound beat at my weary ears. We needed to get home, to our family and our resources, not keep fleeing from O'Shea. Not that I hadn't already known, but we would never be rid of this problem with O'Shea, not until we took him out. Whatever it was that he wanted from Carmen was something much bigger than we had been led to believe.

If we made it through this, Sal needed to reach out to Stepanov and get this issue resolved.

"Get dressed, get Nora. We're leaving," I said, standing and setting the tracer on the bedside table, before moving to put on my shirt and shoes.

"They're coming?" she asked, but moved to stand anyway.

"On their way. We're not sure how long. Leo's talking to Kia now."

Somehow, I was fully dressed and standing back in the little common room a few moments later; my movements from one moment to the next seemed to blur behind my thoughts. Carmen was up now, her own curly hair back in a bun and a bag on one shoulder.

"Found it," I said as Leo looked up with questions in his eyes.

"You need to go now before they're close enough to follow," Kia said via the speakerphone.

"Ingrid's getting Nora and then we'll hit the road," I said just as the door to the room Nora had been sleeping opened. Ingrid held her close, her eyes wide with concern.

"Still sleeping," she mouthed to me.

The five of us moved quickly to the cars. My car had already been deemed too noticeable to use in our journey home, but Leo and Carmen had come in her old Saturn sedan she had yet to get rid of. The thing was ancient in comparison to any of our cars; the windows still had to be rolled down manually with a crank instead of automatic, but it was far easier to disregard than mine.

A seat was already securely buckled in for Nora, and Carmen climbed in the backseat with Ingrid as she buckled the still-sleeping girl into it. Leo and I didn't waste time, him moving to the driver's seat while I had my phone at the ready in the front passenger, looking at the maps and footage Kia had sent over to me.

There they were, a caravan of malice and they weren't far either. I wondered if they had pinged the tracer earlier and briefly, so we wouldn't notice the noise and then only put it on consistently once they were much closer. They were closing in fast now, and we needed to be gone an hour ago.

"Go now!" I snapped at Leo as soon as Nora was secure. The car was already on and in drive, so all he had to do was gun it and whip out of the long gravel drive, leaving dust in our wake before we hopped out onto the country road that led to the highway.

My heart was pounding as Kia sent me update after update, the sleek black cars gaining on the Saturn we were in, zooming in and out of traffic. Some of them would stop at the safe house to check if we were still there, like the tracer said, others would keep going in case we weren't. I knew it, because that's what we would have done. They were maybe thirty miles behind us at this point, but it was only a matter of time before they gained on us. We just had to hope that before we were visible to them, we became inconspicuous amongst the other traffic.

"Carmen, call Adrian," Leo said, glancing in the rearview mirror to lock eyes with her for a moment before she pulled out her phone.

"Did Kia tell you?" Carmen asked as way of a greeting to her oldest brother.

"Tell us what?" I heard Adrian say, his tone immediately clipped and angry.

"They put a tracer on Ingrid during the shootout. We're being pursued," I said, watching the newly updated images on my phone. They made it to the exit to get to the safe house. As anticipated, about half of them took it while the others kept going. They had to have been going well over one hundred miles per hour. There was no way they were gaining such ground so fast. "They made it to the safe house."

"Shit!" Leo said, the engine roaring as he pressed on the gas and swerved around a minivan.

"How far are you from home?"

"At the speed Leo's driving now, probably forty minutes, maybe less from Lee's Summit an hour from K.C.," Carmen said. I turned around to glance at Ingrid. She was staring at the front windshield of the car. There was no focus in her eyes, it was like she was somewhere else. Thankfully, Nora was still asleep, even with the sound of all the talking.

"Head to the main house," Adrian said, referring to the house that had previously been our father's, but now was where Sal and Adrian stayed when they were in Kansas City instead of Lee's Summit.

"Heard," Leo replied, his brows furrowing as he continued to navigate swiftly through the cars on this stretch of I-70.

"Are you armed?" Adrian asked.

A chill ran down my spine at that question, and Ingrid's eyes snapped over to look at me in the front seat.

Adrian wouldn't ask that kind of question unless he felt like there might be cause to use those weapons before we got to the main house. I knew that was a possibility, which was why I had pulled my gun and set it in my lap when we got in the car instead of keeping it tucked in the back of my jeans, but for some reason, Adrian saying those words out loud, for Ingrid to hear was enough to make my blood run cold and it felt like so much more than simply a possibility. Nora was in this car. We couldn't afford a shootout with her in here.

"We are," Carmen said, and that's when I noticed she also had a gun on her lap, as well as an additional one at her feet.

"I'd rather you get here first, but—"

"They're closing in," I said, having finally torn my eyes away from the back seat to look at the newest update from Kia.

The sound of Adrian barking orders to Travis and some of the other men was drowned out by the whooshing sound that started filling my ears.

The fact that some of the most precious people in the world to me were in this car, zooming down the highway, and being chased by our enemies was apparently something that my brain couldn't fully comprehend. I looked at my little brother, trained in combat, battle-worn and deadly, so cool in the face of all this, even with the love of his life in the back seat of this death trap of metal we were in.

I swallowed back the sick feeling that had come over me, trying to channel the strength I had when I knew Ingrid was in the clutches of O'Shea the day before.

This is no different.

But it was different. I couldn't swoop in and quickly calculate a plan to get us out of this. It was only a matter of time before O'Shea's men got to us on this long stretch of road. Only a matter time, before guns were being trained on this older-than-dirt car.

I glanced at where we were on I-70. Leo had really upped the speed during my contemplation, enough that the occasional car horn could be heard as he cut people off and whipped around semis. Nora stirred in her car seat, gaining Ingrid's attention, and it all fell into place for me.

"Pull over after the bridge there," I said, pointing over at the bridge for Little Blue Parkway exit. It was the exit just before the one we would take to get back to Lee's Summit. I wasn't sure where O'Shea thought we were going, but if we stopped, mildly hidden for a moment, and let them pass, we'd be able to watch and see. Lee's Summit or Kansas City? Where did they think we were headed?

"What?"

"Pull over just after the bridge. We park just out of sight, wait until they've passed, and see where they're headed," I said. Leo's brow scrunched for a moment as he considered my plan.

"Sal had Benny pull the moms from the house for now," Adrian said through Carmen's phone. That was a relief. O'Shea had photos of my mom's house already, had probably staked it out too. Having Benny get them out of harm's way would take one worry out of the equation, one that had been ticking at the back of my head as soon as Adrian had told us to go to the main house instead of home.

Leo pulled over like I said, driving through the sparse grass on the hill until the car was mostly hidden from traffic's view. We couldn't stay there too long. The police would undoubtedly be called on us, but we didn't have to. I looked at my phone for the newest set of images Kia sent me and there they were, the black SUVs that held some of the Irish mob, zooming mere miles from us.

"Any minute now," I whispered, glancing up to look at the cars passing us.

It was unmistakable when it happened. We were all waiting with bated breath, and it was happening before our eyes. As if in slow motion, I watched as five or six black cars weaved through the lanes of the highway past us. There must have been some discussion about where we would head as well, since two cars broke off to head toward the city, and three or four went on the exit ramp for I-670 to Lee's Summit.

"Main forces to Lee's Summit," I said, trying to keep my voice from coming out as a growl.

"Head to Lee's. The men are ready. I'll clear out the two that planned on coming here," Adrian said before the line finally disconnected.

"Head into the thick of it with a kid, huh Adrian?" Leo practically spit, his knuckles going white as he gripped the steering wheel.

"We're behind them now," Ingrid said, speaking the first words in what felt like a very long time. I glanced back at her once again. She wasn't looking at me or even at Leo, she was looking down at Nora and smoothing out the little curls that touched her forehead.

"Let's move before they get too far ahead," I said, turning back to Leo.

He didn't need to be told twice, gunning it and spitting loose bits of concrete and dust in our wake as the Saturn zoomed back down the hill behind the bridge and onto the highway. The screaming of car horns and breaks could be heard behind us, but Leo, seemingly unfazed by this, just sped away. As he changed lanes to get off on the exit, I got another image from Kia. I hadn't been looking at them for a few seconds, now that I knew where they were, but something told me I needed to take a look.

My eyes widened, my mouth opening to tell Leo and warn the others, but it didn't matter.

Two shots fired, shattering the back windshield, which rained down over the three in the back seat. Ingrid immediately hunched over Nora, who startled awake at the loud sound of gunfire just as the tires screeched with Leo abruptly switching lanes.

Nora's cries and the terror in Ingrid's eyes brought me back in time for just a moment, when I saw a similar fear on my mother's face, but they were mine and Leo's cries from the backseat. I wanted to vomit. I wanted to scream. I wanted to cry too. But instead, I dropped my phone, rolled the window down beside me, and quickly flicked the safety off my gun.

CHAPTER 25

INGRID

"Who was it?" Leo demanded, eyes flicking between the road before him where he continued to weave through traffic and the rearview mirror where two black SUVs were recklessly trying to pursue us.

"The cars that stopped by the safe house!" Carmen said, gun in her hand as she twisted in her seat to see through the jagged remains of the glass.

I wanted to see what was happening, but I so desperately wanted to keep Nora from seeing anything. At this moment she was scared from the loud sound and being woken abruptly, but that could easily change.

We were helpless and worthless in this situation. Completely useless to the other three and nothing but targets. Carmen, sweet, loving Carmen looked like some sort of badass with her gun aimed out the back window, face set in a determined glower beside me, while I could do nothing more than hunch over Nora and hope that kept the sights and sounds away from her.

"Call Benny!" Leo screamed, but just then one of the SUVs pulled up next to the car, the familiar look of one of O'Shea's men behind the wheel. I didn't know their names, but recognized the wild blond hair and the feral look in his eyes as he reached his arm out the window, gun at the ready; but Enzo was already there. The sound of the gun going off was deafening in the car, Nora's cries became louder, but I was entranced as Enzo's bullet didn't hit the man, but the barrel of the gun in his hand, forcing it from his fingers where it fell, disappearing as we continued flying down the highway.

O'Shea's man slowed the car with the shock of losing his weapon, and probably hurting his hand, giving Leo the opportunity to speed around a semi and make it to the exit ramp, while they were still trapped surrounded by other cars.

"Ingrid! Call Benny!" Leo said, snapping me out of whatever shocked trance I was in.

I was the only one who could. Enzo and Carmen were ready to shoot the enemies behind us if they caught back up to us; Leo was driving. I was it.

Enzo's other hand reached out, his phone in its grasp for me to take, and I did. Our fingers touched and eyes locked for only a moment, but it was long enough. This was a nightmare scenario, but he was determined to get us through it, all of us. They were a team, and they were folding me into it. I had made the declaration at the Airbnb before, but this would be another solidification that my words were true.

I took his phone.

I choose you.

I pulled up Benny's contact, my hands surprisingly not shaking.

I trust you.

I put it on speaker, even though Nora's cries and the wind whipping in the windows were nearly deafening.

"Did you make it to the main house?" Benny asked, though the question clearly faltered as he heard the commotion in the background.

"Three or four are headed to Lee's, two are behind us. We lost them momentarily, but they'll catch up. Where are your men?"

"Ingrid?" Benny asked.

"Everyone else is busy keeping us safe," I snapped.

"Breakers or the gym? Where are they anticipating you are heading?" Leo asked.

"Breakers," Benny said.

"Tell Travis to head to the mall and be at the ready," Leo said.

I was confused. The mall? Bannister Mall had been dead for as long as I had lived in Lee's Summit. Occasionally, it was used for conventions or other such events, but the majority of it was abandoned and desolate.

"But—"

"Away from the public. Are the businesses closed?" Enzo asked, turning back toward me where I held the phone in one hand and still curled over Nora's whimpering form in the other.

"Mom closed the shop. When Adrian called, he said he was having the guards there send the Good Citizen employees home," Benny said.

A breath of relief left my lungs that I didn't know I had been holding. Knowing Sasha wasn't at the shop and in potential danger made me feel much better, even if that thought hadn't crossed my mind until Enzo said something about it.

"We have about ten minutes on them if we keep at this pace," Carmen said, turning back around and sitting in her seat.

"I'll meet you," Benny said, to which the other three all let a resounding "No!" ring through the car.

"Keep the moms safe," Leo said after the car went quiet with their joint plea.

"I hate this," Benny grumbled.

"You aren't alone in that, Benito," Carmen said, looking over at me with sadness in her green eyes.

"How far are you?"

"Two minutes. Give an update to the men for me? If the others that made it to the businesses don't get any action, I want them joining us at the mall," Leo said.

It was strange that Leo, being the youngest of the Lupo brothers, was taking such authority over this situation, but I knew that was where his strengths were, having been in the military. Enzo was good at numbers and computers and there was nothing here in the midst of this chaos we were in where he could use those skills.

"I'll call," Benny said, his voice sounding torn and upset.

As soon as the call ended, I handed Enzo back his phone. The look in his eyes was molten, not with lust as it had been before. He didn't have to say anything to me; no reassurances needed to be made, because simply his expression told me that he was going to make sure Nora and I were protected at all costs.

We pulled into the abandoned mall parking lot and drove around to the loading dock area. The cracked pavement was sprouting weeds. Trash littered the ground, mostly closer to the building where the homeless people used the building for shelter overnight. Leo pulled the car close to the massive structure and turned the car off. Nora's whimpers had lessened, and I pulled away to assess her for a moment.

"Mommy? What's happening?" she asked, reddened eyes peering up at me.

"We just have to go in here so we can be safe. It shouldn't last too long, and we'll be able to go home," I said quietly, though my voice shook with the uncertainty of that statement. The little lies that I had to tell my daughter to keep her young mind safe from the reality of this world were building up. So much of her life had been blanketed in lies. I didn't want it to always be that way, but I didn't know how to change that for her.

"Let's go," Leo said, getting out of the car, but waiting and watching the surrounding area while the rest of us climbed out.

Enzo and Carmen tucked their guns away, but Leo kept his at the ready. I had Nora in my arms in a moment, and we were heading up to the loading dock when Leo's phone rang.

"Tell me," was all he said when he pressed it to his ear, continuing to usher us toward the door beside the massive metal doors that would open for semi-trucks once upon a time.

I couldn't hear the other end of the conversation, but really, I was so much more focused on getting inside, Carmen just in front of me with the case Enzo had grabbed before we left the parking garage in Chicago strapped to her back, and Enzo behind me. Carmen pulled on the handle to open the door, and it didn't budge.

"Give me one second," Enzo said, his phone now in his hand. He was hacking into the system, I realized after a moment. These locks were electric and could be unlocked by a buzzer inside, so he could easily get into them if he knew where to look.

"How many?" Leo said, now more anxiously looking around, his finger on the trigger as if someone could jump out at any second.

"Try it now," Enzo said to Carmen, and this time when she did, the door opened. Without a moment to spare, we all entered the space. It was a massive room. Concrete floors stretched from the doors into the cavernous darkness before us as far as I could see.

"Eyes closed, Nora," I whispered. She was scared of the dark, but I wasn't sure what she'd see if she looked when O'Shea's men came.

"Is everyone okay?" Leo asked, his voice slightly strained now. That seemed to make Enzo and Carmen pause, the echoey sound of our feet halting and leaving the space deadly quiet while Leo pressed the phone to his ear.

"We took down more than we lost, but the remaining cars are headed your way," I heard Kia say.

Headed right our way and there were only three of us who knew how to properly fire a gun. Only three of us who could protect Nora at all, and I wasn't one of them.

Enzo turned to me, a foreign expression on his face, pained but resigned. He took a few steps forward coming so close I could feel the heat radiating off him, and he reached out his empty hand to place it on Nora's head as it rested on my shoulder for a moment, before that hand moved to cup my cheek.

"I promised you," he whispered, leaning forward and lightly pressing his lips to mine. He held there for a moment, like he was breathing me in, taking in as much of me as he could, before he broke the kiss.

He went to Carmen next, kissing her on the forehead before going to Leo, who still had the phone to his ear. He wrapped his arms around his brother, hugging him tightly, much to Leo's confusion, before he bolted right for the door we had just come through. The light from outside was just as much of a shock as seeing Enzo run toward the danger that we all seemed to freeze, shocked as we watched him slam it behind him. The electronic whirl of the lock settling in place was the thing to moved us all into action.

"Enzo?" my voice sounded panicked as we raced to the door he had just closed and locked.

"What the fuck are you doing?" Leo yelled, pounding on the door. The industrial glass window was dirty, but we could still see Enzo's face as he shook his head at us.

"Get the girls out on the other side to safety. I'll hold them off and take as many as I can," Enzo said through the door.

"This is insane!" Leo yelled, punching the glass one more time.

"Go!" Enzo yelled back, turning away from us toward the empty lot, and leaving the three of us to stare at the back of him.

"Fuck!" Leo screamed, his voice echoing long after he finished through the warehouse-like space.

CHAPTER 26

ENZO

I couldn't let anything happen to them. I couldn't bear to see Ingrid, and especially Nora, traumatized by witnessing what kind of mayhem was about to unfold here, but beyond that, with the odds so heavily favored against us, I couldn't die knowing they would take them, all three of them from us, subject them to horrors I didn't even want to imagine, and then probably kill them.

No.

I was going to keep them from it. Carmen and Leo were destined for one another; that much had been made obvious by the clear and apparent love they'd had for so long, and Ingrid and Nora were a package deal, a team. I would never wish them to part if I could help it.

It was me.

It felt almost right. The middle child, the one without a playmate, the one who tried so hard to keep everything together. I would keep my family together and mostly whole by making this sacrifice. I would do it over and over again if I had to. But I was fairly certain this one time would be enough.

Leo's protests died from the other side of the door after a few moments, and I looked around at the dock to see what I was working with. There wasn't much, as far as cover, but there were several dumpsters on the left side, as well as the concrete stairs. I could make something halfway decent out of that. It wouldn't protect me forever, but it would mean I could take out a few people before they got anything that would harm me.

The abrasion on my head from when Elliot shot at me throbbed, almost reminding me that I was most likely going to feel that pain a bit more, perhaps several times over, before it was all said and done.

I heard the car tires screeching as they turned corners heading my way before I saw them, but when I did it didn't shock me. Three sleek, black cars came racing into the lot, coming to abrupt stops just before they got to Carmen's car.

I was standing and clearly visible to them, but I had positioned myself so I could jump down into the area between the stairs and the dumpster quickly if I needed to. It would provide the cover from their bullets, but also allow me to shoot right back at them.

The door to one of the cars opened and so did the other car doors. Only the drivers remained where they were. Freddy O'Shea came around the open car door. His limp was rather pronounced, the grotesque scarring of his face twisted in what I could only imagine was a smirk as he approached me.

"Ah. Enzo. Trying to distract me from getting what I came here for?" Freddy asked.

"Distract you? I don't plan on even letting you step foot inside that building," I said, smirking as his face faltered slightly. "What are you even here for, Freddy? Ingrid and Nora? Or Carmen?"

Freddy grinned.

"Maybe all three," he said, his voice low and nearly a growl.

"That's not going to happen," I said, my lips curling in disgust, which only seemed to inflame him more.

"I'm tired of all of you Lupos and LaMartinas thwarting every plan we put in place. We had a deal with Salvatore. We should be working together, not fighting against each other like this. Just think how different things would be if we worked together, Enzo? The whole of the Midwest would be ours! Morelli would have no choice but to put Sal in the Capo position with that kind of alliance," Freddy said.

"Morelli will choose Sal for Capo because he earned it, not because we gave in and chose to align ourselves with the likes of Irish scum like you, O'Shea." I spit on the ground before me at the thought. We wouldn't stoop so low to be in alliance with people who sell human beings. Guns? Drugs? Smuggling of other illegal goods? Sure. But stealing, buying, and selling *people* was a firm no.

"Sal doesn't even need to be part of the picture, you know," Freddy suddenly said, his eyes flashing with something hungry beneath the gruesome scars that covered his face. "Where is Sal right now anyway? Off in the main city? Hiding away from all of this and leaving his younger brothers to deal with it all?"

He stepped forward from where he stood beside the car, his limp still there, but it was almost like the adrenaline flooding him from this encounter was bolstering him. The air around him changed, and he seemed like the Freddy we had encountered before. He was a much more foreboding figure.

"It could be you, Enzo. You could have it all," he said after a moment, his mouth widening into a sinister smile. "You're the second born. The middle child. Forgotten and used at their convenience. We could do away with all of them, the spot as Capo would be yours. You've already been doing all of it anyway."

His words were supposed to strike a nerve, to make me contemplate and feel the rush of excitement at being the one in charge. That's what it would have been like for most people in my position, but Freddy didn't really know us. Our families, the Lupos and LaMartinas, were so much more than just people who worked in the Mafia together. We were family. No part of us was more important than the other. The only way this worked was if we stayed together, each doing our parts.

I glanced down at the tattoo on my arm, the six-pointed star standing out against my skin like a beacon. It didn't matter if we were spread out and separated from one another. It didn't matter that I started this completely on my own, going after Ingrid a few days ago. Everything we did was as a unit. It had to be that way for us to survive.

"I'm not sure where you get your information from, but your source has it all wrong," I said, smirking as his greedy expression fell in surprise, because why would anyone ever turn down an offer from an O'Shea. "*We* already have it all."

Almost as if my words set things in motion, a bullet hit Freddy's driver, who stood by his open doorway, square in the forehead. His body dropped to the ground, and everything was still for a moment or two before Freddy's men scrambled. I dropped down between the stairs and the dumpster, my gun drawn, but wondering where that initial shot came from as well. The answer was given a moment later when several more shots were fired, and I could tell they were coming from above.

There on the roof of the abandoned mall was Leo with my rifle, picking off the Irish before they had a chance to even aim their weapons up toward him. Soon enough though, opposing bullets were flying toward me and Leo. The pang of bullets hitting the metal dumpster while the crack of shots fired echoed off the concrete building was deafening. Having Leo on the rooftop made it less likely I would die in this confrontation, but I hoped he had sent Carmen and Ingrid running in the opposite direction from all this chaos with Nora.

Freddy's men were dropping fast, some of them dead, others just severely wounded to the point that they were scrambling for cover, but there were still far more of them than us, and if we stopped for just a moment, like when the ammo ran out of our weapons, they would easily overtake us.

And that's exactly what was going to happen.

My final bullet left the chamber, barreling through the air toward a man so young-looking and untainted, I was certain he was a new recruit, probably barely out of high school, but his aim was good, and he was getting very close to shooting Leo, despite the distance. I could have killed him. I knew I could have, but my bullet planted itself in his arm, instead of his chest or head, and the gun in his hand dropped when his arm went limp, and he screamed in pain.

I was out of bullets, and more black SUVs were rounding the corner, headed toward us.

"Get out of here, Leo!" I screamed over the gunfire.

I don't know if he heard me, but a moment later the distinct sound of the rifle's shots ceased, and a silence took over the space.

In the distance, sirens could be heard, and I knew if we didn't leave here now, all of us would be in for far more trouble than we wanted to deal with. Lee's Summit and Kansas City police could be bribed to turn their heads away from a lot of things, but a gun battle in broad daylight after a highway chase was not one of them. We needed to be gone, and all the footage scrubbed, but instead, we were at a standstill.

"If you give them over to me, we can call this a truce. No harm done, even for killing my brother," Freddy yelled so his voice would carry to Leo as well.

No harm done?

If he thought there would ever be a point where we would relinquish one of us to him, he must have been delusional.

"I think we'll have to pass," I said, now standing from where I had been hiding. If there was a prayer of Leo getting out without being killed, it would be because I distracted them. I didn't have any more bullets, and they far outnumbered us two. I could try to take a few out with my fists, long enough for Leo to get away, before I died.

But I didn't have to. Just as the hoard of Irish, both dead and alive, was fully in my line of sight, I saw a very familiar SUV, one that I had ridden in many times over with my brothers. Adrian stood, half his body out the top of the sunroof, with an AK-47 aimed at the backs of all the Irish there. I must have made a face, because Freddy whipped his head around, eyes widening, before he hobbled over to the driver's door, the man that had that position now dead on the ground beside it, getting in with a resounding snap.

Somehow that seemed to spurn the others into action, some of them doing the same, getting in their cars, tires screeching as they followed Freddy, who gunned it, crashing into Carmen's Saturn with a crunch, before backing up to turn and get out of the parking lot. The sound of Adrian's rain of bullets on the remaining people and cars was quite the symphony, especially when accompanied by the screams of terror. A few more cars managed to get away behind Freddy, but those who were left behind and wounded were abandoned to the wrath of the oldest of us.

Sal stopped the car, getting out in a such fluid motion he looked more like a predator than a man. Those eyes, which rarely looked as malicious as our father's, were burning with hatred so potent they almost glowed. I watched from my strange stage of the loading dock as he raised his gun, shooting some of the remaining injured men straight between the eyes, their bodies falling lifeless on the ground.

Only one man remained. The one who was barely out of boyhood that I had shot in the arm was still whimpering on the ground when Sal and Adrian approached him.

"Are you loyal to O'Shea?" Sal asked, straight to the point. There wasn't time for niceties or formalities.

"I just do what I'm told!" the boy cried.

"Do you have a family?" Sal asked.

"The only reason I do it, Sir."

There was a brief pause, Sal looking up at me, weighing the decision he was making in his mind, before looking back down at the sobbing young man.

"Go back to O'Shea. Tell him if he tries it again, we won't wait for Gregor to get his shit together. We'll salt the earth of every fucking O'Shea there is, so none of them can ever rise to power again. Tell him that, and next time we cross paths, I might help you and yours get out." The desperation in the boy's eyes transformed into mild hope. Like many people that are in the life, this boy was forced through coercion, like Adrian had been by my father. He wasn't the first and he wouldn't be the last. "Go now, or I'll end your suffering right here and now instead," Sal said, pointing his gun more directly at the boy's head once more.

He scurried to his feet from the broken pavement, moving around to one of the SUVs that still had tires and climbing in, despite the broken window that tinkled with safety glass as he slammed the door.

"Your name?"

"Mickey," he said. "Fitzpatrick."

As soon as Mickey was speeding through the parking lot and away, I glanced up to the roof, expecting to see Leo. He wasn't there, of course, and I was now completely unsure of how to proceed. I had no way of knowing where Carmen, Ingrid, and Nora were, and now Leo. Was he hurt up there on that roof? I could also hear the sirens closer now. We all had about two minutes to get in the cars and get out of there before anything physical could be tied to us.

"Get in the car, Enzo!" Adrian yelled, now much closer to me than he had been what felt like moments ago.

"Ingrid," I managed to say, as I took a step closer to the door I had locked behind me when I came out to face the O'Shea clan alone. But I didn't take that step, my legs giving out on me. The last thing I saw was the rush of the concrete coming straight for my face before the whole world went black.

CHAPTER 27

INGRID

My hands were shaking, heart beating wildly as I paced the living room of what Benny and Carmen had said was the lake house. I had never been here before, but I knew about it from things Carmen had said over the years working at the coffee shop. They had invited us a time or two, but I always declined. Funny now to think about all the times I tried to push this family away when they were everything I had truly wanted, especially Enzo.

When he had left us in the dark, cavernous warehouse with Leo, I was certain he was going to die. Of course, he was resourceful, and far more skilled with weapons than I would have thought a man who spent most of his time behind a screen would be, but he went out there with a force of unknown size after us.

Leo, though clearly distraught, had moved quickly, instructing Carmen on the next steps, which I couldn't hear as I stared at the window square in the door Enzo had just walked out, grappling with the fact that he had sacrificed himself for us.

No one had ever done something like that for me before.

Only him.

And I was going to lose him.

Suddenly, Carmen had grasped my arm, pulling me as I held Nora through the darkness with only cell phone light to see by.

"Where are we going?"

"To the front," Carmen said as she pressed numbers on the phone while walking.

"Carmen! Where are you? Did you make it?"

"Come to the front of Bannister Mall now," she said, her voice harsh and slightly out of breath as we walked briskly through the space. It was very eerie seeing this once thriving mall reduced to large empty rooms, no light to be seen except for the few places where there were massive skylights in the ceiling, which only made the shadows that much more terrifying.

"Should I—"

"Leave the moms. They should be fine for now. Leo said to tell you Plan C2. I'm not sure what the fuck that means, but I bet you do." Benny laughed uncomfortably, but we could hear the jingle of keys through the speakerphone.

"I have to get Carmen. We'll be back."

"Ingrid and Nora too," Carmen said.

"Make some biscotti," Benny said, to which I could hear Maria make a delighted sound, before the line went silent.

"Will he make it before we do?" I asked Carmen, not sure why that mattered to me so much, but I didn't want to wait. If we were leaving here, I wanted to *leave*.

"Not sure," Carmen said. Her voice was hard. Harder than it had ever been when we were working at the shop together. This was a different Carmen, one I had never witnessed before. I wanted to know this Carmen too, but at the same time, I wasn't sure which Ingrid I was right now.

Now, after walking through what felt like a mile or more of this dilapidated structure, holding Nora's ears as Carmen shot out the last remaining glass window of the entrance doors so we could climb through, and getting into Benny's car, was I there, at the lake house. Nora had calmed down after I sat on the couch holding her a while longer, telling her we were safe now, and she was happily eating biscotti with Maria and Liliana at the large kitchen island.

I, on the other hand, was nowhere near okay.

I had no idea what happened to Enzo and Leo; even Benny and Carmen weren't sure, though somehow Carmen was staying much calmer than I was.

"Just sit down, eat this," Carmen said, pushing me by the shoulders until I was sitting on the couch, and she was shoving a piece of bread in my face.

"I'm not—"

"Just do it. You're going into shock. Eating will help," she said, though I saw the way she glanced at Benny, worry in her own eyes.

The screech of tires on the street made everyone in the house freeze. There weren't really neighbors close by to the house, it was pretty well secluded here on this part of the lake, and anyone coming this way fast enough to make that sound was on a mission.

"Go to the basement," Benny said, whipping his head around to look at Maria, his mom.

"Take Nora and go," Carmen snapped when both women opened their mouths to protest.

"And the bis-cot-ee?" Nora said slowly, trying to make sure she said it correctly.

"Of course, dear," said Liliana, moving to scoop Nora up in her arms while Maria gathered the snacks and drinks to take with them to the basement.

They had barely made it down the stairs when a car braked hard in the driveway and a moment later Leo and Sal were bursting through the door carrying Enzo, Adrian hot on their heels.

"What happened?" I demanded, surging off the couch to follow them as they made their way to the dining room table.

"Is he shot?" Benny asked, as he and Carmen rushed over to them as well.

"I'm not sure. He blacked out as soon as the Irish had either died or dispersed," Adrian said, while Leo began using a flashlight to check Enzo's pupils, before pulling out a massive knife from his pocket to begin cutting away at his shirt.

When the shirt was removed, several abrasions were there. Some I knew he had gotten when we were in Chicago, but others were new. He probably hadn't even noticed he got them. The wound on his head from Elliot had reopened and blood had been trickling down his face and neck.

"Nothing fatal," Leo said, now leaning over to press his ear to Enzo's chest.

"Could be a concussion."

"Maybe it's shock?"

"He's tougher than that, Benny," Adrian said with a scoff, glaring at his brother, who merely shrugged.

"He hasn't slept," I said, cutting through the suggestions everyone was throwing around.

"What?" Sal asked, finally looking up at me.

"I don't know how long it had been before, but two nights ago was when he came to the Airbnb and he

hasn't slept since then," I said, watching as all the eyes found my face, before turning to look at Sal.

He was seething. So angry I wasn't sure how to feel.

"Patch him up and put him in his room," Sal snapped at Leo, who merely nodded.

"I'll get his room ready," Carmen said, glancing at me with an apologetic look, before she headed up the stairs to where, I assumed, the bedrooms were.

Adrian and Benny made their exit as well, heading toward the basement where Maria and Liliana had taken Nora. And now we were alone. Instead of cowering away from Sal, like I would have before, I pushed past the spike in my heart rate and the way his searing look made my palms sweat and moved closer to where Enzo was on the table. Leo had gone down a hallway, I assumed to grab supplies to clean up Enzo's wounds.

"We need to talk," Sal said after several long, silent moments.

"We can talk here, can't we?" I asked, glancing behind me at him. That was a mistake. His nostrils flared and an angry vein seemed to pulse in his forehead.

"I suppose we can do that," he said, words carefully measured, like he was trying to restrain himself.

This was a side of Sal I had never seen. Adrian was quick to be explosive, the hot-tempered one out of the two heads of this operation, but never Sal. If anything, Sal seemed bored half the time, which almost made him seem that much more frightening. I didn't realize how much more frightening he could become, but I was witnessing it firsthand.

"I need you to explain to me exactly what has happened here. From what Enzo said to me when he was driving to *confront* you, things could have gone either way. Either you are a spy working against us, or you are a victim."

The sputtering sound that came out of my mouth was somewhere between a laugh, a gasp, and a cough. I felt that it had been well established that so much of what had happened I had been an unwitting participant, but apparently it wasn't good enough for Sal.

"I had no idea who I was working for," I said after I composed myself.

"No idea? Never looked up Stately Enterprises? Didn't pique your curiosity when you saw information from Ultima Incorporated, the very company that writes your coffee shop paychecks? Never thought to dig into who you were keeping out, and what information they were trying to get to?"

Each question felt like a vice, wrapping me in the guilt and shame I had already been feeling for being so completely stupid about all of this. Each one increased the pressure, my heart stuttering at this speed, my head spinning. This, every bit of this, had been my fault. If I had only looked before, I would have learned the truth and either been able to get away or tell Enzo. Which would have been better?

"You didn't think it was suspicious at all? No red flags went off in your mind? You didn't *think* to look at any of it? Did you even *think* at all?"

"Of course, it crossed my mind, but I didn't!" I screamed, having let the tension build within me with my sharp intakes of air, I simply had to let it out.

Leo stopped, still as a statue from where he had been crossing the room. The room went silent as a tomb for a moment, and then I was crying.

I could feel my legs giving out on me, the weight of it all and the exhaustion finally taking its toll as I clung to the edge of the table for balance. It was unnecessary though. Only a moment later, and I would have fallen, but suddenly strong arms were wrapping around me and pulling me onto the table.

I sobbed, tears and snot streaming as I pressed my face into the familiar chest, hands caressed my head and back; sweet words were whispered for only me to hear.

"Enzo?" I whispered, pulling away to look at him. He had sat up, presumably from my scream, and there he was comforting *me* when he was just the one laid out on the table.

"Lay back down so I can clean you up, Enzo," Leo said, having come back to the table as soon as I quieted down.

"I'm good, Leo. Sal, we'll talk about it in the morning," Enzo said, his voice heavy with his own tiredness, but not lacking any firmness in his tone.

"She better not skip out," Sal said, pointing an accusing finger at Enzo, who merely smiled as he gingerly moved to get off the table.

"She hasn't yet. I think it's safe," Enzo murmured in response.

The room Enzo led me to was nice. Very nice.

A large bed sat on one side, with a door to a bathroom. There was a leather chair in one corner and, of course, a desk with additional screens. This was definitely his room when they came here, but this time, he didn't have his laptop with him. Hell, I wasn't even sure if his phone had survived everything. Did mine?

I had no idea.

I had no idea where any of our things were.

And … *Nora.*

Enzo caught me around the waist as I turned abruptly to leave the room just after we had stepped in.

"Maria and Mom will make sure she's okay. You need to rest too, Ingrid," Enzo said, pulling me in front of him so I could look up at his face. His eyes were much more sunken now, and bruises and blood littered both of us.

"We need to shower," I whispered, smoothing my hands over the mess of blood and bruises on his torso.

"This way," he said, though his voice came out like gravel.

We undressed each other, taking time and care, especially when one of us hissed in pain, but we managed it. Both of us stood fully naked before one another, his once beautiful body now more like the canvas of a warrior. I was certain I looked terrible, disgusting and covered in my own scrapes and bruises, but that didn't seem to matter to him. It hadn't yesterday when we got to the safe house.

We got under the spray, slowly, tiredly cleaning one another, before we stumbled from the shower. The weight of the last few days—who was I kidding, the last eight months—finally came crashing down around me. I staggered toward the bed. Dark sheets in the afternoon-lit room were like a beacon of warmth, safety, and the promise of sleep. Enzo was right behind me, and still wet from the shower. We both collapsed in a heap, only moving enough to get under the sheets and hold hands before the darkness of sleep overtook me.

CHAPTER 28

ENZO

A knock at the door roused me from sleep. My eyes opened to bright sunlight cascading in from the windows, and I assumed I hadn't been asleep long. It was early afternoon when we fell into bed after our shower. But I was awake now, and there was another knock at the door.

I looked over at Ingrid, who was still dead to the world. Her face so relaxed and beautiful in the natural light filling the room. In that moment, I wanted nothing more than the promise of waking up to that face every morning. But I knew I needed to move and answer the door before they knocked again. It was unlikely someone like Ingrid would be able to sleep through so many intrusions, no matter how tired she was.

I slipped from the bed, quickly scrounging for a pair of sweatpants in the bottom drawer of my dresser. I was pulling them the rest of the way up, while simultaneously reaching for the door handle when it started opening.

"Give me one second!" I hissed, seeing Carmen's green eyes for just a moment before the door snapped closed again.

I took a breath as I leaned against the closed door, imagining Carmen giggling on the other side, before glancing back to be sure Ingrid was both still asleep and covered from sight. When I opened the door, I slipped out like I didn't want Carmen to look in there anyway. I didn't want Ingrid to suffer any more embarrassment than she was already going to be subjected to, even if I would delight in seeing that blush creep up her pale skin.

"What do you want?" I asked Carmen as soon as I stepped out of the room.

"It's lunch. I thought you and Ingrid probably could use some food. You've been sleeping for twenty hours."

I gripped the doorframe, my brow furrowing as I tried to understand what Carmen had said, because surely that wasn't true.

"I think that's a bit of an exagger—"

"It's the next day, Enzo. Nora is starting to wonder why Ingrid is sleeping so much, and everyone wants to debrief about what's been going on," Carmen said. Leave it to her to keep it straightforward. Rarely a sugarcoat with that one, but that is as one would expect with a woman who was raised with all of us.

"Give us a minute."

Carmen smiled, nodding before turning to walk down the hall to the stairs.

When I came back in, Ingrid was already sitting up, the sheet pressed to her chest.

"What time is it?" she asked, glancing around the room as if she was expecting a clock to be visible. I didn't typically have clocks around, because my phone was always at my disposal. Of course, now that I had no idea where my phone was, it seemed like I should have simply had one in my room all along, just in case.

"I don't know. Carmen said it's lunch, so I guess we'll find out when we get downstairs," I said, watching her reaction. She nodded, her eyes not leaving me either, so we simply stared across the room in silence for a beat or two. "Nora is asking about you."

Ingrid's eyes widened, tears springing to her eyes.

"I need to-to—"

"Let me get you some sweats," I said, turning to grab sweats that would be far too big for her from the same drawer I had pulled my pants from while listening to the ragged intakes of breath as she tried desperately not to cry about her daughter.

I brought them over to her, setting them just before her feet on the bed and turning to leave her in peace. I was certain she was realizing the full weight of everything that had happened, how dangerous this life was, how unsafe her daughter would be if they stayed here. Stayed with me. But I was surprised when her hand grabbed mine, stopping me from turning all the way and leaving the room.

"Thank you." Her voice was shaking and soft, her hand squeezing mine was not someone who was running away. I turned back to her, kneeling at the side of the bed so our faces were more aligned, and watched the tears roll down her face. "You kept us safe."

"And I promise I won't stop."

We made our way down the stairs to the smell of something delicious. Carmen and Leo were sitting in their spots at the island with Nora beside them, happily kicking her feet as she ate a sandwich.

"Mommy!" she squealed as soon as she caught sight of Ingrid, jumping from her stool, her sandwich all but forgotten to leap into Ingrid's arms. I knew Ingrid was bruised and sore from the last few days, but that didn't stop her from scooping up her daughter and squeezing her tight against her.

"Were you good for Liliana and Maria?" she asked.

"So good! They gave me snacks and made me a fort of stuffed animals that were Carmen's when she was little. I got so cozy I fell right to sleep!"

Ingrid looked at my mom for confirmation, and of course, she nodded, even when Maria's eyebrows shot up with her smile.

"Your mommy is probably hungry. You ate lots of times when she didn't," Maria said, coming over to them and guiding Nora back to her seat beside Carmen once Ingrid put her down.

The moms made us sandwiches and shooed us to the big table where Sal, Adrian, and Benny were sitting with their own. As soon as I sat and put the food to my mouth, I didn't think, I just inhaled. The only thing that would have made it better was ice-cold water and a hot black coffee to go along with it, but that could all wait.

It seemed Ingrid was of the same mind, her sandwich gone almost at the same time as mine, before she got back up to grab a glass of water, filling one and slamming it, before filling another and coming back to her seat.

"Carmen told us some interesting things while you were sleeping," Adrian said, catching my attention while I was halfway through my third glass of water.

"Oh?" I asked, trying to go through the hazy memories of the past few days and pull out the pertinent information.

Carmen was what O'Shea was after, and it wasn't to sell her. No, he had some other reason for needing her, something that even Salvatore hadn't known. Whatever the reason, it was important, so important that they were willing to go to war with the whole Italian mob for it, because if Sal became Capo, that's exactly what would happen.

"Why do they want her?" I asked, but Carmen and Leo moved to sit at the table with us, so our eyes all fell on her.

"Papa had something. Something special. Something important. Or that's what he told me," Carmen started. Her fingers were picking at her nails, eyes cast down at the wood on the table as if the imperfections there were showing her the past. "He asked me if I would help him keep this very important thing safe." Maria gasped a little as she overheard what Carmen was telling us.

"You agreed?" Adrian asked, his voice quivering as the gravity of what she was saying crashed over him. Bernardo LaMartina had used his daughter to hide a secret. Something big enough that the Irish wanted it. Something Salvatore hadn't known about.

"He was our papa, Adrian. Of course, I agreed," she said, looking up at him, a watery smile playing at her mouth. "He brought me places. I can't remember everything, but I remember a little."

"How old were you?" Ingrid asked, her mind already trying to figure out how and why someone would use their daughter to hide a secret.

"It was right before Papa died."

It was like the air was sucked from the room. We had always been led to believe that Bernardo LaMartina had been killed in some random rival gang issue. At that time seventeen years ago, there was a particularly sadistic gang of people going around, sending messages by cutting pieces of their victims off to keep like trophies. From what our childish brains gathered, it wasn't long after Bernardo died that the gang just simply … vanished. Now it was hard to believe that it wasn't somehow all related to whatever it was Bernardo was hiding. His eyes had been pulled from his head, hands cut from his body, and he was left in a heap at the main house in Kansas City for my father to find, like some sort of twisted warning.

Now, it made a lot more sense that someone trying to get information, that they thought the answer would lie with him and his body.

"There's something, somewhere, that has information Papa didn't want anyone to get their hands on, not even Salvatore, and the Irish somehow know about this?" Benny asked, incredulous.

"Yeah, how would O'Shea know?" Sal asked.

"A snitch?" Leo offered.

"Papa didn't let anyone that close," Adrian said.

"His mistress," Maria said, having come up behind Carmen over the course of us talking, taking us all by surprise.

"Mama! That's not true!" Benny nearly yelled, but Adrian looked solemn, shaking his head when Benny looked at him for reassurance that it couldn't be the case.

"Bernardo LaMartina only had one other woman. She came to our house one night not long before he died. He denied that she was his mistress, but I knew from the way they were talking it had to be a lover's quarrel," Maria said, her voice shaking as she it like she hated to even say the words out loud.

"Do you have a name?"

"She went by April Smith, but her real name was Coleen Smythwick."

Smythwick. Like Joel.

It made sense that if this Coleen knew something about the secrets Bernardo was hiding she would pass it on, because it was just a little bit too coincidental that a man we had recently discovered was one of O'Shea's closest men, would share the same last name. If there was anything that had been pushed into my brain about dealing with the Irish now, it was that there were no such thing as coincidences.

"I need details on her," Sal said, looking at me and I nodded.

"After I scrub the footage, I'll get right on it," I said, but Ingrid started talking right over me.

"I'll look into her."

Ingrid speaking up seemed to make all eyes turn to her.

"You'll look into her?" Sal asked, his eyes narrowing. "Like you looked into who you were working for?"

The air was sucked out of the room, everyone else seeming to hold their breath for a beat or two while Sal glared across the table at Ingrid.

"I needed money, and I didn't *want* to know. I made a mistake. Let me make up for it," she said, her voice calm, but I could see the anxiety in the tension on her shoulders. I wasn't worried about Sal. Right now, he was angry, but he would get over it. And if anything, despite how dangerous and reckless this whole thing had been, it gave us more information on the O'Shea's motivations.

This wasn't just retaliation for taking Carmen back or killing O'Shea's son Jeremy, this was a plot much deeper, and we had finally gotten a crumb. Ingrid and I were good at finding things when breadcrumbs were left behind. This would be monumental.

Sal turned to me now, his eyes scrutinizing.

"Enzo? You trust her?" he asked, and I could see it the moment he recognized my answer on my face.

"I do."

"Oh, thank god!" Carmen said, letting out her words on a breath she'd been holding. "I'm so glad to not be the only girl anymore."

I grinned, looking down at Ingrid, who was now wrapped in Carmen's embrace. She looked surprised, but this was probably just something she was going to have to get used to. My family was always full of surprises.

EPILOGUE
INGRID

"**M**ommy! When do we get to go to the *house*?" Nora asked. The way she said "house" was so reverent, which I completely understood. It had been a dream of mine since we got away from Elliot that Nora and I could have a little house of our own. I never thought it would happen, but here we were, closing the coffee shop for the day, while the Lupos and LaMartinas moved our furniture to the house that used to be Maria's.

We'd be right next door to Liliana and Maria now, perfect for Nora, who could come and go as she pleased via the combined backyard. She'd have her own room, we'd have plenty of space, and best of all, we would be with Enzo.

Since getting back to Lee's Summit, we had barely spent a night apart. Most of the time Enzo had opted to stay with us at my tiny, crappy apartment, but it was clear that everyone preferred that Enzo stay at the house next door to the moms, as they all affectionately called them. I worried at first that Enzo would eventually trigger my trauma from Elliot being near me so much, but he was a wholly different person than Elliot. Instead of waking late and screaming at me if I hadn't gotten food and coffee ready, Enzo was usually up before me, often making sure I had something to eat before I headed to open the coffee shop.

I had been considering talking to Nora about the possibility of us moving in with Enzo, seeing as how we were almost already living together, but it was she who brought it up one night after family dinner.

"Mommy, why don't we stay here all the time?" Nora had asked as I tucked her into the bedroom that had once been Carmen's. The question threw me off guard, of course. I hadn't been sure how to broach the subject with her. My and Enzo's relationship was still rather new, not that it seemed to matter since Nora was absolutely in love with him, but for her, it had always just been the two of us. Moving in with Enzo seemed like quite a big step for her.

"Is that what you'd like?" I asked, swallowing a little thickly.

"You used to talk about 'when we have a house someday,' and I like this house. It has Enzo too," Nora said, smiling widely at me. I couldn't help but smile too.

"We'd have to ask him. This is where he lives. You think he wants us and all our stuff here all the time?" I asked.

"I think he'd like it better than staying at our stinky apartment, Mommy." Her face was very serious at that, and I tried to hold back my laugh.

"You think you want him around all the time?" I asked, and she furrowed her brows at me, looking at me like I was crazy.

"Mommy," she said with complete and utter condescension. "I love Enzo, and you do too."

The truth in those words from my six-year-old was enough for tears to spring in my eyes.

"He's funny, and he makes you smile. He's nice. And you aren't as tired all the time anymore," Nora continued.

"Okay, okay," I said with a chuckle, leaning forward to kiss her on the head.

"So you'll ask him?" she asked, looking up at me with those big blue eyes.

"I'll ask him," I said with a nod, but I didn't have to. As soon as I stepped into the hall, he was there, waiting not-so-patiently for me to close the bedroom door before he pulled me against him.

"Ask me," he said, his voice low and husky as he dipped his head down, lips hovering against mine.

"Enzo, can we move in with you?" I whispered, my lips ghosting over his as I said the words.

"Fucking finally," he said with a groan, closing the distance and kissing me thoroughly.

Now it was moving day, and I wasn't sure exactly what was happening at the house. We didn't have too many things to add, a tiny dining table, our beds and dressers, a small couch, and all my kitchen stuff. But the house was fully furnished already, and I hated to replace the much nicer things with my worn-out bargain items.

"Let me just finish one more thing, Nora, and we'll head over," I said to her, pulling my apron off and turning off the last few lights.

We drove over to the house, Paolo, one of the guards, driving behind me as we did, and when we pulled up, there was still complete chaos happening at the front.

"What the hell do you expect to do with this?" Benny asked, holding up one end of my falling apart couch while Enzo held the other.

"Put it in the house? What the hell do you mean?" Enzo yelled back.

"There's no room in there for this!" Benny complained as they tried to maneuver it onto its side so it would fit in the front door.

"Put it in the basement for now. Maybe Ingrid will want to use it!" Maria said from the spot in the yard where she and Liliana were standing on with their hands on their hips.

"You can just put it on the curb!" I yelled as I opened the door to my car and stepped out.

"Thank god!" Benny said, clearly pleased as he began backing away from the front door, Enzo following, but not happily.

I had gotten Nora out of her seat and was waiting at the curb for them as they set the couch down.

"I don't want to throw all your things away," Enzo said, slightly out of breath as he came over to me. I shrugged.

"It's just things, Enzo," I said, coming closer to him and going on my toes to kiss his cheek. He turned his head just in time for our lips to meet, and I grinned into the kiss.

"You going to help me, or am I moving your girl-friend into your house by myself?" Benny called again, though I could hear the smile in his voice.

"Who set up your exam room for you and got that fancy touchscreen monitor again?" Enzo asked him without turning his head away from me.

There was a grunting sound from Benny, but no further words of protest as Enzo pressed our lips together again.

When we finally parted, Adrian was pulling up with an SUV, I assumed with a load of the few boxes I had packed. We really didn't have much in comparison to

the full house of supplies that Enzo already had. But when I parted ways with Enzo, moving through the yard with Nora, Liliana, and Maria just behind me, it was much different than it had been when I saw it the day before.

Gone were the dated, but well-maintained couches that were Maria's. Now, there was a leather sectional that sat quite nicely in the living room. The round dining room table still sat where it was, but there was also a huge cabinet in there that I had never seen before. Nora raced past me to head up the stairs, already knowing she was going to have Carmen's old room. I was almost worried to go look in the other rooms, not sure what other massive changes there were going to be.

Where was this furniture hiding before?

Enzo stepped into the house carrying a large box from my apartment labeled "bathroom," while Benny was coming back down the stairs, I assumed after depositing a box in one of the rooms.

"What's that?" I asked Enzo before he slipped upstairs, pointing toward the cabinet. He grinned, setting the box down on the table, which was covered in other boxes instead of his usual computer setup.

"You're going to love this," he said eagerly.

"No, *you* love it," Benny said as he walked out the door.

"You'll love it too; he's just being a grump," Enzo said, pulling me to the cabinet. It had four doors that ran from floor to ceiling, the dark wood blending in seamlessly with the other woodwork, making it seem like it had always been there.

Before I could ask any more questions, Enzo opened one set of the doors to reveal a computer setup. The doors hid in the remaining cabinet, and I watched, amazed, as Enzo pulled out a full desk.

"It gets better," he said happily, moving to the other doors. It was the same thing, a full desk behind the doors that he pulled out, before bringing everything to life before my eyes. Each computer spot had multiple screens that could pop out and move to be where we wanted them. He had made a hub, not just for him, but for both of us, right here in the dining room.

I could have laughed at the absurdity of it, if I were not blown away and absolutely giddy at the sight of it.

"How long have you been planning this?" I asked, stepping forward and looking at the intricately placed cords, all neat and labeled for easy use. My laptop was already sitting and plugged in, so I could start doing whatever I'd like at the drop of a hat.

"For a while. I had already plotted out one of these, but it made more sense for us to both have one," he said, watching my face, seeming uncertain about my feelings. I turned to him now, about to tell him how much loved it, when Nora bounded back down the stairs.

"Mommy! There's a new bed! Brand new!" she squealed, tugging on my arm.

"I love it," I said, leaning forward to kiss him, before Nora pulled me away.

Yes, there were more surprises in store. I was a little uncomfortable a time or two, realizing Enzo must have dropped quite a bit of money on things like brand new beds for both our room and Nora's, as well as the cabinets he had custom-made and set up the night before. But most of it, Enzo assured me, were things that were in his apartment before he moved into this house to be close to the moms, and he had just stored it away in the hopes he'd get a place of his own someday.

We bought pizza and beer for everyone who had come to help us, Benny seeming happier once he was fed, while the others happily chatted. It felt joyful and normal, exactly what I had lacked for my entire life, and I was, while perhaps a bit overwhelmed, still much happier than I had been. Even knowing the fight with the Irish wasn't over, we all seemed to bask in one another's presence and the ease with which we all seemed to be able to just *be together.*

This was what family was.

Once everyone left and I had tucked Nora into her new bed, complete with a princess netting that cascaded over the top, I moved to the primary bedroom that we had decided to make ours. Enzo had been sleeping mostly on the couch and occasionally in Adrian's old bedroom before, but now that this wasn't going to be temporary, he opted to make sure we had the bigger room.

Enzo was already in bed, his phone in his hand as he looked at something I could imagine was Mafia-related, but his eyes were drawn to me as soon as I stepped in.

"I'm exhausted," I said, immediately climbing up on the foot of the bed and crawling up to where he sat.

"Me too," he said, setting his phone on the side table, before settling a bit deeper on the bed so our faces were close. "Are you happy?"

"Nora's ecstatic. Did you hear the whole freak out when she saw the new bed?" I asked, smiling at the memory of her curls bouncing and quivering as she looked at it.

"I know. But are you?" he asked, clearly trying to hide the worry in his eyes. I reached up, caressing his cheek, a little stubble having formed there.

"I have you. I don't feel like I could say anything else. I have you," I whispered. His eyes closed briefly, a small, contented smile coming over his lips, before they opened again, and he pulled me closer and pinned me beneath him as he rolled over me.

I loved the weight of him on me, the feel of his skin as my fingers slipped beneath his shirt, and I loved the way he kissed me.

"I love you," he whispered against my lips as his fingers went under my shirt, fingers softly caressing the skin of my side.

This I knew, but I never tired of hearing it. I wanted to hear it every day for the rest of our lives.

"I love you," I whispered back.

BOOK CLUB QUESTIONS

1. Ingrid has clearly struggled with body image for many years. How did her transformation throughout the course of the book make you feel? Do you relate to her?

2. Clearly, Ingrid's role as a mother is paramount to any other role she takes on. How do you think that will affect her relationships in the future?

3. Enzo makes deliberate decisions when he discovers the things Ingrid has been hiding, opting to take a path where she would have an opportunity to explain. Why do you think he chose to do that?

4. What about this book was different than the first? Did you think the differences were good?

5. Now that we know the motivations behind the O'Sheas, what do you think the secret that Bernardo hid could be?

6. What do you think the next book is going to center around based on the pieces of the puzzle you've gotten from this one?

AUTHOR BIO

Chelsea Burton Dunn is a Kansas City native—the Missouri side, not the Kansas side. That matters to locals. Where is that you might ask? Right, smack-dab in the middle of the country. She has two beautiful children and is married to a superb partner, but let's not forget their snuggly cat and eager-eater of a dog.

Having always been a little strange herself, she instantly fell in love with paranormal, supernatural, and fantasy books, movies, and TV shows as a child. Did everyone think it was a phase? Absolutely. Was it? Absolutely not. Being weird is a blessing, not a curse. She's always embraced that part of herself and those around her.

She started writing from a very early age, initially starting and completing one of the *Dead Man's Hand* books in high school. She is a lover of music, having her other love and talent be for singing. She performed on main stage operas in the children's chorus from grade school to high school.

Chelsea loves to delve into the difficulties of life, love, and loss while spicing it up with a little magic and monsters. As she liked to say when she was younger, "the monsters in my head need to come out to play every once in a while," so giving them life on the page seemed appropriate.

You can see more about Chelsea, her projects, and find her social medias by going to www.chelseaburtondunn.com

Discover more at
4HorsemenPublications.com

10% off using HORSEMEN10

9 798823 209649